Figurines

ALSO BY JAMIE BOUD

Envy The Rain

Figurines

A Novel by
Jamie Boud

WITH ILLUSTRATIONS BY THE AUTHOR

THE KNOWN UNIVERSE

Jamie Boud
275 Park Avenue
Suite 7R
Brooklyn, NY 11205

First paperback edition

Designed and illustrated by Jamie Boud

Manufactured in the United States of America
10 9 8 7 6 5 4 3 2 1

ISBN 978-0-9767876-3-1

For Deborah and Arlene

O, what a world of unseen visions and heard silences, this insubstantial country of the mind! What ineffable essences, these touchless rememberings and unshowable reveries!

— JULIAN JAYNES

Dear Guest,

Please be advised that activity in your hotel room may be visible from the outside with the curtains open. We appreciate your consideration of the patrons of the High Line park and the residential neighborhood below.

— *THE STANDARD HOTEL MANAGEMENT*

Printed on gold-embossed stationery, the note reads as an invitation. I kick off my shoes, slip off my dress, and stand naked before the floor-to-ceiling window. I'm not an exhibitionist, not really; I just want to be seen, that's all. To prove Mom wrong. *Turning thirty-eight means you're one step closer to becoming invisible,* she had said. *It's what happens to a woman. You'll see.*

It was just another one of Mom's lame attempts at scaring me into finding a husband and having kids. But it did sting when she said it, and I do worry a little when no one in the park looks up at me. The ninth floor might be too far away for anyone to notice, so I stand closer and tap a few times on the double-paned glass with my fingernail.

Nothing.

The only eyes I catch belong to my pale reflection, hovering above the crowd like a green ghost.

Pulling back my hair, turning side-to-side, I study my face. Push my cheeks, tug a bit of flesh beneath my chin. I cup my breasts, pat my belly, try to reassure myself. Wasn't the desk clerk surprised when she saw my ID?

"Happy Birthday!" she'd said, as she slid the keycard across the counter. "I would have thought you were twenty-four."

She was exaggerating, of course, but I thanked her anyway.

"Don't thank me," she said. "Thank your mom and dad for those good genes."

I could have told her the truth—that the people I grew up calling Mom and Dad have nothing to do with my genes, and there's little to thank them for—but instead, I just took the key and smiled.

Is looking young the same as looking good? As being hot? Other people have told me I was hot—beautiful, even—and sometimes people still do. *You should be a model,* they sometimes say. I rarely admit that, years ago, I had been. When I think back on it now, I can't help but hear the words Mom always said to me: *You're not as pretty as you think you are.* If I ever thought I was pretty, nothing did more to disabuse me of the notion than modeling.

I run my fingers across the window and tap it again. With my knuckles this time, but with the same result. What's it going to take to get someone down there to see me? Perhaps if I run as fast as I can from down the hall and careen full force through the glass, that'll do it. I picture my naked body falling in slow motion, engulfed in a swirl of twinkling shards like glitter in a snow globe.

See me now?

Or how about when I hit the park's boardwalk? A crowd is sure to gather then.

What a shame, they'll whisper, *she had such good genes.*

Startled by a knock at the door, I cross the room and squint through the peephole. On the other side, a delivery man is bouncing in the hall, holding an extravagant bouquet of pale-pink ranunculus, ballooned by the lens.

"One second," I say, throwing on one of the plush white robes I find hanging in the closet.

When I swing open the door, I'm instantly overwhelmed by a floral scent almost too strong to be real—like walking into a fancy soap store. The deliveryman breezes into the room and carefully places the heavy vase on the dresser. I rummage through my bag for a tip and give him the crisp five-dollar bill Mom and Dad sent me for my birthday.

Once the man is gone, I read the notecard: *Happy Birthday, Love, Eric.* Nothing on the other side—no apologies, no overtures. I rotate the vase a few times. I'd chided Eric for giving me half-dead flowers from a corner bodega last Valentine's Day, and it seems that as a result, he's gone overboard. Is he trying to make me feel guilty? Maybe. But no, I'm sure he ordered the flowers before our fight. Who knows why he didn't keep the room for himself, but after I'd spent all week fawning over pictures of the "teacup bath for two" on the hotel's website, I'm glad he let me have it.

The room is small, but uncluttered. Crisp and clean, like a well-appointed makeup trailer. Or a cruise ship cabin, where everything is designed with rounded corners, so you won't get impaled should the ship keel over. The bathtub looks nothing like a teacup, of course. It would be absurd if it did. Taking up half the room, It's more like a terra cotta cauldron. It will be a while before it's full enough for me to cook my bones, so I turn the tap and get it started while calling Mom and Dad to thank them for the birthday card. I call them every Saturday at five o'clock. That's the routine, or it has been for about a year. Any other day and neither of them will pick up the phone. Any later than five o'clock, and Dad will ramble through all the terrible things he imagined must have happened to me—a mugging, a car crash, a murder. How about falling nine stories from a hotel window?

Funny how things change. During the ten years that we went without talking, no one seemed worried about me then. Eric was concerned when he found out I'd been estranged from my parents for so long, even though I hinted at why. "They're still your parents," he'd said, "They raised you. They were there for the most formative time of your life. You can't just pretend they don't exist. You should call them."

The thought had crossed my mind over the years, and I figured I'd get around to it eventually. Still, I didn't expect Eric's words to persuade me so quickly.

The first time I called, no one answered, so I sent a letter instead.

It's hard to remember what I wrote. Doubtless, some poorly polished version of the truth, which was that my life had changed less for the better over the past decade than I wanted them to believe. I know what I *didn't* tell them: that I still couldn't hold an office job, still couldn't keep a menial job either, thus was hoping to pay off debt collectors by trying to sell cumbrous, unwieldy custom dinnerware to the same gay husbands of day traders who'd been buying up creations from my studio mates. I was still trying to mold clay into meaning. Still ambivalent about my boyfriend, if that's what Eric ever was. Still drinking. Whatever it was that I mustered up in my letter, it broke the ice. Dad wrote back, probably omitting as much truth as I had done, which led to a phone call, then another, until we fell into our little routine. It has continued in this way for over a year. Not the worst of my habits, I suppose.

Our conversations can still be rocky at times and inspire fits of rage to rival the old days. More often than not, however, the calls are just dull. Dad only likes to talk about three things: the lawn, the dogs, and God. Mom isn't much better, the way she rambles about the birds that come to her feeder. She gives them names: *Lil' Peeper*, *Tammy Faye*, *Jellybean*, *Rambo*, and so on. It's kind of cute, but I find it impossible to follow along. It's better when I can get her to talk about cooking instead. Since the kitchen was strictly off-limits to me as a kid, I never learned how to prepare anything beyond punching a few keys on a microwave. But after telling Mom I've been trying to teach myself how to cook, she's finally opening up, offering tips and sharing recipes. Real mother-daughter stuff, at long last. She tells me funny stories about Dad as well, something we both can laugh at. Dad tends to overshare with strangers, eliciting varying degrees of discomfort in his audiences, be they a supermarket cashier or a mailman, whoever is unfortunate enough to cross his path.

That's the extent of it, though. Mom has yet to ask me about life in New York. Dad is the same way. I don't know why they aren't interested in what I've been up to all these years, but it doesn't matter—I wouldn't tell them anyway, as I have so little to show for it.

Dad waits for the third ring every time.

"Oh, hi, Rachel, hi," he says.

He repeats himself whenever he's nervous—and he is *always* nervous.

"Happy birthday," he says. "What are you doing to celebrate?"

As tempting as it is to tell him I'm standing naked in front of a hotel window, trying to get the attention of total strangers, I don't want to get off track so soon—especially since I'm eager to know how Mom is doing. If she's feeling better, I can end the call early and relax in the tub, so I get right to it: "How did Mom make out with the doctor?"

"I didn't take her to the doctor," Dad says. "She didn't go."

"Why not?"

"On account of the dogs and all."

"I'm tired of that excuse," I say. "You guys use it for every-thing. Forget about the fucking dogs for once."

"Rachel! Don't use that word. That's not how we raised you. What happened? You used to dance all up in the Spirit."

Doesn't he know by now? When I used to dance, sing, and speak in tongues the way Dad does, I wasn't caught up in any *spirit*. I only ever jerked around in violent spasms that way to sublimate my pent-up frustrations.

I had a lot of them back then.

Still do.

"Never mind all that," I say. "You can leave the dogs alone for a couple of hours. They'll be fine."

"Them critters'll get into everything. Chew my socks. Get germs."

"Put them in the basement."

"They'll get into the sump basin and get sick."

"Find a kennel."

"Them places never do what we say."

"If you mean they don't feed the dogs cottage cheese and peaches, of course they don't."

"That's what they eat, Rachel. Besides, we ain't got money for no kennel, anyhow."

"What about Jack? He'll watch them. He's right next door."

"Jack says he can only come by to feed them and take them for a short walk."

"That's all they need!"

"I keep telling you, Rachel, if the dogs get into trouble, I'll never forgive myself. Your mother don't want to leave them dogs, neither. They're everything to her."

I want to reach through the phone and strangle him. Strangle Mom, too. I'd be doing the dogs a favor. Mom and Dad keep them on a short leash—literally—and are as overprotective of the dogs as they once were of my brother Mike and me. In fact, this whole conversation is starting to feel like an argument over my own childhood. Hearing the dogs yelping and whining in the background isn't helping. It's easy to picture us siblings as two excitable Shih Tzus, dusty, matted, and spinning in circles—deluded, sheltered to the point of suffocated, dancing in the Spirit.

"How about Uncle Nick?" I say. Clearly, Uncle Nick is not the best candidate, with his Parkinson's, paranoid delusions, back pain, and so on. To hear Mom tell it, he's taking so many medications for so many things, he's nearly catatonic. But he's also Mom's older brother and perhaps the only person alive she truly trusts. "All he has to do is sit in a chair and watch TV," I say. "Then Jack can come by to feed and walk the dogs the way he offered to."

"I don't know. Maybe Monday."

"Let me talk to Mom."

While Dad carries the phone to Mom, I adjust the water temperature as it flows into the tub. I glance outside and see darkness on the horizon over the Hudson River—a storm, maybe.

Dad gets back on the line. "Your mother don't want to talk to no one. Her stomach still hurts."

"Take her to the Emergency Room, will you please."

"It'll be dark by the time we get back. I don't like to drive at night."

"Then call an ambulance. If you don't, I will." Am I overreacting? Something feels wrong, but when it comes to Mom and Dad, something always does. "Okay, listen," I say. "Get Mom to the ER first thing tomorrow morning. Don't wait any longer than that. You hear me?" He doesn't answer, but I can hear him muttering—talking to the dogs, maybe. "Promise me, Dad."

"Yes, yes, we'll see."

Frustrated and unconvinced, I hang up the phone and stare out the window. Clouds are creeping closer. Silent pulses of lightning begin to flash along the velvet Hoboken skyline. It's as if the dismal purple clouds that hung over me as a child are coming east to swallow me again. A crack of lightning chisels through the sky. The Hudson River is a murky green, nearly black. The crowd of tourists on the High Line boardwalk grows thin under a light drizzle. When the rain suddenly falls in earnest, the last of them hunch their shoulders and scurry for cover. I trace the angled streaks of rain on the window with my fingertips. The robe slips from my shoulders—no one in the park remains to notice.

The tub is still only half-full as I ease into it. The hot water slowly rises around me. When it's finally deep enough, I submerge my head. The running tap sounds like a torrid rush of river, the white noise of rain. I break the surface, inhale deeply, and re-submerge. Reaching with my toes, I shut off the water and coax the stress from one place to another—from my gut, to my shoulders, to my neck. Eventually, it holds up directly behind my eyes in a gnarled mess, the way it always does.

Growing dizzy from the heat, I eventually climb out. Steam rises from my arms, belly, thighs, as if I am about to spontaneously combust. I read about it somewhere. It happens.

A few guests laugh in the hallway, perhaps headed upstairs to The Boom Boom Room or downstairs to The Biergarten. If I could get motivated to dry my hair and put on my dress, I might follow them. Instead, I pluck a small bottle of gin and a bag of potato chips from the minibar, find the TV remote and nestle into bed.

AWAKENED BY A SHARP KNOCK, I wrap myself in a cold, damp towel and open the door.

"Excuse me, Miss, check-out is at noon."

"What time is it?"

"Quarter past. If you'd like a late check-out, it can be arranged."

"No, sorry, I overslept. I'm not feeling well. Give me a minute."

The bed is littered with snack wrappers and miniature booze bottles. Two Heineken cans lie empty on the left side table, and an empty wine bottle on the right. Shoes, dress, sunglasses, and purse—it doesn't take long to get dressed and collect my things. When I untwist the bedcovers and give them a shake, salted peanuts rain to the floor. There's an unopened bottle of Chivas underneath one of the pillows. I throw it into my bag and side-step the maid, who has been standing impatiently by the door. Waiting for the elevator, I remember my birthday flowers and rush back to grab them. They're so much heavier than they look.

Steam wafts from the streets as I shuffle down 14th Street to the L train. Settling into an open seat, I rest the vase on my lap and hide behind my sunglasses. The train squeals and grunts from the station. As it chugs crosstown toward Brooklyn, I drop my face deep into the fragrant blooms to mask the humid train car's summer stench. Rocking gently, I whisper to myself in rhythm with the train: *Hang on, you'll be home soon. Hang on, you'll be home soon...*

ON THE STREET, while fumbling with my keys, the vase drops to the cement in a slow-motion explosion, water sloshing and splashing as in a soft drink commercial, the porcelain cracking like an ice cube. Hangovers give me a kind of temporary arthritis—I basically don't have the energy to control my muscles enough not to spill stuff. Aside from a few scattered eucalyptus petals, the flowers somehow hang together in a soggy cluster. I nearly topple over as I reach down to salvage them. Once inside, I toss the tattered bouquet onto the kitchen counter and make a beeline to the toilet. The bathroom tumbles and spins. My knees buckle. Out spews a gurgling mire of hotel snacks and minibar drinks in a burning arc of relief.

A𝚃 4:30 in the afternoon, half-asleep, sweaty, and still nauseated, my phone rings. I don't recognize the number, but seeing it's a Pennsylvania area code, I answer.

"Oh, hi, Rachel, hi, it's your dad. We're at the hospital. They're taking your mother in for surgery. The doctor did a rectal exam. His finger came out all covered in cancer!"

ANNA'S JOURNAL
Thursday, April 23, 1951

My name is Anna Rubik and today is my seventeenth birthday. I live in North Charleroi, Pennsylvania, and am a Junior at Charleroi High School. I live in a crooked yellow house in between the railroad tracks and the Monongahela River, in a section of town that people around here call Lock 4. A lady from the *Pittsburgh Post-Gazette* came to speak to our class for career day a couple of months ago. She told us that if we want to be writers, we need to write every day. A dream journal is one way to go about it, she said. But she also told us that reporters must never make things up. Since I want to be a reporter more than anything, I've decided only to write what I know to be true. I'm trying to answer, factually, all the W's that she told us about. I have the who, the what, the when, and the where down, even the how. The last W is hard. The lady said that sometimes we never know why things happen. She said that the journey of trying to find out, though, can be more important than the destination.

For "why", I suppose what I could write is why I spent the last few months at West Penn Hospital, and why I missed so many days of school. The headaches, of course, and the dizzy spells, too, but it started before all that. One day a few years ago —around the time of my thirteenth birthday—my legs became twisted, and my body shook. Something sucked me inwards like a tuft of dust into a vacuum hose. Afterward, silence. My legs were like noodles, twisted, like I said, and I could hardly walk. Panicked. Paralyzed. Ashamed. Was it a seizure like Mother sometimes has? Mother takes medicine for them. She says she had her first one when she was pregnant with me, as if it's my fault. I wish I had someone to blame for mine.

If I had seen it coming, I would have had someone tie me to a chair the way they did to Lon Chaney in *The Wolf Man*.

"Even a man who is pure in heart and says his prayers by night; May become a wolf when the wolfsbane blooms and the autumn moon is bright."

Odd, the things I remember without even trying.

I think maybe God is mad at me about the twisting and the shaking in my legs. In between my legs. I can't explain it, but it feels Wrong, to the point of sinful, which is why I've been avoiding church. I don't want to be in a fight with God, but He started this. Though, refusing to go to school, to church, might be making it worse. The doctor told me that I am not having seizures, and that nothing is wrong with my legs. He didn't understand, and I was too embarrassed to explain about touching myself. That was between me and God, so I let the doctor concentrate on my headaches instead. I still get them, but they aren't as bad as before, and they said I'll be well enough to return to school in the fall. Hopefully, God will have forgiven me by then. Mother gets furious when I refuse to attend mass. I don't dare tell her why.

"I don't need to go," I say. "I've done nothing wrong."

Though, I have, of course. Mother senses it and wants me to confess to Father Galas—tell him all my secrets. *Mea culpa, mea culpa, mea maxima culpa.* I can't.

The problem with my legs—the twisting, the weakness—that's why I wound up at West Penn. My headaches, too, of course. Dizzy spells. All of it. They took x-rays, but I don't remember much about that. It doesn't matter. They said I'm well now and will have all summer to rest.

About the same time as when the twisting started, a girl in my class named Margaret died from the Donora Death Smog. They said she had been visiting relatives in Donora. It's not far —only a couple of stops upriver on the Interurban trolley—but I've never been to Donora, and I don't understand what happened there. I only know Father stayed home from his job at the steelworks on account of the poison air. He said that it was so thick people couldn't escape. Drivers couldn't see. Margaret is the only one I knew, but lots of other people died there as well. How many, I don't recall, but the newspaper said the town ran out of caskets. They ran out of flowers, too. It went on for days until the rains finally arrived on Halloween night to settle the smog.

Margaret didn't die right away, but the smog stayed in her lungs, and she never returned to school. Everyone in my class assumed she'd been plucked from the earth by the hand of God.

My classmates must think of me that way now, as well, since I missed many months of school—plucked from the earth. I have to repeat Junior year, but maybe that's okay. I can reinvent myself in September and become someone new for a whole new class—the person I want to be. Maybe even popular.

Esther bought this journal for me last weekend at the stationery shop in Charleroi to celebrate my release from West Penn. As you enter Charleroi, there's a sign along the road that says, *Welcome to the Magic City*. Esther said it out loud, practically singing, as we passed. I told her I wanted to live in the Magic City rather than Lock 4. Walter and Esther live in Coal Center, but Esther thinks it's an ugly name and likes to tell people she's from the next town over—Daisytown. She thinks it's okay for me to say I'm from The Magic City if that's what I want to do—the same way she tells people she's from Daisytown. But, since I'm sticking to the facts, I live in Lock 4.

Esther is my sister-in-law. She's a lot older than me but not as old as my brother, Walter. He's twenty-six—nearly ten years older than I am. My other brother, Frederick, is old, too. Twenty-four now, which makes me feel like an only child. Walter left home when I was seven. Frederick got drafted not long after that, so in a way, I was an only child for a little while. But Frederick moved back home when he got out of the Army. While he was away, Father rented part of our house to Mr. and

Mrs. Demski, though, which left Frederick without a bed. Now he sleeps on the davenport in the living room. Frederick resents me for it, but it's not my fault. Mr. And Mrs. Demski are from Poland, like Father, so Father will never ask them to leave.

Mother is from Austria, but she speaks a little Polish, too. Mostly when she is telling Father something she doesn't want me to understand, which has been happening more and more.

The lady from the newspaper told us if we want to write, it's good to read a lot, too. So, after we went to the stationery shop, Esther took me to the library, and I borrowed a book. It's called *Cheaper by the Dozen*. I saw the movie, so I know it's about a big family, which I guess is why I borrowed it. I wish I had a bunch of brothers and sisters—or at least one or two near my age. Maybe then I wouldn't be so lonely. Honestly, I don't remember much about the movie, because I'm still foggy and my mind wanders. The facts are that I enjoyed it.

Watching movies is my favorite thing to do. I'm going to watch a movie on TV called *Caravan* tonight. I love my movie magazines. It was reading about the stars in Hollywood that made me want to be a reporter. I plan to move to Hollywood and write for *Modern Screen* or *Screenland* someday. It's been hard to read the stories lately, though, so I've mostly just been looking at the photographs. If you study the pictures hard enough, you can almost imagine them talking to you.

Well, I think that's good enough for my journal's first entry. Writing makes me tired, but I'm determined to do it as often as I can from now on.

A STUDIO VIST
August 29, 2011

I'm about to press the buzzer, but a couple of guys on their way out of the building let me in. A rickety freight elevator jostles to a stop on the third floor. The doors squeal open—fluorescent lights spastically strobe and buzz in a struggle to illuminate the dim hallway. My boots echo as I follow the thick smell of linseed oil and turpentine toward intense white light spilling from an open door. There he is, alone in his studio, sitting on a paint-splattered folding chair, swirling a few drops of red wine in the bottom of a plastic cup.

It must be satisfying for Eric to watch me come crawling back to him for a change. When he looks up, however, his expression is impossible to read. Is he happy to see me? Do I kiss him? Shake his hand?

I step inside and greet him with a meek wave.

"Thought that was you," he says. "Recognized the clack of your boot heels coming down the hall."

He was listening for me, I realize. "Lots of people wear boots."

"Lots of people don't come around so late."

"There were plenty of people here to let me in. You should tell your building mates to be careful whom they allow safe passage."

"I'll put up a sign with your picture on it."

"Make sure it's a pretty one."

"I have a lot of those." It's hard for him to admit he is happy to see me, but I know he's been waiting for me to come.

"Thanks for the flowers," I say. "They were beautiful. There's still one bloom left."

I want to apologize for emptying out the minibar. Still, it's better not to mention it in case he doesn't believe I did it alone.

He refills his cup from a bottle resting on a card table. I hunt for a clean cup amid a mess of cracker crumbs and cheese husks, and he fills my cup, too.

It wasn't so long ago I helped Eric find this place. He was skeptical when I told him I'd seen a listing for a workspace in Chinatown—he thought Manhattan would be too expensive. But, when we came to look at it, he decided it was perfect and signed a six-month rental agreement on the spot. As soon as Eric had completed a few canvasses, we gave the studio walls a fresh coat of Gallery White, clipped spotlights to the overhead pipes, and set a date for his first show. This is his second one since then, and a lot more paintings are hanging on the walls this time. Landscapes, mostly—images culled from his childhood home in northern Michigan. Up North, he calls it. Many of the scenes could just as easily be drawn from my own childhood home in Daisytown. The grasshoppers, the fireflies, the bees. Dysfunction lingering longingly around the linseed and the colored paste, like a masher at a lace bra.

Trying to maintain an air of nonchalance, I stroll the perimeter.

"Sell anything yet?"

"One," he says.

He shakes open a trash bag and begins sweeping crumbs into it using a postcard invitation. When he's done sweeping, he tosses the stack of remaining postcards into the trash, too.

"I can't do this anymore, Rachel," he says.

What does he mean? Us? Our relationship? The way we continuously try to pick up as if nothing's wrong?

"I don't have the showmanship for the art world," he says. "I never did."

I'm relieved to realize he's not talking about us after all. Then again, our relationship might be something he's already given up on—old news, not worth mentioning. I crush my cup and toss it into the bag.

"No one wants to see this earnest bullshit," he says, waving dismissively at his work. "People want brightly-colored jokes. Pop culture references. One-liners, punch lines, comicbooks. John Currin, Eric Fischl, Jeff Koons. Half the time I can't tell if I'm in a gallery or a toy store."

As he launches into the same post-show rant as last time, my eyes drift to one of his paintings—a figure, seen from behind, walks a sandy path through a grove of scrub pines. A blue heron is loping in the distance. "This is new," I say, walking up to it and leaning in for a closer look. "Is that me?"

It turns out the painting is so new that it's still wet and smudges when I absentmindedly graze it with my fingertip.

"It *was* you," he says, softly—admonishment tempered with something I can't identify, something akin to pride.

He hands me a cocktail napkin, and I rub the bit of oil paint from my finger.

"I should have warned you that I was working until the last minute. Nothing is dry."

An apology wedges in my throat like a bite-sized lump of leather-hard clay.

He retrieves a paintbrush from a footlocker in the corner of the room and carries it to the painting.

"I wouldn't care so much," he says, "but it's the one I sold." He pauses, his brush hovering above the canvas, studying my fingerprint. He tilts his head to the left, then to the right. "I think you made it better."

Abandoning the touch-up, he crosses the room and returns the paintbrush to the locker. The lid drops with a thud.

"Listen," I say, continuing to wipe my finger long after it's clean. Out, out, like Lady Macbeth. "I need to ask for a favor."

"How much do you need?" he says.

I wasn't expecting to be so transparent.

"I'll pay you back," I say. "You know I will."

"What do you need it for?"

"It's my mom…"

He doesn't wait for me to say anything more before pulling a wad of cash from his pocket. "I suppose that painting you smudged is a collaboration, now, right? It's only right to share the profits." He laughs and begins to divide the cash but stops himself. "On second thought, take it all. Consider it an advance payment for the bowls you promised."

I don't remember promising him anything. But it's gratifying to know that anyone is interested in my pottery—even someone who may or may not be more interested in me than the work itself. I haven't sold a piece of fired clay in over a year. Could be it's because I haven't fired a piece of clay at all in over a year, though there is a back catalog of unsold pieces that the studio's owner has been storing for me as a courtesy until I can afford to pay rent again. Nothing like the early pieces Eric likes so much, unfortunately. After I'd given him one of the first pieces I ever made—a small bowl with a messy glaze—he asked me to create a whole set in the same style. I remember saying I'd try, but it was hardly a promise and I never got around to it.

"I don't know when I'll have time," I say. "I have this family shit going on."

"Understood. No rush. But that's the deal, okay?"

"I don't even have access to my workspace anymore."

It would be better to owe money—with interest, yet—but either way, cash or ceramics, it will take forever to pay him back. He must realize this.

"Take it," he says, wagging the bills at me.

I try to gauge how much it is.

"Six hundred and fifty bucks," he says as if reading my mind. "More than enough for a plane ticket."

I wave it off. "My ceramics aren't worth that much."

"Okay," he says, feathering the bills and plucking out a fifty like a flower petal. "Minus what you owe me for the minibar."

He loves me. He loves me not.

ANNA'S JOURNAL
Thursday, March 5, 1953

All I think about is Stewart. He must be wondering where I've been. Did he try calling? Now that I'm home, I hope he tries again. I'd dial him myself, but Mother will throw a fit if she catches me on the phone. It's infuriating how she forbids me from placing long-distance calls and only allows me to use the telephone while supervised. I've graduated high school! I'm not a child. And what good is a supervised call anyway, when Stewart is the only one I want to talk to? I wouldn't have anything if it weren't for him.

A letter has no guarantee of reaching him, either. Mother tore the previous one from my hand and burned it on the stove. It used to be merely the phone bills that upset her, but now she doesn't want me contacting Stewart in any way. A new letter may get burned, too, but I'm trying not to care anymore. Soon enough, I will be moving to Washington, DC, where I'll be entirely free to do as I please. At long last.

It's frustrating to be moving further away from Stewart than I already live. Still, I have found a good-paying job that should allow me to save money to move to Los Angeles by winter. The position is nothing glamorous—not a newspaper job, as I had hoped. I'll merely be a typist. Nevertheless, I'm tickled thinking about finally setting out on my own.

Father tells me spring is beautiful in DC and wonders if I won't find a husband amid the cherry blossoms. A "career man," he says. Father is so clueless about my devotion to Stewart. He tries to ignore it whenever Stewart's name comes up, but I can see it makes him uncomfortable. He's afraid of him. Afraid of us. Of what Stewart and I have. No one understands.

In any case, Father and Mother are both glad to see me working. Mother is worried, of course. Despite my assuring her I will be living in a women-only hotel, she still insists I come home every weekend. Eight hours on the bus, can you imagine? I will do what I can, but it's a lot to expect.

Perhaps I can persuade my roommate, Helen, to travel with me once in a while. She's a girl I met in steno class from nearby Charleroi—the "Magic City." I've always been jealous of the town's nickname, but soon I'll have no reason to be. The Capitol City will be my home. After that, the real Magic City: Hollywood!

It feels like a dream.

In the meantime, I've been biding my time with the same old routine—reading, listening to the radio, watching TV. Plus, my new favorite activity: painting!

I've been taking a painting class at the MonValley YMCA. My teacher says I have a real talent and wants me to enter an upcoming show at the Pittsburgh Arts and Crafts Center. He thinks I have a good chance at a ribbon.

His praise made a classmate of mine so jealous that she hid my tube of Prussian Blue (my favorite color), and I had to threaten her with the blunt end of my paintbrush to get it back. She refused, saying that she didn't have it and that I'd used it all up myself, but I know better.

The teacher separated us and gave me another tube of paint. The whole class has been staring at me ever since. Fortunately, I get so lost in my art that I'm usually able to ignore them.

Esther fell in love with one of my paintings in particular, so I promised to give it to her after the art show. It feels good to know she likes it. I've thought about posting one to Stewart, but I'd prefer to deliver it to him in person.

We'll see.

Saturday, after I had another nasty argument with Mother, she wanted me out of the house. When Frederick said he was going to the movies with some friends, Mother told him, "Take your sister." I don't know if Frederick was mad to have his little sister along, but he didn't seem to be. I didn't have anything nice to wear, and science fiction double features are not my type of films, but Mother insisted.

What a mistake! Though I did like Dana Wynter in *The View from Pompey's Head*, this new film of hers, *Invasion of the Body Snatchers*, was too frightening to watch. Sitting in the darkened theater, surrounded by so many silver faces staring dumbly at the glimmering screen, I wondered if some space devil hadn't snatched the souls of our entire group. I worried an alien was about to invade my body, too. I begged Frederick to bring me home, but he refused. His friends had a big laugh, which only seemed to prove my fears right: they *were* possessed. I couldn't stand it and rushed from the theater, missing the second show entirely. (*Atomic Man* was the name of it. I wouldn't have liked it.)

Outside, I became as alert as the neighbor's cat when he escapes the house. Nearly flat to the ground, I alternately crept and darted in short bursts on my way to the trolley, wary of creatures swooping down from the open skies. Even the shop window dummies were telling me to run.

Trust me, it was a long journey home.

It will be some time before I'm ready to leave the house again. Mother pitched a fit when I refused to go to church the following day. She called me a sinner. Maybe I am, but what does she know about it?

I must find my way to California to be with Stewart before I burst. I've already fallen behind schedule because of being sick. More headaches and occasional dizzy spells. Mother has long accused me of making up my problems to duck out of chores, but she must believe me now—I've been in the hospital twice already. The only thing that makes me feel good is knowing the delays are over and I'm on my way. Soon, I'll be with Stewart. That's all I need.

It's getting late, and Frederick told me to shut off the TV set. He hates when I leave it on after the programs have signed off for the night. But I find the dancing snow comforting. The soft breath of its static, too—as if Stewart is here beside me, whispering my name, just as he did on the day we met.

My window curtain is glowing as bright as the TV screen. I just now peeled it aside and found a full moon shining perfectly round like a miner's headlamp, the trees casting shadows as crisp as a summer afternoon.

Honestly, it may as well be the afternoon, the way I'm still so wide awake.

It won't be long before the television programs return, and the first train of the morning whistles past the house. Then I will finally sleep and dream of jumping aboard one of those trains and riding it to California. Oh, the joy of a life with Stewart!

I don't know if I'll hear from him before I've settled in Washington. I don't have a phone number there yet, but I'll call him soon as I do. Meanwhile, I really must find a way to get a letter to him. It would be so lovely to have a reply waiting when I arrive at my new home. I'm absolutely breathless until then.

HURRICANE
August 29, 2011

Hurricane Irene is barreling up the coast and makes booking travel to Pittsburgh impossible. Flights are getting canceled, and bus service is spotty too. Even the subways are scheduled to shut down.

I've been on hold with Greyhound for fifteen minutes when Eric calls. He persuades me to hunker down at home until the storm passes. "They've downgraded it to a tropical storm," he says, "but it's still looking like a direct hit." He asks if I'm prepared and offers to bring me bottled water and snacks. "Maybe a flashlight, just in case."

"Beer, too," I say.

An hour later, Eric arrives with provisions and helps me move books, table lamps, and plants away from my apartment's drafty windows. By the time we're finished, tiny cyclones are already strewing trash and small tree limbs up and down the street. Outside my window, a sneaker tied to a telephone line kicks higher and higher like a kid on a swing.

"Mind if I stay until the storm passes?" Eric says.

"I think you better."

Winds ramp up and rattle the windowpanes with howling gusts. Rain blows sideways, and street lights flicker. The lights in my sublet dim sporadically, too. We know it's a bad idea to stand near the windows, but we're both transfixed.

After a while, the rains ease, and the winds stall. A faint sunbeam struggles through gauzy clouds. It seems a lot of fuss for it to be over so soon, but then Eric reminds me it's just the eye.

Neighbors from across the hall tumble down the hallway and into the street, their laughter breaking the eerie silence. Eric suggests we follow them outside, but before I pull on my boots, my phone rings.

As soon as I hear the unfamiliar voice with a too-familiar Allegheny Plateau accent on the other end, I know what she's going to say: Mom is dead.

"Your father is taking it hard," the voice tells me. "He's hysterical and upsetting the other patients."

It's easy to imagine Dad shaking and wailing, collapsing like a marionette on slack strings. I think I hear his distant voice crackle through the phone line, crying for Mom, bargaining with God. Or am I hearing my neighbors in the street? I picture Mom lying perfectly still in bed, a random television program playing in the background—weather forecasters cutting in to report on the hurricane. I want to ask the woman to put Mom on the phone—to say the things I'd been hoping to say and hear the things I'd been hoping to hear. *I always loved you, honey. I never meant all of those things I said. And did.* All of it impossible for her to say, ever, including now.

"You need to come get Homer," the voice says, again.

"I'm three hundred miles away in the middle of a hurricane," I tell her, my lungs dangling breathless like two storm-tossed plastic bags. "Have you spoken to my brother, Mike?"

"Yes, he told me he's in Arizona. He said I should call you."

"My cousin, Jack, lives nearby. I don't have his number, but my Dad should know it. Call me back if you can't get ahold of him."

As soon as we hang up, the gusty winds return and the windows clatter a nervous Morse code.

Laughter echoes in the hallway as my neighbors return from outside. Keys jangle in their lock.

Three girls live across the hall, their rooms divided by hanging bedsheets. One of them sells grey-market Xanax shipped from Pakistan, and I ask Eric to see if she has any. He comes back with two.

Water trickles in through the rotted glazing and books get wet. Eric shuffles them further into the room while I wash down one pill with a fresh can of Guinness and collapse onto the couch, prepared to devolve into mush.

Eric downs his own pill, picks a random book from the pile and settles beside me. It's a science book someone in the building had thrown away—the kind that tries to explain particle physics to people like him. I'd already read it and I flipped through the pages of the book with him for a few minutes, explaining what I'd learned. That while most particle interactions can be explained with the Standard Model theory that was developed in the 70's, what modern physics is really waiting for is a Theory of Everything that would link together all the physical aspects of the universe. Einstein's theory of relativity is a stab at it, but it focuses on gravity, the oldest known force field, while a true a Theory of Everything would pull in non-gravitational forces as well.

Looking up from the book I see Eric watching me as I ramble. He has an expression that I wish I couldn't read. I know what he wants to say. I pray that he doesn't say it, so that I don't have to say it back. *He's not even my boyfriend, I tell myself, no matter how he feels about me, I owe him nothing but ceramic bowls.* In a sort of tacit compensation, I nestle closer to him, thinking about the force fields that pull me toward then away from him. As the pill kicks in I feel my own particles begin to unravel, floating in a loose cloud like a swarm of drunken fruit flies. Will the Theory of Everything nudge Dad out of the hospital? Will some force field they haven't yet discovered or invented bring my mother back? Wherever she is, wherever *they* are. I don't even know where I am at this point. "I should have left days ago," I say.

If we had a third pill, I'd take that one, too—disperse the swarm entirely, become empty space, turn my brain off. "I can't get on a plane," I say, mumbling now.

Eric gently pats my leg, likely numb himself. "Don't worry," he says. "When the storm passes, I'll drive you to Daisytown."

I can barely nod.

WE MISS the exit and make a few wrong turns, getting us lost on the backroads for nearly an hour, looking for the only motel near Mom and Dad's house I can remember. Looming in the distance, thirty-feet above the road is a landmark: ADULT-

MART OPEN 24 HOURS. A few yards farther, a lighted sign glows dimly by the roadside: THE KING'S INN. The most important sign of all hangs blinking in the ramshackle family-owned motor park's office window: VACANCY.

Despite its stained rugs and bleach-faded bedcovers, this musty motel in the middle of nowhere turns out to be expensive. Since it's either this or a night with Dad, there's no choice.

Eric tosses the key on the table and drops onto the bed.

"Relax," he says, patting the bed, inviting me to lie down beside him.

"I need to wash my hair," I say.

He shrugs, stretches out, and turns on the television.

It takes the old set a few minutes to warm up, and, when it finally does, the picture is faint, nearly white.

A small mirror hangs over a particleboard dresser, but the lighting is so poor my reflection is just a silhouette. Turning on the desk lamp is only marginally better. I hold my hair in a ponytail, then brush it out with my fingers.

It's like I'm twelve years old, again—as if I'm fussing with the awful home perm one of Mom's church friends gave me, which left me too embarrassed to be seen at school. I remember trying desperately to tame the fried curls before the school bus arrived. When it did, Mom blocked me at the door and slathered a handful of congealed bacon grease into my hair, rubbing it in like shampoo. *You don't like your permanent? Well, how do you like it now?* Spent the rest of the day sweating under the hood of my winter coat.

Suddenly ill at the prospect of Eric meeting Mom, I have to remind myself he won't actually be meeting her at all. None of my boyfriends ever did, and now none of them ever will.

Rusty-orange water trickles from the showerhead. Feeble white suds gather around the corroded drain as I bend beneath the limp stream to rinse the shampoo from my hair. It takes forever and doesn't leave me feeling much cleaner.

By the time I dry off, Eric is sleeping. It comes so effortlessly to him. Everything does. It's annoying.

Nestled under the covers beside Eric, I surf through the TV channels and pause on a real-life mystery about a man who murdered his entire family. I watch for a minute or two but decide I better switch to cartoons.

ANNA'S JOURNAL
Friday, April 30, 1954

E xciting news! I've enrolled in modeling school here in Washington. We'll see how it goes, but I may even try the acting class they offer. Imagine me, an actress? Surely it would be better than the dreary secretarial pool where I have yet to make a single friend. Not even Helen seems to like me. When I told her that I was expecting an urgent call from Stewart in California, she snickered and wanted to know how I knew him, but I wouldn't say. I've learned no one believes it.

She's jealous, of course, like all the other girls at work. Jealous of my modeling classes now, too.

They must think I can't hear them and the awful things they say. Maybe it is a blessing, maybe it's a curse, but I hear everything. Mother is convinced I exaggerate. She says, *what other people think of you is none of your business.* She doesn't know. These women are as cruel and petty as the girls I knew in high school.

I try my best to ignore what I hear and content myself with time alone in the park or at the movies. I often watch a picture three or four times in a row and would stay longer if the theater manager let me. I saw *Salome* that way— again and again, imagining Stewart beside me in the theater the entire time, holding my hand, anticipating the plot with gentle whispers. I may go back to see it this weekend—if I can get out of bed, that is.

My sleeplessness is returning, and my days are inverted once again. Constant headaches too. When I can't sleep at night, it's as if hundreds of faces surround my bed, jockeying for my attention, fighting with each other to be heard. Every one of them has an opinion of me, and none of them is good. The worst of it is, I'm inclined to agree with them. My employers seem to agree, too. I was reprimanded by the office manager for missing so many days of work. When I do make it in, it's a struggle to stay awake.

Mother said that if my restless nights continue, I should go back to the clinic or West Penn. I can't imagine it, but if things continue this way, I may have no choice. If only to catch up on my sleep. I need to be at my best before traveling to California— to make sure these troubles don't continue to follow me. California is meant to be a clean start. The sun, the palm trees, the vast, endless ocean. A whole world for Stewart to show me.

I have never seen the ocean before, other than in the movies or on TV. A few of the girls from work went to Rehoboth Beach for a weekend, but they didn't invite me along. Well, they did, but only because Helen and I were together at the time, and it would have been awkward for them not to. They were relieved when I declined. It would have been nice to go with friends, but I would prefer to have Stewart show me the ocean for the first time rather than tag along as an afterthought with that catty bunch.

Unfortunately, I haven't managed to save any money yet, so I'm afraid I can't say when I will leave. It is hard to account for my money. All I ever do is see a movie once in a while. Modeling school, I suppose, but that's an investment. Bus rides back and forth to Pennsylvania are an expense, but I haven't been going nearly as often as Mother wants me to. Twice a month is all. I hardly eat, so that's not it. I'm beginning to suspect Helen may be a thief. I need to be on my guard. She may well be intercepting Stewart's letters, too. I really wish he would call. I am lost without him.

I shouldn't complain so much. Things are going well otherwise. I can finally focus on my future without all the fighting at home. Things are so much better than they were; there's no denying it. And when I finally move west, I will look back and laugh at all of these silly concerns.

I must be patient. I must keep faith that everything will work out as planned. God will arrange it. In the meantime, I carry Stewart's picture with me everywhere I go and pull it out whenever I feel alone. That is to say, I look at it often.

HOMECOMING

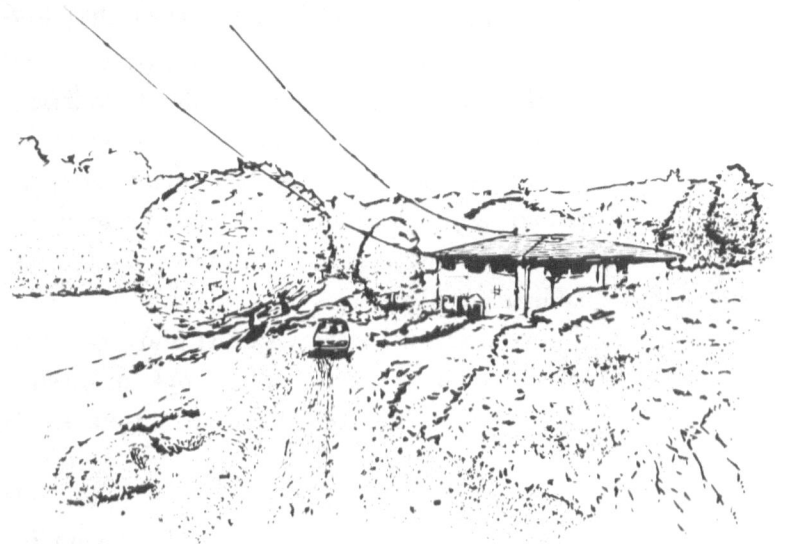

T he house in Daisytown, where I grew up, sits along a serpentine road, full of blind hills and unpatched potholes. Gravel and grit pool at the shoulders. You can practically mark the miles with roadkill—raccoons, possum, feral cats. The houses are built in clusters of two or three, separated by miles of farmland (and from what I see now, natural gas wells too). It's not the kind of road you'd want to run away from home on. I know because I've tried.

The only halfway-successful attempt I ever managed was when I took the school bus home with Lorelei, a classmate of mine. I was a depressed loner, for sure, but it wasn't as though I didn't have any friends. Lorelei was my best and closest. A loyal confidante and co-conspirator who loved helping me circumvent Mom and Dad's strict rules. "Are you sure you're listening to Christian music?" Mom once asked when I brought home an old Sony Walkman Lorelei had given me. "Yes, Mom," I said, ejecting the cassette and showing it to her. The cassette had been labeled by Lorelei with a red magic marker in bold, loopy letters: "Praise and Worship." Of course, if Mom had listened for herself, she would have heard Duran Duran, Van Halen, Talking Heads—but I knew Mom would be too afraid of getting an ear infection to put on the headphones. Unfortunately, she worried I might get an ear infection, too, and made me swab the headphones with bleach so many times they eventually stopped working. Distorted voices overlaid with static, like tuning in an overseas signal from a shortwave radio. It didn't keep me from listening, though. I listened all the time.

My plan with Lorelei seemed so easy I don't know why we hadn't thought of it sooner: When school let out for Easter break, I would ride the bus with Lorelei to her house and I'd never go home.

Unlike Mom and Dad, who scrutinized my every move, and hissed like territorial cats whenever they sensed a friend of mine draw near, Lorelei's parents were too wrapped up in their failing marriage to pay much attention to what their kid was up to. As a result, I was able to sleep at Lorelei's house a few nights in a row before Lorelei's mom even noticed me. I sat quietly, eating a bowl of Cheerios for dinner, when she finally did. When Lorelei explained my situation to her mother, the stories Lorelei told were so appalling—exaggerated, I'll admit, but not by much—that her mom was tempted to call Child Protective Services. But Mom and Dad had already figured out where I was by then, and Dad showed up at the front door. "We're going to change," Dad said. "We'll go to family counseling, things will be different, you'll see. I promise." It was all a bluff meant for Lorelei's mother, but she bought it and apologized for not contacting him right away. She whispered an apology to me, too: "Sorry, honey. If things get bad, you're always welcome here."

As I climbed into the car with Dad, I was filled with the same sense of dread as I feel right now, arriving twenty years later with Eric.

Everything is just as I remember it: the house, the hedges, the sizzle of tires rolling down the steep gravel driveway. I can't believe it's been over a decade. Although our routine of Sunday calls began about a year ago, I had yet to visit. I'd promised Mom I'd be here for Christmas. I'm early, but too late.

Feeling unprepared for my worlds to collide, I ask Eric to wait in the car while I run inside to get Dad.

The two dogs are also familiar as they scramble out the door, barking wildly and biting the air as I approach. They aren't from the same litter as the six I grew up with, but they may as well be.

Dad calls after the dogs in his usual way but, other than his voice, I barely recognize him. His head is nothing but loose skin draped over a skull, sparse thatches of colorless hair at its sides, a few wisps on top. His body, shrunken and bent into a question mark like a dried worm. When did this happen? When did he get so old?

I help corral the dogs as Dad secures them on a leash. We hug and I'm surprised to find the years have made him shorter than me.

"Your mother kept asking after you," he says.

"I'm sorry I didn't get here in time," I say.

He wipes his cheek with the back of his hand.

"She wanted to see you."

"I wanted to see her, too."

"I hoped she'd make it to the Rapture."

"We'll talk about it later, okay? We're running late. We're supposed to meet the funeral director at noon."

As he shepherds the dogs into the house, he pauses to pluck a bug off the screen door and place it gently in a bush like a sleeping baby. I've seen him squish so many insects beneath his thumb or under his shoe, it's odd to see him treat this one so gently. Almost lovingly. Turns out, it's a stink bug.

"If you squish one," he says, "the stink attracts more."

We never had a problem with stinkbugs that I can remember, and Dad explains they've been making a slow march from the south since the time I left home. Now they are legion. Like a Biblical infestation. An early sign of the Apocalypse. One of many.

"I can't find my car keys," Dad says, patting his pockets as he circles through every room. "I lose things all the time, Rachel, all the time."

"Forget about your keys, Dad, Eric will drive us. He's waiting in the car."

"Who's that?"

I realize I don't know what Eric's title is. And that I hadn't told Dad I'd be bringing someone. I never expected I would.

"Rachel, I need to take my car."

"You're in no condition to drive."

His damp cheeks balloon out and then pucker in like a sock puppet.

"Of course I am," he says. "How do you think I've been getting around? Besides, you have to stay here with the dogs."

"Forget about the fucking dogs for once."

"I told you I don't want to hear you using that word. It's awful, just awful. What happened to you?"

"Dad... Dad...We don't have time for this. We'll leave the dogs here for now. They'll be fine."

"We'll take them with us," he says. "Leave them in the car is what we'll do."

"It's a hundred degrees outside. You can't leave the dogs in the car."

Why is it perfectly okay to leave the dogs in a hot car but not the house? We could argue about it all day. Except we can't; we don't have time. As it is, I have to wait for Dad to use the bathroom. Twice.

When he's finally ready, I see a paper towel poking out of his trousers.

"I have seepage," he explains, tucking the paper under his waistband.

"Okay, never mind, I don't need to know about it. Let's get going."

Watching Dad load the dogs into the backseat of his car, I lose the will to argue.

I call out to Eric. "Come on, my dad is driving."

Eric climbs out of his car and gets into the backseat of Dad's, alongside the dogs.

"I've told you about Eric before, right?" I say, even though I'm sure I never have.

"I don't remember, Rachel. I told you I have Alzheimer's."

When did Dad turn into a medical professional with an opinion? Whatever is wrong with Dad, it isn't Alzheimer's. Not yet, anyway.

Preparing to back out of the driveway, Dad looks over his shoulder and asks Eric if he is my boyfriend. Caught off guard, Eric doesn't know what to say, as I didn't. It's a tricky question these days. Still, Dad is confused enough without adding our own confusion to the mix, so I interject with the simplest answer—Yes—and toss Eric a shrug. Eric is pretending to be too busy fighting off the dogs to notice.

Once underway, it's as if we are tuning in mid-broadcast to a Sunday radio program.

"Jesus used to talk to me all the time," Dad says. "I would hear him clear as day—the way you and I are talking now. Flashes of light and tingles up my spine—that always meant Jesus was about to speak. But it don't happen no more. That's not to say I don't talk to him. I'd been praying he would take me before he called your mother home. I don't want to live without her..."

As he speaks, the car drifts from one side of the street to the other, going too slow when the road is straight, too fast around the bends.

"Careful, Dad!"

"I'd always planned to be with your mother for the Rapture," he says. "We were supposed to get called up together. When the preacher predicted the world would end in the year two-thousand, I never left your mother's side in case I had to grab her hand. I can't get to Heaven any other way..."

"Focus on the road, will you please? You're going to get us killed."

We park under a tree, and Eric offers to wait outside with the dogs, so they don't die in the heat. More likely, he wants an excuse to be alone. Not that I blame him. Fifteen minutes with Dad is a lot.

A DOZEN CASKETS clutter the dim wood-paneled showroom. Somber grey carpet deadens the sound, but Dad's reedy voice still carves a crisp line through the still air.

"Peggy told me not to take out any loans," he says. "She's going to pay for everything."

Aunt Peggy is married to Uncle Nick, who lives, basically, next door, while Peggy lives hundreds of miles away from him in Arlington, where she works as an insurance adjuster. She says she and Uncle Nick can't divorce because she's Catholic, but I suspect it has more to do with the survivors benefits from Uncle Nick's police and military pensions she's expecting to get. She must be furious Mom died before Uncle Nick did.

I suggest we call Aunt Peggy to be sure she wasn't just speaking from the bottom of a wine box, but Dad is adamant.

"She's on her way from Virginia right now with her checkbook. That's what she told me."

Dad says this over and over as the funeral director threads a meandering course through the maze of caskets. He describes all the available options, explaining every possible combination. It feels as if we're car shopping.

When we hit an inexpensive and understated model with simple, clean lines, I ask Dad what he thinks.

"That's fine for a man," he says, running his fingers along the casket's open edge, but he prefers the one next to it. "Now, *this* is beautiful."

It's a steel casket, airbrushed pink and rose gold, lined with yards of pink frosted crepe. There is a cartoonish pink rose embroidered on the lid's lining. The whole thing is small enough to be a salesman's sample and appears to be designed for a five-year-old beauty pageant contestant. Despite how thin and frail Dad says Mom became, I can't imagine she would fit inside of it.

Clued to Dad's taste, the Funeral Director leads us to a top-end casket made of mahogany and lined with maroon silk.

Across the underside of its lid is a gold sash embroidered with a huge white cross.

"It's too expensive," I say, thinking this should be obvious.

Dad stiffens. "I told you, Peggy will pay."

"All the more reason not to go overboard."

"But I want Dorothy to have a nice casket. I know she's in heaven, I know it's just her body, but I still want her to have a nice casket."

While I try to steer him toward something more realistic, Eric comes inside.

"Where are the dogs?" Dad says.

Eric tells him not to worry, that he cracked open all the windows, and there's a gentle breeze under the tree.

Although Dad claims he leaves the dogs in the car himself, he is horrified and runs outside to check on them.

I seize the opportunity to get Eric's opinion. "You're the only one thinking straight," I say.

"Am I?"

Eric talks it over with the funeral director, and together they negotiate a reasonable price for a middle-of-the-road number. The best-seller, we're told.

True or not, it looks good to me, and, once Dad returns, the funeral director and I work on persuading him that it's the best option.

"I guess so," Dad says. "What do you think, Ernie?"

"Eric, Dad. His name is Eric."

"It's perfect," Eric says.

I'm prepared for deliberations to continue for at least another twenty minutes if not all day, but for some reason "Ernie"'s opinion seems to carry weight.

The funeral director leads us into his office to take care of the paperwork.

"All perfectly standard," he assures us, sliding a small stack of papers across his desk.

After Dad signs the pages, and initials them in a half-dozen spots, the Funeral Director slides them in front of me and indicates where he'd like me to sign, as well. As if I am a reliable alternative, should Dad fall through with his payments. It's hard not to laugh. Sure, Dad is dirt poor, but at least he owns a house. Probably not worth much more than what the funeral will cost, but it's something. What am I supposed to do, pay with ceramic bowls?

I sign, anyway, and once everything is settled, I get on the phone with Aunt Peggy to give her the grand total: six-thousand, nine-hundred dollars and change.

Even though Aunt Peggy earns more money than anyone else in our family and likes to imagine herself as its grand matriarch, she is stunned.

"I don't have that kind of money," she says. "Two thousand dollars is the best I can do."

I'm not surprised and hang up to give Dad the bad news.

"I don't understand," he says. "Peggy said not to worry."

"Well, unless you're willing to reconsider cremation, it looks like you'll need a loan after all."

The funeral director says we have time to figure it out. He even offers an extended payment plan. "But the gravediggers need their money in advance," he warns. "Seven hundred and fifty dollars in cash. They won't touch a backhoe without it."

Even with the money from Eric's painting still in my pocket, that's a lot of cash. But Dad stays calm for a change and mentions an envelope hidden in his house.

"What envelope? Where did it come from?"

"Never mind," he says.

We return to the car only to discover one of the dogs—maybe both—has soiled the backseat. Dad doesn't appear surprised—he says they do it sometimes—but I'm mortified.

Using a few leaves torn from a nearby tree, I try to clean the mess. Meanwhile, Dad takes a handkerchief from his back pocket and wipes the dog's fur.

He's about to slide the handkerchief back into his pocket when, thankfully, Eric spots a grocery bag clinging to a nearby bush. "Here, put it in this."

With the car as clean as we can get it, the three of us squeeze into the front seat and head back to the house.

"Jesus don't talk to me no more," Dad says.

WHILE HUNTING for his secret stash, Dad finally explains where it came from: Mom had been saving money from her social security checks to replace the matching easy chairs in front of the television with a pair of recliners. Years of watching the Home Shopping Network, Lawrence Welk, and any number of Christian programs took its toll.

The only reason they never got around to buying the replacements is that Mom was too agoraphobic to leave the house, and she didn't trust Dad to pick something out on his own. Over time, she amassed close to a thousand dollars. Money for a place to recline after all.

Not keen on a repeat performance from the dogs, I suggest Eric stay with them at the house while I take Dad to the cemetery to deliver the money.

"I guess that'll be fine," Dad says, tentatively handing Eric the leash. "But don't let them get into nothing."

Dad walks to the driver's side of his car before I stop him and tell him I'm driving.

"You? You don't know how to drive."

He's right, more or less.

Prohibited from driving as a teen, I didn't learn until years later when I followed an old boyfriend to LA, whose car was a souped-up death trap I had no business driving. But with my shoes off, feeling the gentle resistance of the accelerator against my bare toes while bombing along the Pacific Coast Highway, I felt invincible.

That was years ago, however, and my license has long since expired. In other words, I am a rusty, unlicensed driver behind the wheel of an unfamiliar and equally rusty car. I feel anything but invincible. But it will take a lot more than that to make me a worse driver than Dad. "Trust me," I say, "I know how to drive."

AT THE CEMETERY, Dad gives me a tour of the family graves, pointing out his parents' headstones—two grandparents I never knew—and finding those belonging to a few of his siblings as well.

A couple of yards away, I spot Mom's parents. If it hadn't been for Grandma and Papa, I likely would have killed myself years ago, and I feel obliged to pay my respects.

I think of Grandma, rocking me in her lap, singing Hungarian lullabies. And of Papa, my true savior. I could always escape to his garden and help him thin the corn, plant beans, or pick tomatoes. In the off season, we would sit and watch professional wrestling through the static of his TV. He would leap from his chair and shake his fist at Andre the Giant, or Jake the Snake, yelling in his thick accent, "You dirty rotten animal!" Mike and I would roll on the floor laughing. My last visit home was for Papa's funeral. Not much reason to visit after that.

Dad is calling to me. "Over here Rachel, over here." He is pointing to the far end of four adjacent plots. "This is where your mother will go," he says as I approach. "And that one is yours."

Under different circumstances, I'd tell him I'd rather have my ashes flushed down a toilet, but all I say is that he should sell my plot. "I'm not going to use it," I say. "And you need the money."

"I don't want to be buried next to some stranger!" he says. "Though, I suppose if you and Eric get married, he'll be the boss of you, and he might want you buried somewhere next to him. I might not need mine, either. Not if the Rapture comes. We'll see. Are you and Eric getting married?"

He doesn't give me time to think about it, much less answer.

"I would like you to give me grandkids," he says. "There's Alexander, but I never see him. You know how they are. You'd do a better job. You don't have much time. Maybe it's too late already. Your kids could come out retarded, like your nephew."

"Dad, what have I told you a million times about using that word?" Blunt, and Mike's kid Alexander is merely "on the spectrum" and responding to treatment, last I heard, but Dad has a point. Getting too old to have a kid doesn't bother me, though. What bothers me is getting old at all, with nothing to show for it. Looking at my own gravesite doesn't help.

"Let's pay the man and get going, okay? It's hot out here."

Inside the poorly lit cinderblock office, a man with a neck like a roast ham sits behind a dented steel desk chewing an unlit cigar. Dad says hello and proceeds to overshare, the way he always does. He tells the man that Mom didn't have a bowel movement in the ten days leading to her hospital stay. He explains that the doctor examined her, rectally, and said: *Cancer! She has cancer!* He describes her suffering, assisted bowel movements, and ultimate death, in lurid detail.

"I have to wear paper towels in my underwear," he says out of the blue. "And I can't hold my urine, either."

He mentions wearing a penis clamp and claims, falsely, again, that he has Alzheimer's. The man rocks back and forth and listens politely as if he's heard it all before. If he's ever met Dad, he probably has.

"Do you have the money?" I say.

Dad has been carrying the envelope in a folder filled with paperwork, but when he opens the folder, the envelope isn't there. He lets out a yelp and dashes out of the office to retrace his steps. Darting from headstone to headstone like a spooked rabbit, his hands raised, praying to God, he pleads for the Lord to give him his money back. One of the groundskeepers pulls next to us in a rusting pickup truck and asks what we're doing. It must look as though Dad is the priest of an exotic cult, trying to raise the dead. When we tell the groundskeeper what happened, he plucks an envelope from the truck's visor and holds it up. "Like this?"

Dad squeals with relief.

"Found it over there," the groundskeeper says, pointing in the direction of the family plot.

Dad drops to his knees. "Thank you, Jesus, thank you, thank you."

"God was with you today," the groundskeeper says as he hands me the envelope.

"Don't encourage him," I mutter, as I count it to be sure it's all still there.

ANNA'S JOURNAL
Saturday, June 9, 1955

I thought of Frederick the other night when I heard the whistle of a distant train. The cry grew louder and louder until it barreled through my skull, ear to ear, and I was swaddled in billows of thick white smoke. The smoke lifted me and carried me behind the train as it trundled along the tracks bordering our front yard.

Passing our crooked yellow house, I noticed Mother outside, tending her precious roses. I called to her through the smoke, but she didn't turn around.

Frederick was there, too, my dear brother, standing and waving as the train carried me farther up the riverside, through heavy woods and rocky hillsides, past the great mills and coal tipples, northward to Donora. *"Next to yours, the friendliest town in the USA."*

All these years later and I'm still afraid of Donora. Yet, there I was, heading straight into the Death Smog.

The train stopped, and a carpet of smoke laid me on the platform, surrounded by gray silhouettes, the poison air drifting down and draping me in a blanket of death.

In the last second, before I succumbed, I woke and thought I saw Frederick's face, friendly and familiar, looking over me. But it wasn't him, it was a doctor.

"How are you feeling?" the doctor said.

I wasn't feeling anything.

Frederick is set to visit me this weekend with Mother. I've asked him bring me my journal. Loose pieces of paper such as this are too hard to keep organized. And I'm certain writing in my journal will help in my effort to mend my memory—a way to restructure my thoughts and shore up my life. I can't remember exactly where I've hidden the journal, but I'm certain Frederick will find it. If not, I've asked if he will buy me a new one. It seems to be what people want from me, anyway—to start clean.

I suppose it's what I want too, although it's hard to say. The past few days, I haven't wanted anything other than to lie in bed and listen to my heartbeat. Sometimes it nearly bursts my eardrums with each ferocious beat. Other times it's as quick and faint as a baby bird's.

However, like the twitching leg of a squashed bug, something moved in me today, and rather than listen to my heart, I sat up to write for the first time—not the very first time, of course. Still, I must say, that's how it feels. And now, writing is once again all I want to do.

Writing these few lines is helping, already, because I suddenly remember walking past Mother's roses before getting in the car to come to this place. The memory is a delicate one, and if I think too hard on it, it slips away, but it's a start.

Mother told me the doctors would attend to the continued

clanging in my head. At times, I swear it felt like the entire steel mill where Father and Frederick work was bashing, smoking, and sparking in my poor skull. (How can they bear to work in that place?)

"They will take x-ray pictures and find the cause," Mother said.

Did I receive them? Are x-rays like a freight train through the skull? Like the atomic bomb from the war, flattening everything in my head with the enormous power of a white-hot plume? Will it cure my headaches? And the weakness in my legs I've been too embarrassed to talk about?

Whatever they did, my head doesn't ache anymore, but now it feels as though it's filled with river stones. I wasn't expecting to feel this way. Perhaps there's some truth to what Mother says —that I'm too sensitive. I was only meant to be here one day, but it's been at least a week, maybe longer, and I'm still recovering. They say I'm doing well, but I'm getting impatient. I have things to do! If I had my way, I'd have no need for my journal after all, and when Frederick comes to see me, it will be to take me home. I pray that it's true. If not, I'll need to ask another favor of him. Stewart has invited me to live with him in California, and I intend to go as soon as I can arrange it. However, he won't know about my recent troubles and may well be trying to reach me. I need to get word to him so that he knows my circumstances. Stewart needs to know I haven't forgotten him. When Frederick looks for my journal, I'll have him search through my movie magazines where I've hidden drafts of my letters. Perhaps he can find Stewart's phone number there for me. Frederick must promise not to read anything I've written!

And Frederick must promise not to tell Mother what he's up to either. She is so determined to keep Stewart and me apart and will tell Frederick all sorts of lies. I've discovered Mother can be quite persuasive. Frederick best keep his mission a secret from Father, too. Although Father only seems upset by the cost of my long-distance phone calls, it is best not to risk getting him involved. Can Frederick be trusted? What choice do I have?

The nurse here, Nurse Winthrop, has just now arrived to get me out of bed and take me outside. Not long, just enough to stretch my weak legs and get a lungful of fresh air on the way to the dining room for supper.

The property here is quite beautiful—rolling fields of farm-land sprawling endlessly into the sun. But I feel so weak and exposed under the cloudless expanse of sky. If they'd let me, I'd find a quiet corner inside, draw the curtains, and read or write all day and night. But they won't allow it and are quite insistent. Perhaps if I had my paints, I'd feel differently about stepping outside. Maybe Frederick can bring those as well? If they'll allow me to have them, that is. I don't see why not. A little painting will surely help in my recovery.

Nurse Winthrop is getting impatient, so that's all for now.

FUNERAL

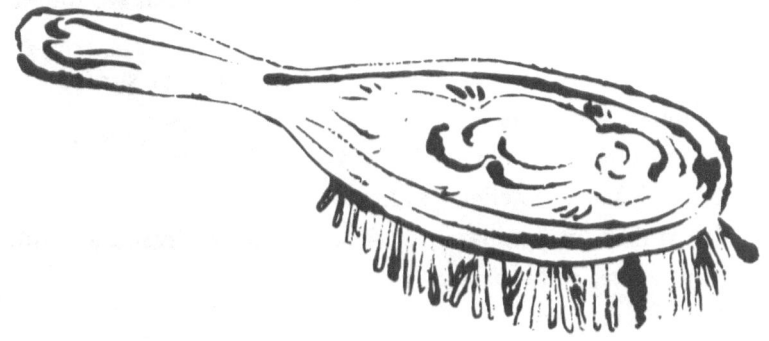

We arrive early at the funeral home to discuss last-minute concerns with the funeral director. Dad pulls a hairbrush from a paper bag and asks for it to be placed inside Mom's coffin. I can't tell if it's the same hairbrush I remember—the one with the metal prongs—but it would still hurt if you got hit with it, and it's disturbing to allow Mom eternal access.

The director assures Dad he'll see to it and, after glancing at his watch, suggests we spend a few private moments with Mom before the mourners arrive.

As the Funeral Director walks away, I consider following him to get the brush back, but when I see Mom's elaborate wig, I stop myself. She'll need it.

Wig, makeup, mauve-colored press-on nails—it's my first-time seeing Mom in years, but I'm sure she never looked this way. Nothing left of the cruel mother who wielded the brush, scarcely a wisp of the sweet mother who shared her recipes. Just a shell—a hollow Easter egg. As a result, I find it impossible to cry, though I was never sure I would. More surprising, Dad doesn't cry either, only reaches out to touch Mom's waxy hands, as if hoping for a last chance on a plus-one to Heaven.

But, if Mom does float away, it's not clear where she'll wind up. And, during our final phone conversation, Mom wondered about it, too.

"Even if the Rapture came this second, I'm not sure I'd be called home," she'd said.

"Why would you say that?"

"Oh, you know, Rachel, you know…"

She trailed off, apparently wanting me to respond with something like, Yes, I know.

But I didn't. I waited.

"I was a toughie," she finally said, almost in a whisper.

Far short of an apology, but it only takes a centimeter of continental drift for the world to shake. I couldn't bring myself to absolve Mom, however, if that's what she wanted. I couldn't bring myself to say anything at all.

Aunt Peggy and Uncle Nick are the first to arrive—still rather affectionate, considering their circumstances. Behind them are Jack and Maggie and their little boy, Owen. Uncle Nick is helped along by each of them in turn. Maggie helps Nick from the car, Peggy helps him along the cement path, and Jack helps him up the stairs, while Owen darts in and around them all like an untrained miniature shepherd.

"I still can't believe how much this is costing," Aunt Peggy says to me without first saying hello.

I ignore her and greet the rest of the clan. Although Mom had told me Uncle Nick was failing, he's far worse than I expected. The Uncle Nick I knew had been a DC cop and, before that, a Marine. He could be just as overbearing and controlling as Mom, and at six-two, 240 pounds, he was even more terrifying. Thankfully, he never hit me the way Mom did —despite plenty of opportunities while I was living with him and Aunt Peggy in Arlington. Occasionally, Uncle Nick even slipped me a twenty-dollar bill.

Living with them wasn't ideal. But at least the mattress on the floor of Maggie's room was more comfortable than the random squat floors and park benches I'd been sleeping on in Pittsburgh. I hadn't spoken with Mom or Dad in over a year at the time, and regardless of whether or not they'd given up on me, I'd given up on them. I needed to escape Pittsburgh, and without money or means, Arlington had been my only real option. Who knows, I might have stayed longer if it hadn't been for Aunt Peggy's aggressive effort to mold me in all the ways Mom had tried and failed.

"You're going out like that?" Peggy would say whenever I left their house to catch the Metro to DC to sneak into bars and clubs.

A change of clothes could only mean taking off a pair of black Capri tights and pulling on a torn pair of fishnets, but, regardless, the conversations were always the same.

"Wear a bra, at least."

"What's the point? I don't have anything to support. You told me so yourself."

"Maybe, but it's only because you're so skinny. You don't eat enough."

"I eat plenty."

"I don't like to imagine what kind of trouble you're getting into when you stay out all night."

"I'm not getting into any trouble."

Not true, of course. I was getting into the same trouble I got into in Pittsburgh. It was the same trouble I'd eventually get into in New York.

"Tomorrow, I'm taking you to the Dress Barn," Peggy said when she'd finally had enough. "I'm going to buy you a nice suit so you can look for a decent job. Then I expect you to start paying rent."

Eventually, I did find a halfway decent job. And I did start paying rent. Only not in Arlington, and not to Aunt Peggy.

I say hello to Uncle Nick and give him a kiss on the cheek, but I'm not sure he recognizes me. Even after everyone takes turns explaining who I am into his one working ear, he still looks befuddled.

Dad's sister Norma and her children and grandchildren arrive, with a couple of neighbors behind them. Then a handful of people Mom knew from church. Finally, Mike shows up. Even though his hair has been replaced by shimmering beads of sweat and his Army dress uniform is cluttered with more flash and stripes than I remember, he's still easy to spot. Without a hug, kiss, or even a handshake, we say hello. I introduce him to Eric, who appears to have forgotten I have a brother—if he ever knew in the first place. The two of them nod to each other and shake hands.

"Where's Dad?" Mike says.

"Over there."

Dad stands restlessly next to the open casket babbling all sorts of gory details to anyone who will listen. Mike heads over, but his patience with Dad is even shorter than mine and, after a few minutes, Mike excuses himself to make the rounds. When Eric walks off to use the bathroom, I invite Dad to a downstairs coffee room.

"I can't," Dad says. "Someone will come, and they won't know where I am."

"We'll only be a minute."

I steer him down the narrow staircase to a small, paneled room.

Beneath a couple of framed historical photos from the Pennsylvania Railroad is a Formica countertop with two pots of coffee sitting on side-by-side warmers. One of the pots may be decaf, but there is no way to tell. I pour some into a Styrofoam cup and hand it to Dad. It is scalding, but he gulps it in a series of frenetic sips.

"Easy, Dad, you'll burn yourself."

"Someone might come, and they won't know where I am."

"You keep saying that. Who are you expecting?"

"I don't know. An old school friend, maybe."

"No one will leave without seeing you. Drink your coffee."

It's useless. Dad's brain spins so fast it bends time. My thirty seconds are his twenty minutes. He takes three more panicky sips before handing me his cup and racing upstairs. It occurs to me he wants to stay near Mom's hand, just in case.

I follow him back upstairs and scan the small crowd, searching for Eric. As I do, someone strolls up beside me and puts his arm around my waist.

"Rachel, beautiful Rachel," he says, squeezing me tightly before I shimmy loose and turn to see it's Reverend Furman. "How long has it been?"

His slick hair is dyed the color of walnuts, and he smells of drug store cologne and cigarettes. However, I only smell it briefly before his wife's perfume rolls in like a mountain fog. She's well-preserved, seventy-something, in a tight sweater over a torpedo bra. False eyelashes, fake nails, and broad strokes of blush. I think her hair is phony, too, though it is hard to tell because of all the hairspray. Either way, it's a fire hazard. She and Reverend Furman host a Christian radio program. "Nine hours a week," they boast.

"How about you?" the reverend asks. "How's the modeling going?"

"I'm nearly forty, you know that, right?"

"Has it really been that long? Well, last I heard you had quite a career going."

I'd call it more of a stint than a career, and it wasn't anything I'd intended to do. But I've never been good with plans—especially at age twenty-four, sharing a five-hundred square-foot walkup in the East Village with two roommates who weren't good with plans either. I literally walked right into it.

I'd spent the previous twelve hours at a rave in the Meatpacking District and was overly caked-up-made-up and underdressed in an outfit I'd been wearing since Friday. While rummaging through my bag to see if I had the $1.99 for a fried egg on toast and a cup of coffee at La Bonbonniere, I ran headlong into Damian. (To this day, the most fastidiously groomed straight man I've ever met.) I apologized for bumping him and continued across West 12th Street.

"Hold on," he said, trotting up beside me. "Have you ever done any modeling?"

I figured it was a line—and not a very original one. Whenever I wasn't receptive to a come-on like that, whoever said it would usually have a sudden change of heart and blurt out Mom's old line: "You're not as pretty as you think you are." I braced for it.

"Seriously," he said, pulling a letterpress business card from his £3000 bespoke suit from Davies and Son on Savile Row. (I still remember where it was from and how much it cost because he wound up telling me so many times thereafter.)

As I paused on the sidewalk to read his business card, Damien, coolly professional, explained he was a modeling agent.

"Where are you headed?" he said. "Let me buy you breakfast. I'd like to talk."

Over Bloody Marys at Florent, he asked, almost as a passing courtesy, as though he cared, how old I was. I told him twenty-two. "Let's say you're twenty, a student at FIT." Besides a semester at community college and a couple of ceramics classes, I hadn't studied anything anywhere, and I was painfully self-conscious about it. "Better yet, Columbia, you're brainy." If he cared at all about my real story, he didn't ask. "Five-eight? Let's say you're five-ten."

He made it all sound like a game. Let's make a young person feel old! Let's cover up a truth I didn't even know was inconvenient! Let's turn Rachel into a hottie, on paper! Because she isn't right in real life.

(I would later discover "brainy" was just a way to avoid getting me pegged "Heroin Chic." Which is undoubtedly how Damien would have branded me if the phenomenon hadn't been on the cusp of such a huge backlash.)

"Ever been to Germany?" Damien asked.

Munich was where they sent new girls to gain "experience," he said. No, I'd never been to Germany. I'd never even been on a plane before. But nothing was holding me to New York and. before I knew it. I had a brand-new passport (my first) and an economy-class ticket on a redeye flight from JFK.

Munich, to Milan, to Paris, it's all a blur. Same routine, different languages. Regardless of what city I was in, the editors and stylists could always find something to criticize—my hair, my weight, my height. If they spoke to me at all, that is.

The only people who weren't reliably insulting were the photographers. All they ever did was snap a few pictures, say a few salacious things, and invite me to dinner. "He's well connected," Damian told me over the phone about one in particular. (Meaning I wasn't.) "Who knows, you might get him to pay for a nose job."

Nose job? No one had ever criticized my nose before—not even Mom.

Growing ever lonelier and more disillusioned, my physical insecurities at an all-time low, I was ready to return to New York. But my contract had me on the hook for all my expenses —agency commissions, rent, meals, transportation fees. Unless I could land a lucrative gig that covered all my agency's deductions, plus the cost of a plane ticket, I was stranded.

I spun my wheels for another two months before something finally came through that fit the bill: an ad for an obscure

French jeans company. It was a surprisingly fun job and almost made me change my mind about leaving, and I sometimes wonder what might have happened if I'd stuck it out a little longer. But as it was, I returned to New York precisely as I'd left it: flat broke, and alone. Are you a model? Nope.

I simply tell Reverend Furman it was a long time ago.

"You don't look forty," says his wife.

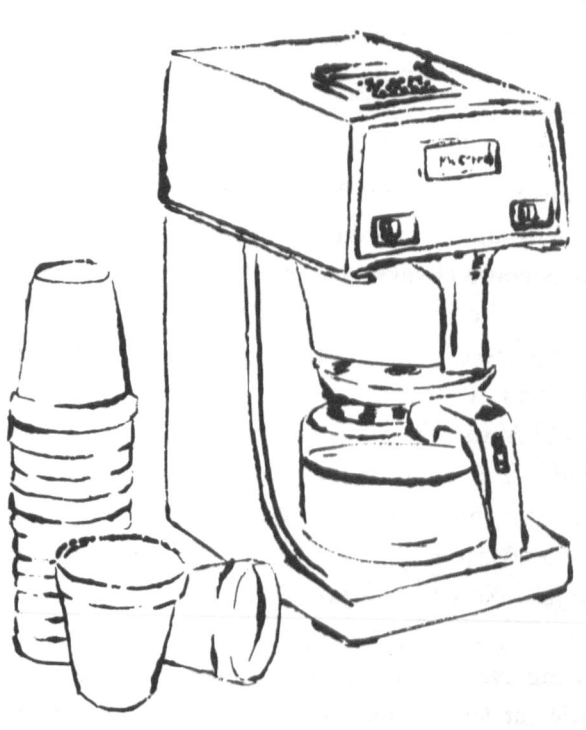

THE FUNERAL DIRECTOR shepherds the guests into a small wood-paneled side room where folding chairs are arranged around a podium.

"I'm afraid my wife and I won't be able to sing today," the reverend says from behind the podium. "We're both suffering from sore throats—have been all week. But I brought along this CD player here, and I thought we could start by playing a few of Homer's requests."

The room is so stuffy, and the CD player so underpowered, that when the preacher hits PLAY, the air barely moves.

"I invite you all to sing along," he says.

Dad's warbled notes are all I hear as Dad sways and sings, *"Just a closer walk with thee..."*

The song ends, and the reverend changes CDs.

I lean over and whisper to Eric. "After all the money Dad gave to his church over the years, he can't sing one fucking song? His voice sounds fine to me."

Eric says nothing. He rubs my back to calm me down, but it feels condescending, and I inch away.

When the last song is over, Reverend Furman positions himself behind a podium.

"Before we go any further," he says, "I'd like to ask if anyone here would like to stand and give testimony."

Dad is eager to speak, I can feel it, but he doesn't want to be the first one—certainly not the only.

"I believe a few among us may have fallen away from the church," the reverend says. "You may have gotten busy with your lives and drifted away. It happens, I know. But I look you in the eye today. I testify to you right now as an ambassador to Jesus Christ. If you pray to God with a sincere heart and ask his forgiveness, I can guarantee he will answer your prayers. If anyone wants to come up here and repent, we're here to welcome you home."

Everyone's eyes scan the room, hitting a speed bump when they get to me.

Dad has been praying for me to collapse into a puddle of contrition for years. I begin to suspect he may have conspired with Reverend Furman to put me on the spot.

Dad leans toward me and takes my hand, gives it a gentle tug as if to raise it for me, but what does he expect me to say? To speak even a single word would be like slicing open a water balloon—decades of anger, frustration, and disappointment gushing forth and drenching the room. *"And another thing..."* I hear myself saying. I'm not subtle about jerking my hand free.

At the peak of awkward silence, one of my cousins stands. "I would like to give testimony," he says.

Barrel-chested, suffering from scoliosis, he rests his weight on a crooked hip, rubs his pencil mustache, and clears his throat.

The Reverend, reluctantly it seems, turns his gaze away from me and, with a strained smile, encourages my cousin to continue.

"I'm thankful for knowing Dorothy and Homer," my cousin says, nodding toward Dad. "And I'm thankful for knowing their family, too. We never knew no sinners." He pets his mustache again and cinches his pants. "We only knew Christians. And for that, I am forever grateful."

Next, Aunt Peggy stands and reminisces about the days when she and Mom were much younger—when Mom still left the house. "We were like sisters," she says. "We had the same taste in everything. We used to love going to Scenery Hill together to shop and to look at the Christmas decorations. One of the gift shops was selling the cutest hand-painted birdhouses, and I just knew Dorothy would love them. It wasn't easy, but I managed to buy one and have it wrapped without her noticing. Come Christmas day, when we exchanged gifts, we both couldn't believe it. She had bought me the exact same one!"

The long silence makes it clear no one else has anything to say, so Dad finally stands for his turn. He draws a long breath, clasps his hands, and begins.

"Dorothy was the greatest," he says, before closing his eyes and bowing his head for a moment. He looks around the room to be sure people are listening. "First time I ever saw Dorothy was in church. She was so beautiful, I knew right away that I wanted to date her. I couldn't stop thinking about her. So, after a couple weeks, I asked her father if I could date her. But he wanted to know I was serious. Oh yes, I told him, I was never more serious about anything in my whole life. He said I seemed like a good boy and that it would be okay. So, I gave Dorothy my pin, and we started dating."

He pulls a handkerchief from his breast pocket and pats his eyes.

"At first, Dorothy would only let me kiss her once a week. Not until she turned eighteen—three days before we were married—did she say it would be okay to kiss her once a day. Every day, she let me kiss her one time. It was that way for years and years. Eventually, she didn't like it so much and would only let me kiss her once a year—on my birthday. But with her in the hospital and all, well, she was too weak to push me away no more, so I kissed her all the time. Only on her cheek so as not to make her sick, of course, or sometimes on her hand, but they were kisses all the same. I must have kissed her a million times." He begins blubbering. Can barely speak. "What will I do without my Dorothy?"

I wonder if there's been any word from Stewart. If he calls or writes, someone must let me know immediately! It's been so long I worry he's forgotten me. At least I have an address for him now, thanks to Frederick.

Words can't express how much it means to me to have seen Frederick the other day. Even if he couldn't stay long, I'm so thankful for his visit. And that he brought my journal! I knew Mother would try to prevent it. She hates for me to have any private thoughts or a life of my own. I only wish Frederick could have visited me without her so we could've spoken more freely. But it's good that Mother got to see for herself that I'm well enough to go home. I guess I understand why Father didn't come. I assume Frederick and Mother have relayed all the news —what little of it there is.

After Frederick and Mother left, I had an interview with Dr. Abrams about it—about going home. Dr. Abrams' neck was choked tight at the collar, and his head big, round, and red like a birthday balloon. It was difficult not to stare at him as he spoke, expecting his head to pop. It was so distracting, in fact, that when the questions came, they caught me off guard, and I wasn't prepared. I'm afraid I may have blurted out some things I shouldn't have. Next time, I'll know not to answer his questions at all. How did he know to ask such things in the first place? Mother has no doubt been telling him tales. Nevertheless, when Dr. Abrams finally got around to asking me what I plan to do when I go home, I told him the truth straight away: I will rest.

I am utterly exhausted. Sometimes merely lifting my head uses all my energy for the day. Nevertheless, they insist on keeping me busy here. It's the most mundane work, too, mending curtains in the sewing room. Mother must be laughing at that one. She's out to teach me a lesson, I know it!

In any case, after a good long rest at home, I will look for a proper job. I didn't mention to Dr. Abrams that I plan to earn money for California, of course. Even when caught off guard, I know better than to reveal such things. Mother has done such a thorough job of polluting the waters regarding Stewart that the mere mention of his name provokes smug expressions from whoever hears it. I understand why Mother doesn't want me to be happy—jealousy—but why is everyone else so determined to stand in my way? Jealousy too, I can only assume. I see so much more around me than I wish I did.

Once home and well rested, I plan to start painting again. Mother will surely suggest I take more secretarial classes at the YWCA, but isn't it clear by now? I'm not cut out to do clerical work. I'm an artist! I hope to one day make a living with my paintings. Esther thinks I can. She mentioned it in a letter I received from her the other day.

I wrote her back and told her to go through my paintings and pick one out for herself. She can have the picture that won the ribbon if she still wants it. It's the only one I have that's nicely framed. The way back is covered with a dust cover of Kraft paper, and labeled with the Art Center's very own label, makes me feel like a professional. I must learn to do that, myself. The painting needs to be handled carefully, of course, but I trust Esther. She is so good to me—so encouraging.

Sadly, it has been such a long time since I painted, it will surely take real effort to get back into it. As much as I hate to admit it, I think I will need an office job to start.

I'll have Frederick drive me to the employment office as soon as I'm home. Hopefully the agency can find me a situation far from dull and suffocating Lock 4. In Pittsburgh, possibly. As long as they don't suggest I return to that den of she-wolves in Washington DC, I'll go anywhere.

The mere thought of my last days in DC still infuriates me. The girls I worked alongside were so jealous of my modeling classes that they conspired with the waitress to put something in my soup. By the taste of it, they may well have tried to poison me. For all I know, it's what made me sick and could be the reason I'm here. They laughed like it was a joke, but it was no joke. It caused such a scene when I smashed my bowl to the floor that the waitress banned me from the place. By that point, I had run out of sanctuaries. When was that, anyway? It's such an unusually vivid memory, yet feels so long ago.

No matter, I don't expect to go back to DC ever again. Good riddance to all of them. It is what I'll say when I finally leave this place, too. To the patients, the nurses, the doctors—Good riddance!

Get this: Nurse Winthrop took me for a bath last night and had me dress for bed. She was treating me like a child, and I'd had enough. I became irritated and snapped at her. Who wouldn't? I know how to wash. I know how to dress! Like two match heads, her eyes flared from her face, glowing white with derision. I feared the entire room would go up in flames. I was stunned to hear her scold me in a language I didn't understand. Polish? Hungarian? All I know is she sounded just like Mother. Her face became mother's face, mocking me through the fire of her eyes, cackling like a witch. I tried to swat away the face, extinguish the fire, but Winthrop grabbed my wrists and stared me down. "Stop acting up," she said. "Now, you do as I say and dress for bed!" Gradually, her eyes receded back into their sockets like turtle heads, but they continued smoldering. She then had the nerve to call me arrogant. Me?

I expect that now I will forever be on her bad side. Fine. She'll forever be on mine. And she won't be alone. (You know who else I mean!)

It's not all so bad. I very nearly had a decent conversation this afternoon while sitting with Olive, who is my friend in the day ward. The way Olive goes on about the Mitchell Ghost Bomber reminds me of Frederick and how he had been obsessed with that news story, too. He scoured the papers each morning for weeks after it happened.

Like Frederick, Olive has a lot to say about that plane crash —about how the Monongahela River is hungry and swallowed that Army plane whole. The Army will never find it, she says, because the river digested it.

I recalled Frederick's theory—about the polluted river causing the plane to sizzle and dissolve before anyone had a chance to look for it. Digested, in a way.

Olive told me about the Johnstown flood and how an entire town got digested by millions of gallons of water from a broken dam—houses, churches, stores, bars, a library, a railroad station, and people. I think Frederick would like Olive if he met her. Perhaps I'll introduce them next time Frederick visits, though

I'm not sure, yet, whether Olive can be trusted. She has issues—
and coming from me, that's saying a lot. She told me her step-
grandpapa had his way with her a few too many times and it
messed with her head. She said it as matter-of-fact as I'm
writing it now. Olive has facts. Olive said Monongahela means
"falling banks," but I knew that already because we learned it in
school. Olive also has opinions: when I told her that we can see
the Monongahela from our yard, and that my brother, Frederick, was in the Army, she accused me of being a Communist spy.
She became suspicious of me. And I in turn, of her. But I trust
her more than I do most other people around here. And there
aren't many I can talk to.

I stopped listening to Olive, though, as I imagined myself
standing at the edge of the Mon and its falling banks, watching
them crumble into that lazy expanse of murky water. The Mon
is hungry, I thought, and will swallow whatever it's fed. I closed
my eyes and saw the bank collapse under my feet until the river
flooded and consumed me, too. The water continued to rise,
swollen and brown. It overtook our house, engulfed the tracks
and the trains. All of North Charleroi devoured, bones and all,
like the Johnstown flood. Like that plane and its pilots. Nothing
left but ghosts.

The longer I'm here, the more faded all the spirits of North
Charleroi will become. Soon nothing will be left of it, and
nothing left of me. I must persuade Mother to let me come
home. I wouldn't be here if it weren't for her. She and I can't
speak to each other; I'll need Frederick's help. He's on my side. I
look forward to his next visit. Soon, I hope.

LEFTOVERS

T he sun blazes high above a treeless hill dotted with headstones—some crooked and pockmarked, others freshly chiseled. Beyond them, parched fields stretch to the horizon. The air is thick and still, the voices soft. It's 10 a.m. and way too early in the day to bury a mom.

I tell Eric he doesn't have to be a pallbearer if he doesn't want to be. But who else is there? Even with two men from the funeral home pitching in, they are still one man short. Eric makes six—an even split between people who knew Mom and those who never met her.

Each man grabs hold of a brass handle, and together they march the coffin twenty yards from the back of the hearse to the edge of the hole.

Reverend Furman stands upon a patch of Astroturf beside the casket and sops his ruddy face with a handkerchief. He looks ready to faint. Everyone does.

As he recites a simple prayer, a woman hands out roses from a wicker basket. And, with a final Amen from the reverend, I lay my rose upon the casket like everyone else.

Quite a few flowers are left, and the woman offers them to me. Eric suggests I take them home and dry them—as if by the time the petals turn dark and brittle, something will make sense.

Dad wants to ride in Eric's car because that's the car he arrived in, but I persuade him to ride in Mike's rental instead. "It's air-conditioned," I say.

Mike is annoyed.

Good.

The caravan snakes out of the cemetery and proceeds down a desolate country byway like a band of travelers heading for a better life. As we drive, I lean my head out the window and inhale deeply, taking in the twinned scents of pasture and death.

Several miles later, an incongruous space-age neon boomerang flickers near the edge of the road. On it is an arrow pointing to the far end of an expansive gravel parking lot, where a dilapidated shack sits in desperate need of repair. According to Dad, Hugo's Restaurant is where people always gather after a funeral. Its apposite sheen of utter desolation makes me think he's right. Plus: there's nothing else around.

Rickety dining tables are pushed together and covered with shabby vinyl tablecloths to create an ad-hoc banquet hall. After claiming seats, everyone forms a line to load up paper plates from the buffet—a hodgepodge of roast chicken, mashed potatoes, coleslaw, salad, spaghetti...institutional loss on a chafing dish, each one its own warmed beacon of mourning.

"Looks good," says Eric.

"Good enough to eat?" I say.

We carry our plates back to the table and sit down across from Mike.

I'm not hungry and can only pick at my food, but it's not long before Eric heads to the table for seconds.

"We need to talk about Dad," Mike says.

"Not right now."

"It's either here and now or over the phone. I'm flying back to Phoenix first thing."

"That was quick."

"I was just here, Rachel. I came to visit Mom while she was alive."

"I tried to come, too. The hurricane."

It sounds lame. If I hadn't procrastinated, I might have beat the storm. I feel ill.

Eric is about to sit, but I push him aside so I can get to the bathroom.

"Matthew 4:19" is scrawled in fine-tip black Sharpie across a piece of plywood cut out, crudely, to resemble an Ichthys, which is hung over the back of the Ladies' door. Squatting in front of it, then turning to bend away from it in my nauseous haze, I remember relatives, maybe my Papa, talking about casting for smallmouth bass in the Mononga-hela. The ones that got away. Over the toilet, my stomach contracts like a crushed paper bag. I retch with nothing to give, sweat beading my head in a filial-obligatory ring of laurels. I run the tap and splash cold water over my face. I can't believe this place doesn't have a liquor license. A broken mirror hangs over the basin, and I turn away to avoid my reflection. As I stare at the lavender paint peeling on the walls, Eric knocks.

"You okay?" he says.

Without a word, I open the door and hustle past him.

Half-familiar relatives to my left, lukewarm pasta to my right, I cut a line to the exit and stand outside in the sun.

Eric follows and, moments later, Mike does, too.

Mike taps a cigarette from a fresh pack and offers it to me. Despite having quit, not to mention the incipient nausea, I can't resist.

"I have something to show you," Mike says, lighting our cigarettes before marching to his car.

He grabs a paper bag from the back seat and tosses it to me. "What's this?"

"No way was I going to let her be buried with that thing," he says.

I hand it back to him. "What are you going to do with it?"

He takes a few steps to the edge of the parking lot and hurls Mom's hairbrush, the one with the metal prongs, deep into the woods.

———

WE HAVE Hugo's reserved for two hours, but an hour of strained small talk proves more than enough time for everyone. When I ask the two teenage servers to wrap up the leftovers, they refuse.

"Sorry, no," one of them says, "we can't be held liable."

For what, I can only guess. Wrapping the food would be as simple as putting cardboard lids onto the tinfoil chafing dishes, and I'm ready to do it myself.

"Sorry, but you can't," says the other server. "It's the law."

"Bullshit."

"There's no need to swear, ma'am. It's not up to us."

The manager emerges from the back room. "What's the problem?" he says.

"There's no problem. I want to take our food home with us, that's all."

"Sorry, it's been outlawed."

"What are you talking about? I've worked in restaurants my whole life—catering jobs, too."

"Honestly, a restaurant in town gave leftover food to a homeless shelter last year, and everyone got sick. They don't allow it anymore."

"So, you're going to throw it away? I doubt it. You're either going to eat this food yourselves, or put it back in the kitchen and serve it to the next group of suckers stupid enough to walk through the door. We paid for it, and we're taking it with us."

Eric steps up beside me and tugs at my elbow. "Forget it," he says. "It wasn't expensive. Who wants to eat leftover corn on the cob, anyway?"

"Don't you get it? Dad could live off this crap all week," I say. "Where's Mike? He's the one who booked this place."

I load a paper plate with as much chicken as it will hold. No one stops me. "Here," I say, handing the plate to Eric before grabbing another and piling it with more chicken.

Eric follows behind me as I storm to the car.

The preacher and his wife are idling in their luxury sedan. Reverend Furman rolls down his window. He's laughing and shakes his head. "The prodigal daughter," he says. "Still as feisty as ever."

Prodigal daughter? What a joke. This isn't my home. Never was, and never will be. And I'm no one's daughter.

Before I have a chance to hurl a slimy chicken thigh at the reverend, Eric clutches my wrist.

Yanking my arm free, I stare Eric down.

He doesn't say anything but stares back at me. Judging me, it seems.

"What?" I say.

He tosses a lip balm tin into my lap. I had given it to him to hold for me as we were getting ready, and now he's using it like a dog treat—a way to make me sit. I resist.

But once we're moving, I begin absentmindedly rubbing my finger around in the tin. The balm feels reassuring on my lips, creamy and warm from the heat. A mile later, I'm calm.

"You're not obliged to stay, you know. I can fly home."

"Don't worry about me," says Eric. "I'm fine. The worst part is over."

ANNA'S JOURNAL
Friday, March 22, 1957

I used to take pride in my ability to concentrate—painting for hours, rendering exquisite detail with the most deli-cate brush. However, if I was given a blank canvas today, I'm not sure I would know what to do with it other than to paint it like the side of a house. Some people do that. I found an old *Life* in the day ward, which featured an article about "the greatest living American artist" who dribbles paint over the canvas like a child. I'm afraid I'd be hard-pressed to do even that much these days. Ideas are there, I suppose, but they have nowhere to go and build upon each other layer after layer, resting low against the floor of my skull like a pile of rugs, heavy and dull. Perhaps the painter in the magazine suffers the same problem—when there is no more room in his head, the pressure builds until his ideas burst forth in an explosion of paint.

The x-rays don't help much in this regard. Men get them on Tuesdays, the women on Thursdays so, yesterday, Nurse Winthrop came to escort us to the basement of the cottage next door.

As a child, classmates used to invite me to places. "Come here, Anna, come with us." When I went, they would turn and run. The women here are the same—the same as in school, the same as in Washington, the same as everywhere. Constant stares and whispers. Barely stifled laughter. The only difference now is that I'd *prefer* to be left behind.

Sitting next to Nancy on a long wooden bench outside the x-ray room felt familiar, the way a recurring dream might. Not a real memory, that is, but I'm not sure I have those anymore. Despite the routine of coming here every week, I can't describe what goes on in the room. It's as if the yellow door is a portal into a tin-colored fog that feeds on memories. Beyond it lies the end of the world.

Nancy's leg was bouncing with nervous energy, her fingers weaving a cat's cradle without any string. Her breath was like kerosene from the sedatives. Everybody's is. Not the pills, but rather the liquid they inject us with now and again. The smell is everywhere, soaking our clothes, spilling into the toilet bowls, escaping from our mouths like a poison mist. The sedative must have made Nancy delirious because she turned to me and asked if I was telepathic. She said she could often hear me through the television.

I told her it's not me. It can't be. My head is stuffed with the sawdust of a Raggedy Ann doll, and it takes all the concentration I can muster for thoughts to merely travel from my skull to my mouth, never mind broadcasting one through a television set.

Perhaps if my old acting aspirations ever materialize, I can look into the camera and send Nancy a message. Until then, she will have to wait.

For now, my only performances are during my presentations. I gave one the other day. Or rather, Dr. Abrams gave a presentation of me. Like a show-and-tell object that he brought with him to class. But at least I got to act.

When he questioned me about Stewart, for instance, I acted as though I didn't know what he was talking about.

"Why are you smiling, Anna?"

Was I?

"Who tells you not to eat, Anna? Is God still telling you that?"

I don't know how he got this idea unless, perhaps, I'm telepathic after all. Maybe he heard me through the television. More likely, Mother has been filling his ears with more nonsense—scheming to put me away forever.

I heard about a man, 65 years old, who had lived here twenty years before he finally killed himself.

I'll be home next week for my birthday. I wouldn't have known it was coming if Nurse Winthrop hadn't reminded me.

"I hear you'll be spending your birthday at home with your family," she said.

Another birthday? How can it be when time never seems to pass? I swear I can count a thousand seconds within one tick of the day ward's clock. Outside is different. Out there, the hour hands spin faster than a hummingbird's wings.

When I'm home, I will convince Mother how vital it is I stay home for good—while I'm still young enough to have a life.

Before I know it, ten years will have passed, and there will be nothing left for me to do but follow that old man out a window. I lied when Dr. Abrams asked if I've ever thought about it. I'll lie the next time, too.

As I sat next to Nancy waiting for my turn in the x-ray room, a problem arose—something to do with the machine or maybe a patient, I don't know, they wouldn't say. We sat for several minutes until a nurse came to tell us we would be taken back to the Delbert Cottage until the problem was fixed. The news caused Nancy to scream and flail, demanding her treatment. She threatened to jump out a window. Guess that goes around here, the easiest way, after all. We were in the basement, so it was hard to imagine. I pictured Nancy falling through the dirt to the center of the earth where the dinosaurs live. An attendant encased her in a bear hug and dragged her backwards into a safe room down the hall. A nurse followed and closed the door behind them. It would have been more horrible to see if it weren't so commonplace around here. The muffled screams faded as the rest of us were shuffled up the stairs and back to our cottage.

Nurse Winthrop calls it Building 3—"C'mon now ladies, back to Building 3"—but its official name is Delbert Cottage, and I refuse to call it Building 3. It's bad enough I come from Lock 4.

The interior walls of Delbert Cottage are painted what Olive calls, "Holiday Turquoise," but there isn't much else on the walls. Not much else in the room at all— a card table with some uncomfortable wooden chairs, one rocking chair with a worn-out cushion, a couch. There's a piano, but no one ever plays it. Above the piano is a color litho-graph of the main hospital building. It seems silly to hang a picture like that. We all know what the hospital looks like. They should hang a picture of palm trees, instead, to fit with the color of the walls. Better still, a painting of the California coast, so I can look at it and imagine I'm where I'm supposed to be rather than where I am.

They're telling us we won't go back for our treatments until next week.

Later in the day, Nurse Winthrop and a few attendants rounded us up again, this time to walk us to the dining room. Nurse Winthrop insisted I wear a dress, the way Mother always wants me to do.

"This isn't the Barbizon Hotel," I said.

I say it a lot, and it seems to annoy her, but it's true. I know about the Barbizon Hotel from my movie magazines. It is where all the starlets in New York City live. It's similar to the women-only hotel where I stayed in Washington, DC. Only the Barbizon is much classier. The lobby floor is made of polished marble, not like the porcelain tiles at the entrance of the administration building here at Oakville. No, indeed, Oakville Hospital is no Barbizon Hotel, and I felt entirely justified to dine in my trousers. I wasn't hungry, in any case, and told her so.

"I am content to sit where I am," I said.

Nurse Winthrop turned cold. She told me it is not healthy to sit all day.

"You don't want to end up catatonic like Henrietta," she said.

I'd never heard the word before, but I've seen Henrietta. She sits in the day ward and rocks all day long, the chair chipping away the silence.

Once, the sound of her rocking burrowed into my ears so deeply, I took off my shoe and slapped Henrietta across the head with it. My reward for the effort? For getting up and *doing* something? An injection deep into my already bruised arm and sent to bed for observation—kerosene wafting from my pores.

Nurse Winthrop soon lost patience at my refusal to eat and called for reinforcements to escort me to the refectory. I didn't wear a dress, in any case. I wore what I had on, jeans and a blouse as always, and when she began to shove me toward my plate, which I was ignoring, I ate exactly one canned pea and one diced carrot.

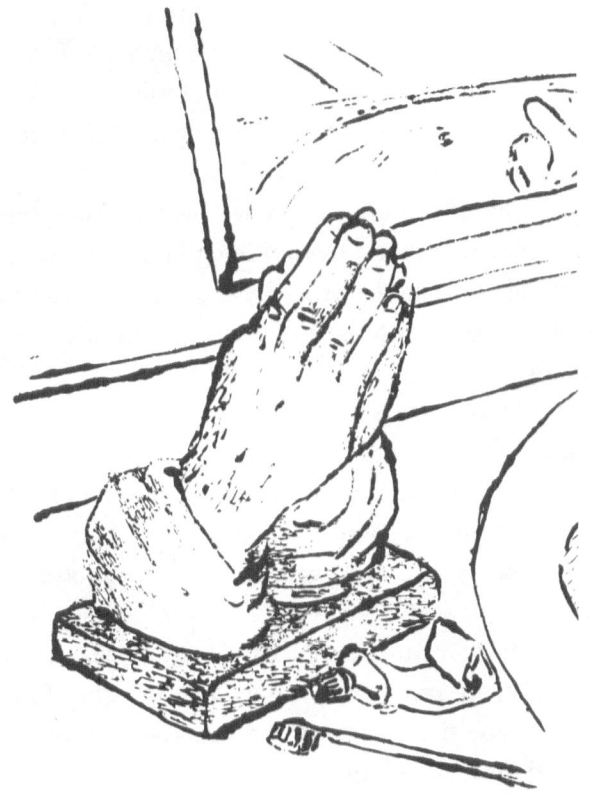

B ack at the house, with the dogs walked and fed, Dad instructs Mike to sit on the couch next to Eric and me.

"I want to tell you all something," he says.

"Unless you're going to tell us we've inherited Mom's secret millions, it can wait," says Mike. "Why not pop one of those anxiety pills I got the doctor to prescribe for you and take a nap?"

"No," Dad says. "I need you all on the couch."

Mike kicks at my leg, and I slide over to give him room.

"What pills?" I whisper to Mike as he squeezes beside me.

He rolls his eyes. "Don't even think about it," he says.

Dad pushes his easy chair in front of us and sits down with a notebook in his lap. One of many that litter the house. He pats the notebook several times before dropping his face into his hands, like an actor preparing for a one-man show. Theater of the Absurd. The two dogs circle Dad's chair and scratch at the well-worn carpet before curling at his feet.

Nearly a minute of silence passes before Dad's expression whips into a melodramatic froth. Rising up in his seat, he looks up and extends his palms to the sky like a figure wailing to the heavens in the corner of an Old Master's painting, the performance begins: "I had a vision..."

The dogs whine dissonantly.

"You mean you had a dream," I say.

"Not a dream, a *vision*. Sometimes visions come to me in my dreams, that's how they work. But that's not important. What I'm trying to tell you is God spoke to me. He showed me four chairs."

He points to four imaginary chairs one by one.

"In the first," he says, "sat a young version of me, four or five years old—maybe six. Around when I ran barefoot over a piece of glass and needed all them stitches. In the next chair sat another me. I was a teenager with all my blond hair, like in the picture over the fireplace."

He points to the mantle. I don't have to look to know the picture he means. A framed photo of him and Mom standing in front of Papa's black Chevy Stylemaster, holding hands with broad smiles. By the late 70's, that car was a junkheap rotting in the back pasture that Mike and I would play in, but the photo attests to its previous glory. I used to stare at it as a kid and wonder why Mom and Dad never smiled like that in real life. Maybe they would have been happier if they could have afforded a car as cool as the Stylemaster. Although it's black and white, it is obvious Dad's hair had been blond—*the color of white corn,* as he likes to say. The same color mine was when I was a little girl.

He often tells me my hair is the reason he and Mom chose to adopt me—he could pass me off as his *real flesh and blood.* He still talks about his disappointment over how it gradually darkened to brown. But his own hair became brown in time, too. And now it's turning gray.

"I must have been more like twenty," Dad continues, "because I was dressed in my Army uniform. Nineteen fifty-nine is the year Jesus saved my soul. Must have been right about then. In the third chair, a version of me sat all grown. Maybe forty. That's when I was fat. I don't like to be fat. People shouldn't be fat. Anyway, in the last chair sat another me the way I look now. But, listen, this is the important part: we were sitting before Jesus as he judged me through all my life's phases. Jesus shook his head and told me I wouldn't get a house." He takes his palms to his thighs and sinks inward, his head rolling down on his spine, moving his eyes to the floor before looking out at us to see who's paying attention, rocking slightly in the threadbare easy chair.

Aside from the Rapture, a house in heaven is another one of Dad's obsessions. Not metaphorically, but a real house on a real street in the ultimate gated community. Whether it's a mansion or a cabin depends upon merit. God doles out crowns, too—fourteen, eighteen, or twenty-four karat gold. If you're exceptionally well-behaved, you might even get one set with a jewel. But don't get your hopes up, you have to be Billy Graham-level exceptional to earn something like that. So says the reverend. I think of Furman's oily grin in the parking lot and shudder, momentarily, with nausea.

"I did some bad things—terrible, sinful things," Dad says, curling like a pill bug with each forward rock, looking heavenward with each backward one. "I need to confess."

He rocks and rocks and rocks, his confidence wound up like a catapult.

"Don't tell us you murdered someone," Mike says with a chuckle.

"Murder? Oh my, no. I could never murder someone."

Dad whoops, and the dogs wail in solidarity. His Greek chorus.

"So, what's so important?" I say.

"Remember my janitor job at the mental hospital?"

"No," says Mike.

Sure he does. Mom liked to say, *"One of these days, they're going to keep your father at that hospital."*

Mike and I believed it.

"The supervisor called me to his office one day and says, 'The guys tell me they found this in your locker.'"

Dad wipes the spittle from the corner of his mouth with the back of his hand.

"The supervisor was holding a dirty magazine. It had pictures of men. They were rubbing all up on each other, doing dirty, filthy things. Wicked, sinful things."

He shuts his eyes and trembles.

"I told the boss the magazine wasn't mine, the other guys must have been playing a trick. I would never look at something like that. Never..."

If the magazines weren't his, why is Dad including this story in his family confession? Over the years, Mike and I often speculated about Dad's sexuality. Mainly from how he interacted with Mom or, maybe, how she reacted to him. When some minor transgression of his set her off, she'd say, "You want me to tell the kids about you?" And the way she made fun of his sketchbooks filled with colored pencil drawings of angels and princesses—things a little girl might draw. All of them had blonde bouffant hairdos and wore pastel-colored dresses and high heeled shoes. I loved them.

Dad opens his eyes to look at each of us. He repeats: "I would never, ever look at pictures like that."

He seems to be trying to tell us something without telling us anything at all.

Mike is in another world, his arms clenched tightly across his chest, face frozen. He probably remembers his own stash of magazines and how Mom wrenched his arm from its socket when she discovered them.

"Whether or not they were yours, it's no big deal," I say.

"Well, that's not all…"

Mike scowls. Glances at his watch.

"When your grandfather had his accident, your mother and I took care of him. He couldn't shower or nothing. I went to his house to help him with a bath, and while I washed him, he complained about being lonely. He missed your grandmother—missed loving up on her and all. 'Well, György,' I said, 'maybe you ought to masturbate'…"

The room falls deathly quiet. My ears are ringing. *What did he just say?*

"Your grandfather sat naked in the bath, see, so I reached down and started rubbing him to show him what I meant."

The screen door startles me as it slams shut. The dull thud of a car door, tires spinning in the gravel, and Mike is gone.

"Anyway," Dad goes on without acknowledging Mike's departure—as if he'd been expecting it.

"You don't have to finish your story, Dad. We get it."

"Your mother didn't sleep in the same bed as me after that—never again." I was surprised to hear that they ever had slept in the same bed. From as far back as I could remember, and this was long before Papa died, they slept separately.

"Wait, you told Mom about this?"

"I had to. I needed your mother's forgiveness."

Forgiveness? From Mom? No chance.

"Your mother stopped talking to me for a good long while.

And Jesus stopped talking to me, too. He used to talk to me all the time, clear as I'm talking to you right now, but not since then."

He covers his face and shakes his head as if reliving the precise moment Jesus hung up the phone.

"God will forgive you," I say. "All you have to do is open your heart and ask. Isn't that what you tell me?"

"I ask all the time, but He doesn't answer me."

He crumples forward into a full-blown sob.

Eric is silent, staring ahead expressionless, impossible to read.

Dad's rocking slows, his breathing steadies.

"I feel a little better," he says. "Confessing helped. I should tell everyone else about it, too. My sister and brother, Reverend Furman..."

I picture him telling everyone he knows, everyone he meets —bank tellers, grocery store clerks, the mailman.

"That's not a good idea," I say.

He's not listening.

———

WHEN I CATCH Eric nodding off on the couch, I nudge him awake and consider telling him he's been dreaming. If only he would believe it. If only it were true. Instead, I suggest he go back to the motel.

"I'm going to spend the night here with my dad," I say. "I'll call you in the morning."

He doesn't try to persuade me to go with him the way I expect him to—the way I hope he might. He must be as eager to escape as Mike had been. He collects his things and I walk him to his car.

"Be careful of deer," I warn him as he turns the key.

"I'll be fine."

"Sorry that you had to sit through all that," I say.

"Don't worry about it. Your dad is a nutty old man, that's all."

True, but before he was a nutty old man, he was a nutty young man. And, from the stories he tells, he was a nutty kid even before then. "He shouldn't be alone right now," I say.

"I agree."

The car's tires edge across the gravel as I follow alongside. Eric taps the brakes.

"Do you want me to stay?" he says.

Not until his taillights disappear over the hill do I wish I'd said yes.

But it's better this way. I need a chance to absorb everything that's happened without worrying about what other twisted nonsense Eric might be exposed to. Or trying to read his thoughts—is he bored, does he regret coming, does he see me differently?

Standing in the front yard, I kick off my flip-flops and clutch the grass with my bare toes. With time to have a real look, I realize the house isn't as unchanged as it first appeared. It's ragged at the edges and paint is peeling down to bare grey wood in places, a crack migrates through the cement of the front stoop, teeming with ants. The entropy of a perfectly still house in a perfectly still town. Like a fading photograph.

The incessant hum of Dad and the dogs gradually morphs into the sound of babbling water as I cross the backyard and approach the creek dividing the house from the hill.

Over the rusting cow bridge, I pass what is left of the small barn where Mike used to hide his Playboys, before the arm-socket incident, that is. I would sit on a milk crate and flip through them myself sometimes, marveling at the voluptuous bodies so alien from my own, the triangles of dark bushy thatch curling beyond my grasp. The barn is choked with weeds now and will soon decay into nothing.

The hill is steeper than I remember, and I put my flip-flops back on before attempting to clamber through the overgrown thistle.

It's hard to believe Papa's cow, Zsa Zsa, used to graze on this slope. Or that Grandma, in her final years, thought Papa met women here. It's something Mike and I often laughed about—the thought of Papa meeting women in the woods. Mom would laugh, too, but not about Papa. Whenever it came up, Mom would look at Dad and say, "Are you meeting women there, too, Homer?" She'd let out a loud cackle. "No, you don't meet women, do you?"

Dad, turning red, would say, "I'm married to you, Dorothy. I don't want no one but you."

Small grasshoppers arc in all directions until I reach the hilltop where I turn and look out over the property, so peaceful and verdant. Mom and Dad only ever owned the acre of property their house sits upon. The field and hill behind the house—twenty acres total—are shared with Uncle Nick. Once Dad and Uncle Nick are gone, it will be a nightmare to tease out who owns what. There's a smaller strip alongside the house that once belonged to Mom's sister, Aunt Emily, but much to the family's annoyance, she willed it to the church. I overheard Reverend Furman offering to sell it to Dad for five thousand bucks. As if taking five hundred dollars to play CDs weren't insult enough.

The sun inches lower, and the clouds glow orange and warm. The trees cast long shadows over where Papa's cornfield used to be, where green beans once grew in absolutely perfect rows.

When I close my eyes, I am back with Papa, picking beans, planting potatoes, hand-watering tomato plants one by one.

If this were all I ever knew—all I ever saw—I might think, what a beautiful place to grow up.

The screen door slams behind Maggie as she walks out of the back door of Papa's house. It belongs to Jack and Maggie now, but it will always be Papa's house to me. He built it sometime in the '30s with a few of his friends from the coal mine—all of them paid with Papa's homemade dandelion wine. He made it every year—and was the first thing I ever got drunk on.

Maggie notices me on the hillside, and waves as I trot down in long strides to greet her.

Funny to see her surrounded by chicken coops. She used to call me a hillbilly whenever her family came from Arlington to visit during the summers.

"I don't know how you stand to live in Daisytown," she'd say.

But now it seems I'm the cosmopolitan girl living in the big city and Maggie is the country girl living down on the farm.

If you can still call what's left of Papa's place—a yard full of trampled vegetables—a farm.

"I let the weeds and vegetables grow in equal proportion," she explains. "Japanese style."

The smaller one of Maggie's two dogs barks wildly, bouncing in a nearby pen.

"His name is Buckshot," Maggie says as I walk over to pet him.

She tells me Jack's childhood dream was to own a purebred beagle—loyal, smart, and true. The kind of dog to take on hunting trips. "But Buck is afraid of loud noises," Maggie says. "The little guy would rather sit around the house eating pizza all day than hunt. But Jack only hunts once or twice a year, anyway, and spends much of his own time sitting around the house eating pizza, so it's not as big a problem as he makes it out to be."

The dog is wild for attention.

"Sorry, Buster, I don't have any pizza to give you," I say, rubbing his dirty white belly while he squirms in the dirt.

He pops to his feet, slobbers, and smiles, revealing a set of teeth that look as though they were put in his skull upside down.

I call him Buster a few more times before Maggie corrects me.

"Buckshot," she says.

"Looks more like a Buster." All beagles look like a Buster to me.

"Call him that if you want, I don't care. But don't let Jack hear you say it."

I give Buckshot a few hard pats before heading toward the other dog, a retriever of some kind, whose eyes roll back in his head, pink and white. A gooey string of spit trails from his mouth. He nearly strangles himself at the end of a taut zip line when he senses my approach.

"You better not," Maggie says. "Arrow killed one of the chickens a couple weeks ago, and he hasn't been the same since tasting blood. We're trying to figure out what to do with him. He's dangerous."

On one side of the garden sits a homemade chicken coop and, on the other, a makeshift duck house. Between them rests a blue plastic wading pool filled with milky water.

"Watch the duck shit," Maggie says.

"Where?"

"You're standing in it."

I kick off my flip-flops, pick up a tangled hose, and wash my feet.

Inside, things aren't any better. The couch in front of the TV —the same spot where we'd watch wrestling with Papa—is now surrounded by catalogs, crayons, hunting magazines, and trash. Half-eaten bags of cheese puffs are scattered randomly, surrounded by dusty orange crumbs ground into the rug like flea powder.

Maggie kicks a few of Owen's toys out of the way and leads me to the basement door.

"Come downstairs, I want to show you something."

At the bottom of the stairs, the wall to Grandma's old

canning closet, where she used to store pickles and stewed tomatoes, is half-demolished. A pile of construction debris rests on the floor like a beaver dam.

Penciled on an exposed stud are various measurements and notes written in Hungarian. They start in neat lines but get messier and messier as the workers presumably got drunker and drunker.

"Check it out," Maggie says, pointing to a layer of makeshift insulation comprised of dozens of empty beer cans entombed since the 1930s. "Jack thinks they might be worth something."

Next to them is a pile of old newspaper clippings. I pick one up.

Whenever Mom told stories of growing up with a belligerent drunk for a father, I had to remind myself she was talking about Papa because I never saw him that way. It was before my time.

Hard to know what happened—even the newspaper clippings are vague: *Area Man in Critical Condition After Mysterious Beating.* All we know is that they found Papa tied to a telephone pole outside the Miner's Club.

After a month in a coma, he came home with a steel plate in his head. He used to let me tap it.

"Crushed like a clay pot," he said.

He quit the coal mine, went on disability, built up the farm, ran Zsa Zsa in the pasture, and never drank again. Mom must have been relieved by his reformation, but it drove her nuts that Mike and I never saw his hard-drinking dark side.

"You think Papa is so great, but you don't know."

I think of Mom and how she changed over the years, too. If I'd ever gotten married and given Mom a grandchild the way she'd wanted me to, the kid might have only known Mom as the sweet old lady who liked to feed birds and cook. That's how it goes.

ANNA'S JOURNAL
Friday, February 7, 1958

If I ask Frederick about Father again, I hope he won't get so upset. He'll have to forgive me—I'm never confident about what is a dream anymore. If I ask about Father tomorrow, and someone tells me he's dead, it may be like I am hearing it for the first time. I may react as I did today when Dr. Abrams mentioned it—by saying nothing, feeling nothing. Dr. Abrams says that he told me Father died last week, and I appear to have forgotten or blocked the memory of being told. Father's death merely marks time—another event to remind me I've been here too long.

When Dr. Abrams prodded me about my feelings, I told him what he wanted to hear—that I was sad. I suppose I am. Sad but relieved. It's no secret Father didn't like me. Nothing anyone says will ever convince me otherwise. Did he ever come to see me here? During my brief visits home, did he welcome his little girl? What did I ever do to make him so cold other than to be born? He can't blame me for that.

Still, I'm sorry I wasn't kinder to Frederick when he came to pick me up for the funeral. I shouldn't have threatened him or said the things I said. I wanted to go with him—honestly—and regret now I didn't. However, it became imperative that he turn the car around and return me to Oakville. I can't explain it. The spindly gray branches of bare trees looming over us like a cage, the narrow road cutting a straight black line through the wet white snow. The silence between us. Suddenly, I wasn't sure where Frederick was taking me and felt an urgent need to turn back.

I pray Frederick doesn't become afraid of me the way Father was. I want nothing more than to go home again. Next time he comes for me, I will go. Happily. Quietly. And I will visit Father's gravesite for a proper goodbye.

Meanwhile, the doctor here has arranged to move me to a new ward. I'm not sure why. The worse-off patients are usually placed upstairs in Delbert, and the cured are sent home, so I'm not sure why the lateral move. But, as far as I can tell, I've only gotten worse since my arrival. That is, I once had a future— ideas, plans, goals—but they've wiped them all away. Maybe that's why they are moving me? Another step toward the ulti- mate end of erasing me altogether. Building 5.

Life here is so dull, there's not much of a me left to erase. The routine is stifling, and they make it impossible to break free

of it. I sometimes think the buildings are charged with magnet-
ism, the floors swabbed with glue. Mother never thought I was
any good at sewing, but I've become quite skilled at mending
curtains and tablecloths. I'd use the sewing machine to make
myself a dress if I thought I would ever have a decent place to
wear it. A seamstress is not my ideal situation, but it's better
than kitchen work. No jobs for models here. No jobs for artists
or writers. There is a room with typewriters, however, and they
occasionally allow me to use one of them to compose my letters.
Some days I sit and stare at the blank pages struggling to
remember what all the keys are for. A few days ago, I sat at the
typewriter listening to the slow tap-tap-tap of another woman
beside me. An eternity passed, but I finally began to do the same
—a slow, quiet tapping, one letter, then another. Ten minutes
later, I'd managed a whole word. I struggled that way for what
felt like hours. But eventually I was blazing away at my old
secretarial pace—explaining my predicament to Stewart, telling
him everything that's been happening and why I've been so
absent. Then, without warning, Nurse Winthrop came in to pull
me away. "Time for work," she said. It felt like she was about to
tear the letter from my hands and burn it on the stove the way
Mother used to do. I yanked the page from the machine and
folded it up before Winthrop had the chance to read what I'd
written.

   With Father gone, I am feeling more inclined to go home for
extended visits. I'd like to go back for good. I've promised
Mother I'll do as I am told. I'll do my chores, go to church, wear
whatever she wants me to wear. I miss my room. I miss Frederick. Most of all, I miss having a life. Or, at least, a future.

   Here at Oakville, there are only fleeting moments when I
can pretend my life is anything more than merely existing. But
they do come. The other day Olive managed to sneak lipstick
and a compact mirror into the ward. One of her visitors had
brought it for her. They don't allow us to have lipstick—espe-

cially since the day Henrietta smeared some all over the day ward walls. But Olive got her hands on a tube and offered to give me a makeover. "Like in your magazines," she said.

After circling my lips with the vivid hue—Cardinal Red, it was called—she touched a dab to each of my cheeks, working it in with her thumb the way Mother did when rubbing dirt from my face as a little girl. (And still tries to do from time to time!)

When Olive had finished, I faced Olive's compact mirror and felt I was looking at a complete stranger. The sophisticated woman staring from the other side of the mirror spoke to me and said: "The sun should see this beautiful face. Step outside and join the world."

"But, where is the world?" I asked.

Thousands of miles from this place, certainly. And no map to show the way.

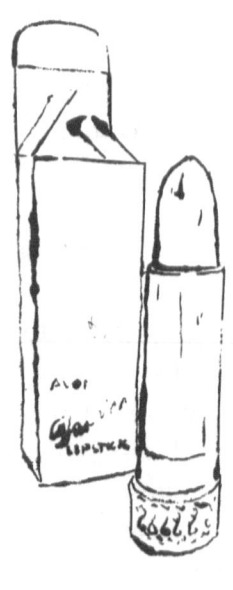

I thought of where I might wear lipstick and pretended I was talking with a friend of Frederick's that he'd wanted to introduce me to—I've forgotten his name.

"Why yes, I believe a movie would be nice," I said.

Olive and I acted little scenes like this until Winthrop discovered us and spoiled our fun, confiscating the lipstick, and compact, and making us wash. "Dress for dinner," she said, sounding like Mother, again. But I was already dressed, wasn't I? And had my makeup done, too! "You look like clowns," she said. Winthrop, as I've said, has it in for me, I know that. But what does she know about style, or personality, or creativity, or charisma, with her drawn, humorless face and her stiff, white costume?

When I'm home, I'll go to town and buy a Cardinal Red of my own. I'm a woman, now—too old for Mother to tell me no. I'll buy a lovely dress from the best shop, hop on the train and flee once and for all. Disappear. Towards a city, I should think. Somewhere with a lot of people and big ideas. Pittsburgh, perhaps. Not Washington DC, of course. Maybe New York! The Barbizon!

I've heard Frederick speak of disappearing, too. If he ever does, he must take me with him. I don't care where. Any place. He needs to come soon, and we'll escape together.

BOX OF THINGS

The dogs bounce and whine as I carry a couple of grocery bags through the front door. They circle my ankles and nip at my pants.

Dad is at the kitchen table, scribbling into one of his notebooks. Embellishing his latest vision, perhaps.

"I thought you left without saying goodbye," he says.

"Went to the market with Maggie," I tell him. "Got you a few things."

I notice the hallway is cluttered with boxes and strewn with bags. They spew from my old bedroom like the detritus of receding floodwaters.

"What's all this?" I say.

"I cleaned off your bed so you'd have a place to sleep."

Peering into my old room, the cleared mattress looks like an open raft afloat on a sea of junk—out-of-season holiday trimmings, religious books, records, assorted thrift-store knick-knacks. None of it is mine or ever was. Mom threw everything I left behind in the backyard fire pit years ago. Mike had told me about it shortly after it happened. He said that while he was home on leave and staying with Papa, he and Papa smelled smoke and the two of them walked to Mom and Dad's house to investigate.

"What are you doing, Mom?" Mike had asked.

"I don't have a daughter no more," is all Mom would say.

It meant I didn't have a mother, either, but that was nothing new.

Mom's overly dramatic fire ceremony happened during, or maybe shortly after, my first semester of community college. Mom and Dad were mad at me because I'd stopped taking the bus home every weekend the way they expected me to. To avoid listening to them yell at me about it, I stopped calling, too. But when I suddenly found myself doubled over in pain and the school doctor recommended I have my gallbladder removed, I didn't know what else to do. I thought they might have enough sympathy to give me the insurance information I needed to get it done. But Mom seemed to relish the news. "That's God punishing you. That's what that is," she said. "God is punishing you for not coming home no more, and for everything you put us through. We can't do nothing for you. We're not going to help you." I asked to talk to Dad, but Mom wouldn't put him on the phone. "What do you want to talk to him for? He says the same as me: It is God's will."

At the time, enough of their religious gunk still clogged my mind to believe it might be true. Maybe God was punishing me. For what, though? Disrespecting Mom and Dad? Drinking Mad Dog and smoking pot? Dancing to the devil's music? For merely doing the same things everyone else around me was doing? I hadn't even had sex yet—although who knows what Mom and Dad imagined. I was furious. The pain subsided to a degree without surgery, but I found it harder and harder to concentrate on my classwork, and my first semester grades were an embarrassment. So much so that when the student loan check came through for my second semester, I dropped out and used the money to pay three months' rent in advance on an apartment I found listed in the *Pittsburgh Post-Gazette* sight unseen.

One night, after an all-ages show at The Electric Banana, I invited a bunch of kids back to my new apartment. It was only a matter of days before the place was overrun by a rotating cast of anarchist street punks, skate rats, crusty hippies, and high school kids looking for a place to crash whenever they stayed out all night. Graffiti covered every wall, the bedroom door got a hole kicked through it, cigarette burns dotted every surface and butts were crammed into every nook. I managed to sleep in my own bed once in a while, but not very often. Most of the squatters didn't even know whose apartment it was. I started to forget, myself.

Without a private room to escape to anymore—nowhere to think quietly or cry—drugs became my only sanctuary. I was a fidgety wreck without them. Since I ate free sandwiches at my restaurant job (my first) and easily shoplifted whatever else I needed, most of my meager paycheck went toward buying whatever was on hand: LSD, mushrooms, ecstasy. The invading marauders who were living rent free in my new so-called home, stealing half my stuff, sleeping in my bed, were more than happy to sell me whatever I could afford.

As cheap as the dump was, after three months, I couldn't afford to pay the rent and the landlord kicked everyone out. After that, I resorted to sleeping on friend's couches, on benches in Schenley Park, amid the graves of Homestead cemetery, in squats, movie theaters, wherever. Without a place to stay, it was hard to keep a job. Still, I was finally free, and vowed never to ask Mom or Dad for anything ever again. And I didn't.

On the advice of a fellow squatter, I got public assistance to pay for gallbladder surgery. Feeling the constellation of faint scars on my abdomen, I'm reminded of what the doctor had asked me: "Does anyone else in your family have gallbladder issues?"

"I wish I knew," I said.

The discharge nurse came into the recovery room with a stack of papers. "I need you to sign a few things and then you're free to go."

"Can't I stay a little longer?" I asked. "I don't have anyone to take me home or to watch me." I couldn't imagine trying to recuperate on a park bench.

"What about your parents?"

"I don't talk to them anymore."

"How about a friend? A roommate?"

"No."

"Nobody?"

The nurse shook her head. It was all so pathetic, I began to cry.

"Okay, honey," said the nurse, "we can arrange for you to stay until tomorrow."

With clean sheets, free food, and a television, it was like a luxury vacation.

Seeing how Dad has now gone through the trouble of pulling Mom's things from my old room, I'm tempted to finish the job with my own bonfire. Burn all of Mom's stuff in a ceremonial funeral pyre. *I don't have a mother no more.* Instead, I tell Dad I plan to sleep on the couch.

Unpacking the groceries and putting them away, Dad follows me into the kitchen to see what I bought. Canned goods, mostly—things that are easy to prepare and won't spoil for years.

"I can't bother with this stuff," he says, picking up a can of ravioli from the counter. "Your mother don't like me to mess with the stove."

"Eat it cold then. You don't even need a can opener—just pop the lid."

He squints at a label. "It's no good, Rachel. It gives the dogs diarrhea."

"Why don't you take the dogs for a walk?" I say. "I'm going to use some of the leftovers from Hugo's to make us Chicken Paprikash. How's that sound? Mom's recipe."

"How'd you learn to cook? I never knew you to cook."

"There are a lot of things I know how to do, Dad. A lot of things I've had to teach myself."

AFTER DINNER, I pull the pillow and sheet from my old bed and carry them to the couch. Along the way, I trip over one of the boxes in the hall.

"Ray-shell?" Dad calls to me from his bedroom. Mike wasn't kidding during Dad's "visioning" session: he persuaded a doctor to prescribe Dad Lorazepam, and it causes Dad to slur slightly. As Mike predicted, it is all I can do to keep my hands off the pill bottle. If it was in the medicine cabinet instead of sitting on Dad's dresser, I'm sure I would have downed one by now. Maybe two. "What—what you doing out there, Rachel?"

"Nothing, Dad. Go to sleep."

While tidying up the hall, clearing a path through the boxes, I notice a small one with my name written faintly across its top in what appears to be Dad's handwriting. I scan the boxes surrounding it—Christmas ornaments, Easter decorations— nothing else with my name on it. The box is old—the cardboard is warped, and the tape that once sealed it is no longer sticking. Mom had done such a thorough job of erasing all traces of my existence, it's difficult to imagine how a box like this survived. Where has it been, and what's inside?

Evidence of a daughter, after all. Old report cards, school photographs, a couple of ribbons for perfect attendance. Mike and I never missed an opportunity to get out of the house.

Choir programs, the buffalo nickel Papa gave me, and a medal that I won at an Arts and Crafts show in Pittsburgh. I had painted a circus troupe in "Astonishing detail for a teenager," the jury said. I included the six family dogs, dressing them in tiger, seal, and elephant suits, and painted Mom as ringmaster, a stern grimace set on her face. I assume Mom destroyed it in the fire long ago. (She never liked it.) I also assume that Dad hid these keepsakes in his closet, where she never went, for all these years.

Having tried for essentially my entire adult life to forget about my childhood, I'm surprised at how fascinated I am by these relics. I've moved so many times, I've never been able to hang onto anything for very long. Once you lose something, no matter how you feel about it, you want it back, be it a complicated mom or a useless tchotchke. I wonder if it's time to reassess the past, revise history, and face the person I used to be.

Thumbing through the pictures, stacked together like a flip-book, I notice the smile on my face fades with each passing year—from genuine, to forced, to pained, to where I could finally no longer fake it. Missing is my senior class photo —the one of me straining hardest to smile—but I remember what it looked like. My eyes were closed. Mom wanted the photographer to create a composite—take the open eyes from one shot and superimpose them onto the half-smiling face of the other. He said he couldn't do it—or wouldn't do it—so Mom scratched out the closed eyelids on the smiling photo with a pushpin and drew over them with a ballpoint pen. It looked like something the FBI might find in a psychopath's lair. Mom must have burned that one. Or had I destroyed it myself?

The report cards tell the same story: All A's in First Grade, becoming mostly D's by graduation. The only good marks are in Art and Music. I used to enjoy singing, and I was good at it, too. Good enough to be selected to represent our school as a soloist in a regional choir program. Unfortunately, since it involved an overnight bus trip to Pittsburgh, Mom said no.

You just want to meet boys, is all you want to do.

No, Mom, all I wanted to do was sing. I wasn't interested in the choirboys. (And they certainly weren't interested in me.)

Digging deeper still, I find a prom picture next to the crushed remnants of my tacky corsage. Who knows why Mom and Dad changed their minds at the last minute and let me go to my prom, since they allowed me to go nowhere other than school and church. Probably because I went with Mike's friend, William, the son of a Methodist minister. Mom and Dad always talked about me marrying a preacher's son, becoming a school teacher, building a house on the strip of land beside the house. Methodist wasn't good enough to marry, of course, any more than that marshy strip is fit to build upon, but by some Easter miracle, William was considered safe enough for a prom date. Barely.

When William arrived at the door, he wasn't invited inside and was made to wait on the porch, Dad making menacing eye contact the entire time it took for William to slowly sink onto one of the sun-faded plastic chairs, after which Dad went inside and slammed the door without another word to him. The six dogs nearly barked themselves to death, frustrated over not being able to chew a fresh pair of ankles. One of the dogs got so excited, he puked—as I had already done from nerves while getting ready.

Mike's ex-girlfriend lived up the street and she gave me her old prom dress to wear. It was entirely too big, but Mom took it in for me. I watched over her like a hawk while she adjusted it, checking to make sure the waist wasn't too tight, the skirt too long. I shudder with fresh embarrassment to see the boxy cut, the hideous pleats, the shoulder pads, the puke-lilac satin in the old photo. Listing underneath the teased, feathered helmet of hair that Mom had White Rain-sprayed into a colossus, and teetering atop a pair of thrift-store heels, I am frozen in the frame alongside William and his tonight's-the-night grin. The prom itself wasn't anything special—a small affair at a small school—but merely having the opportunity to pretend I led a normal teenage life was exhilarating.

My friends knew how overprotective Mom and Dad were, so they were shocked to see me walk through the door. A few of them rushed over and gave me a group hug.

When I wasn't dancing with William, who turned out to be as awkward on the dance floor as he was on my front porch, I danced with Lorelei.

"I can't believe you're actually here," Lorelei said, as we held hands and spun around the dance floor.

No one could. Especially me.

I still can't.

It was past curfew when the prom let out, but I didn't care. Sweaty palm in sweaty palm, William walked me to the car. Between pools of light from the street lamps, he paused to kiss me.

I leaned in and kissed him back.

"No, no, no!"

It must be a voice in my head, I thought, but before I had time to look around, Dad leaped from behind a bush like a jilted lover, grabbing me by the arm and jerking me away.

"What are you doing here?" I said. "Are you spying on me?"

"I saw this boy kissing all up on you. I saw everything," he said, batting away the lingering fog of teen romance with his one hand, gripping my arm tightly with his other. "I told you eleven-thirty. It's past midnight. We raised a decent girl..."

William wanted to run away, I could tell, but I assume he wanted to do more kissing. Maybe other things too. I know I did.

"Stop it, Dad, you're hurting me!"

Flapping in the light, my arm looked like the bleached fossil of a small bird. I feared it might snap.

He relaxed his veiny grip, and I broke free. But what could I do? Run?

I looked helplessly to William as his lustful optimism collapsed into soggy disappointment.

"I better go," William said, gesturing toward his car while avoiding Dad's wild glare.

"Yes," Dad said, "leave us be." Beads of his spittle caught the light like gnats. "Rachel is a decent girl," he said—and continued saying it long after William was gone. "We raised a good girl."

Home from the prom, I lay in this same bed and cried so hard I'm surprised the pillows aren't still wet.

Deeper in the box, I find some fabric—two little dresses, both heavily creased from being undisturbed so many years. One is white cotton with lace trim, the second, a faded yellow sundress with delicate flowers hand-embroidered along the neckline. They are tiny, made for an infant. For me? Must have been. But who made them? There are no baby photos of me wearing them.

Finally, at the bottom of the box, is an envelope. The name Virginia Rubik is written across it in ballpoint pen. The name is unfamiliar. Maybe an old teacher of mine?

Attached to the envelope with a rusting paper clip is a receipt of some kind.

Mom used to tell me I cost a thousand dollars.

That's what we paid the adoption agency for you, we spent a thousand dollars.

Whether she meant to tell me that I was expensive or I was cheap depended upon the situation. But either way, the receipt from Catholic Charities of Washington County is for only eight hundred dollars. Looks like she rounded up.

Putting the receipt aside, I open the envelope and pull out a dozen folded pages relating to my adoption. Things I've never seen before. Things I never knew existed.

Mom always told me my biological mother was dead, but the stories about how she died changed constantly. Sometimes my birthmother died of pneumonia, and other times she died in childbirth.

After that, no one wanted you, Mom would say. *They told us your mother was trouble and that you'd be trouble too. Turned out, they were right. You're lucky we found you. We're the only ones who would take you...*

Dad interjected from time to time with cryptic information about my origins, when the topic came up. *If it weren't for me we would never have found Rachel!* But they always shut that conversation down as soon as it started. I begin to wonder if my birth mother had even died at all. If not, where might she be? And why did she give me up?

The papers don't offer many hints—my weight and temperature on various days at the orphanage, what I ate, and so on. There's an accounting of the things I arrived with, including two dresses. On the bottom of one page, someone wrote:

Baby Rubik loves to be held.

Baby Rubik? Is that Virginia Rubik? Is that me?

If it is, whoever wrote it should have written it larger because other than to be held down or held back, I can't remember being picked up and held by anyone.

Not at all.

Ever.

ANNA'S JOURNAL
Wednesday, September 16, 1959

H ome again, only to discover Mother has taken over my room. My one true sanctuary, gone. Frederick has moved into Mother and Father's bedroom, while Mother insists on sleeping in mine, expecting me to rest alongside her in my tiny bed. It makes no sense. I need my room!

Frederick relinquished his bed when he left home long ago. His return was meant to be temporary until he found a place of his own. Why doesn't he move in with Mr. And Mrs. Demski if he's so desperate for a bed?

Oakville wiped me clean from the inside, and now Mother is trying to erase me from the outside. Not only has she taken my room, but she has thrown away all my old movie magazines. My pictures of Stewart, as well. She had no right. Those were my personal things!

She defended herself by claiming she assumed I had forgotten all about Stewart—that since my hospital stay, he'd been washed from my life. They certainly worked at it. However, Stewart's voice persists, like a muffled old radio from another room, or another world. A world that was once so crisp and full of promise and is now creased, torn, and faded. Hollywood seems farther away than ever from dreary Lock 4, where the trains are all coal cars, and the boats are all barges. Farther still from Oakville, where the dismantling began.

Still, I'm wondering if I wasn't better off there. At least they had a job for me at Oakville. Tedious work, certainly, but I fear it's all I'm capable of anymore. My reeducation has been so complete that, even if the placement agency finds me a job, my clerical skills have wasted away. When I see my old practice pages from steno class, it's like trying to read the curling trails of a woodworm.

I WAS READING *Peyton Place* in bed when Mother stumbled home from bingo last Friday night. She and Frederick quarreled—he's convinced she'll be hit by a train one of these nights while crossing the tracks near the churches. (St. Jerome's on Tuesdays, Mother of Sorrows on Fridays.) He described it in such detail that I began to wonder if it had already happened. When Mother finally walked into my room, I couldn't help but feel a twinge of disappointment that it hadn't.

"Don't come in," I said. But Mother did, anyway, and collapsed onto the bed beside me, fully dressed.

"Stop rustling the pages," she said to me, the same way Frederick often does. And again, just like Frederick, "Turn out the light."

I surrendered and carried my pillow to the davenport, which was cramped, hard, and cold. How did Frederick sleep on it every night for so many years? A short while later, I moved to Father's old overstuffed chair, where I may have fallen asleep for a minute, but it was no good, either. In the end, I carried my pillow to the hallway by the front door to lie on the floor where it was cool.

I had only been asleep an hour or two before Frederick kicked me awake, annoyed that he couldn't get by. He stepped over me, stomping his feet by my head, continuing to scold me under his breath as he walked to his car, but I couldn't hear him by then because I was hollering at him for waking me up. I can't even recall what I was saying—they were just sounds. I watched them erupt from deep in my gut. It happens that way sometimes. I can be utterly still on the inside while watching myself throw a fit.

With Frederick gone, I carried my pillow to Mother and Father's bedroom. "Frederick's room," Mother calls it now. I see why—the bed smells just like him. Like the Rolling Rock that seeps from his temples, and the residual Pall Mall smoke that blows from his open mouth as he snores. The acrid smell of the steel mill, too, that clings to his skin like the Death Smog.

I waited for Mother to get up in the morning, and when she finally did, I returned to my room and went to sleep alone in my familiar bed. It is the only spot that fits. Like Goldilocks.

ON SUNDAY, Mother insisted I go with her to church. I'm trying to be good and do as Mother asks. I clean the house, do the dishes, and so on—anything to avoid going back to Oakville.

But church still scares me. I don't need to understand Latin to know I am being judged. God hasn't forgiven me for all I've done, and I'm sure He never will. Everyone at church knows it, too. Mother only managed to persuade me to attend by telling me Father Galas was gone, and they have a new priest now. There is an excitement at church that I've never seen before, having something to do with a young Catholic man from Massachusetts, who the priest says is going to run for President. He says a Catholic hasn't run for president since 1928. It seems to give the congregation something to look forward to. Still, it was difficult for me to join in their excitement as I held my breath for the length of the entire service, expecting the font of holy water to explode like a hydrant, roaring forth in a torrent of judgment, soaking my head, trickling into my ears like rain.

I grew dizzy and left before the second syllable of the final Amen. *Dominus vobiscum.*

Mother found me outside and showed me off to a few of her friends, church ladies who all go to bingo and get sozzled, doubtless bad-mouthing their husbands and belittling their children the whole time. They are all fawning over a photo of the man they hope to vote for next year and they ask me what I think of Mr. Kennedy.

"I don't follow politics," I said.

"But isn't he handsome?" they said.

They told me how good I looked, too, and how happy they were to see me again. A phony flock of liars, all of them. Mother wanted me to wait so she could introduce me to the new priest, but I couldn't hold still any longer and left them all behind.

Waiting at the railroad crossing, watching the long string of coal cars pass, I imagined jumping aboard one of them like a hobo. But a better idea occurred to me: dive beneath the steel wheels and be done with the blackness for good. When we were children, Frederick taught me to put pennies on the tracks. I've seen what those wheels can do.

Breathless from the walk, I entered my room, sat on the bed, and slowly tapped my head against the wall.

Is this my life now? Is this all that's left? A greasy gray spot on the wall, a rhythmic thumping? It's almost enough to make me long for Oakville.

Almost.

What I really yearn for is a home of my own.

But where would I go? Stewart has grown bored, and I've lost all faith in his attraction to me. Am I ugly? There is no way to tell. I have no visitors. The mirror lies, and I've stopped looking at it when I brush my teeth—what I see is too scary. At the hospital, the doctors are old men, barely interested in me as a patient, much less a mate. The attendants are all made of brick, and the male patients are sequestered in a separate building entirely—some of them criminals.

Meanwhile, here at home, I'm a ghost. With Stewart gone, there is no one else. I doubt there ever will be again.

Honestly, I don't care much about men. (And the feeling appears mutual.) I know for sure there were boys in high school who wanted me. One boy, Albert, who had a locker near mine, would do a hammy impersonation of Mario Lanza when we passed in the hall. *"Be my love, for no one else can end this yearning..."* He said it razzed his berries to turn me red. Another boy, Dean, used to take the trolley all the way to North Charleroi with me, even though I knew for certain he lived in The Magic City. I would catch him looking at me, but we never spoke. High school boys were all so young and foolish they left me cold. Why would I bother with them when I had Stewart? The boys' attention made me sure of my looks, however, and my suspicions were confirmed by the jealousy it stirred from the other girls.

I wouldn't be doubting myself now—or care much about my looks one way or the other—if I hadn't agreed to let Frederick set me up on a blind date with his friend from work. It was a disaster before it even started. So much so that I don't even remember the man's name. Peter? I'm not sure. Why bother to keep a man's name in my head when there's so little room inside of it as it is. What I do remember is that the man lives in California—the town in Pennsylvania a few miles south of North Charleroi, not the state. Nevertheless, Frederick used the location as a means of persuasion: "Peter lives in California, just like your friend Stewart," he said.

California, PA, is nothing like Hollywood but, still, if I'm honest, the coincidence is what made me agree to the date. I should have known it wouldn't be enough.

Peter showed up at our door in a nice shirt and a run-down car, bearing a graveyard bouquet of aging, distressed white carnations. I never went to prom but if I had had the chance, a wilted corsage like that, compared to the gorgeous roses Mother grows, would have put me right off the idea all over again. Clean-shaven but for a Clark Gable mustache, he had fresh razor cuts on his face, which glistened with the trickle of forehead sweat belonging only to the truly nervous. He tried to kiss me on the cheek and, diving out of his way, I hit the passenger-side door jamb with the side of my head, creating a bump that we both tried unsuccessfully to ignore. I put my cool hand to my throbbing head and prayed for the evening to end.

As he started the car, Peter said, brightly, "You don't seem crazy." Which is the kind of thing people only say (e.g. "You got a haircut! It looks...great!") when they mean the opposite.

What had Frederick told him? *What other people think of you is none of your business.* But I was suddenly embarrassed, self-conscious, angry. Peter was ashamed, too, of his gaffe. He was bumbling and apologetic and, at times, appeared frightened. There was no climbing out of it for him.

We dined at a busy Italian restaurant in Charleroi, and the crowd made my discomfort all the worse. Everyone appeared to be murmuring the same as Peter had said, *"She doesn't seem crazy,"* while they nonchalantly slurped their minestrone and stabbed at their pasta. They were pretending to ignore me. Yet, I could feel them watching, waiting for me to do something out of the ordinary. Merely holding my fork the wrong way would have been enough for them to cry out: "Ah, hah! There it is— crazy! We knew it all along!"

I tried to control my thoughts, but the lights were too bright, and the silences between us much too long. When Peter did speak, it was about his work at Homestead Steelworks. The lengthy strike was over, and he was thrilled to be back at work —and with a raise.

"It was the longest strike as there's ever been," he said.

"A hundred and sixteen days," I said. He was surprised I knew that, but how could I not? Frederick has been talking about the strike for months. Frederick thinks the strike was a bad idea because the country is importing steel now, but Peter is jazzed to have been a part of it. "Better pension, better health insurance. It's a good job for a guy like me."

I focused on the rough edges of Peter's calloused hands and the yellowed tips of his fingers. I glanced at his eyes only once the whole night. They were yellowed, too. There was something defeated about his eyes, which darted to and from my face with something that could have been shyness, could have been shame. His eyes, his hands, the acrid steel-mill cologne, the conversation—all of it reminded me too much of Frederick. Peter is simply an old man from the mill, already at the age of twenty-five, nothing special. True, Stewart is an actual older man, as well, but he is cultured and refined. Why wasn't I seated across from Stewart, instead? Better yet, why wasn't I nestled beside Stewart in a velvet-upholstered banquette at Musso and Frank's, listening to enchanting tales of exotic travels and making plans for our future?

"Where would you like to go for our honeymoon, Anna? Como? Catalina? Havana? Mustique?"

"Anywhere, my darling. Anywhere!"

Peter sensed I was miles away. He reached across the table, shook me by the wrist, and startled me back to the restaurant. I looked down at my own hands with their jagged hangnails. I studied the fraying sleeve of my cardigan and watched a drop of red sauce seep into my skirt. Suddenly, I felt as if I had transformed like Cinderella after midnight. What did Peter think? I shouldn't have cared so much, but I'm embarrassed to admit I did.

It was raining when we left, rattling like pots and pans on the roof of the car. Tires on the wet road whooshed past us as Peter turned the key. Downtown Charleroi is no Hollywood, but the lights of The Magic City glowing through the fall mist were romantic, I must admit. Yet, it's because it was romantic, I still couldn't bring myself to look at Peter. He was not the one for me—not at all.

"You don't have to go home right away, do you?" he said as we drove. "Why don't we take a drive? I know a nice spot where we can park and talk some more."

Talk. Ha! I knew what he was really asking. Still, it was nice to feel desired by a man, any man—to be wanted by someone. I need someone to know me. Someone somewhere, to understand me even just a little, love me just a little. There should be a dozen men trying to court me. Maybe there will be. If Stewart abandons me as I fear he will, Peter might be the first of many.

Later, I lay in bed, remembering the windshield wipers of Peter's car going clack-clack-clack as he drove me home. I saw the wet blacktop rolling under the car tires like newspapers through a printing press. The night ended even quicker than I had hoped it would. Even now, as the sun begins to rise, I can still hear the wipers ticking off lost time with each clack. It never stops. It wasn't only a newspaper rolling from beneath the car's wheels; it was my life measured out in miles. Flattened dreams, scrolling behind me.

I should have allowed him to kiss me. Why not? I need to start living before it's too late.

Eric arrives from the hotel in the morning and I start to cook breakfast. Dad sits at the dining table, scribbling into one of his notebooks. Volumes of brittle, honey-colored pages line his shelves. The bindings are wrapped in aging cellophane tape curling at the corners. A black crust creeps under the edges of the tape like dirt beneath a fingernail. Written on unevenly cut pieces of construction paper, and attached to each cover with more layers of the crusty tape, the word: VISIONS.

I don't know if he's transcribing another vision, but I know better than to ask. The dogs settle at his feet, and he reaches down to pet them.

"Cheng has these growths, see?" he says. "Look here."

"I'm busy, Dad."

"Like little strawberries," he says. "Come look."

"I can't. I'm cooking."

He turns to Eric. "Look here, Ernie. The dogs got these growths from eating strawberries."

I want to scold him for feeding the dogs strawberries, but what's the point.

"They're skin tags," Eric says. "Nothing to do with what they eat."

"No, it happened to me, too," Dad says. "I once ate strawberries, and my nose turned red and got all bumpy like this—like a strawberry. I'm allergic to anything red—tomatoes, raspberries, strawberries, beets..."

Eric chuckles. "Where are you getting your strawberries? Willy Wonka?"

"I'm telling you, it's true. Look at my nose."

It's hard to deny his nose looks like a strawberry—with blackhead seeds against a red berry nose. But that's how it has looked for as long as I can remember.

As we settle at the breakfast table, a sparrow lands on the windowsill looking for Mom's handouts. It searches the well-pecked wood for sunflower seeds before flitting away in disappointment. A bag of Mom's birdseed still rests on the floor. I open the window and scatter a handful of it onto the sill. It's funny, the kindness that nonverbal creatures can inspire in you. Even in Mom. She probably liked me best before my mouth learned to form words, when it opened only for handouts like the birds.

Before we eat, Dad begins a long, rambling prayer. He's heard a lot of sermons in his life—some of them multiple times on vinyl—and he does his best to mimic their tone and inflection, but he may as well be speaking in tongues.

"Dear blessed Lord God, king of the universe, you are my rock and fortress. Your only son, Jesus, suffered so, so much for us. You raised your beloved son from the dead, and made him Lord an' all. We turn to him now in prayer and ask that he shine his light on us during this sad, sad time. I miss my Dorothy so much. I keep wanting to tell her something, but then remember she's with you now. Rachel is all I got left. She and Mike are all I got since you called Dorothy home. What will I do without my Dorothy?"

Good question, what *will* he do? Mom and Dad were married for over fifty years, constant dysfunctional companions through all of it. As difficult as their relationship was, they were about as intertwined as two human beings can be. Dad's loneliness is profound and I feel his emptiness as if it's my own. I squeeze his hand.

"I hope you bring Rachel home again, soon," he says. He's looking at Eric when he says it. There's a fine line between Dad's prayers and his everyday conversation, so it's difficult to tell who he's talking to. "You two look handsome together," Dad says—still focused on Eric. "I hope you two get married and give me grandkids someday. I'll be your dad. You can call me Dad. Like, when I married Dorothy, her father became my father, and Dorothy's mother became my mother. That's how it works."

"Let's eat," I say. "We have a long drive ahead of us."

Dad takes a bite of toast, but his mind is still grinding away. "Maybe it's too late for Rachel to have kids," he says.

"Drop it already, will you?"

He eats a little, complains I made the coffee too strong, but he's obsessed.

"If Rachel has a baby at her age, it might not turn out good. But you two could adopt."

I take a final swig of coffee, stand up, and begin to gather my things.

"C'mon, Eric, you ready?"

Eric rushes to finish what's on his plate.

"Wait!" Dad jumps to his feet. "I have something for you."

He runs into my old room and returns, carrying the box of my old things in one hand, and a green plastic grocery bag in his other. "I've been saving all this stuff for you," he says. "I told Dorothy she shouldn't be doing what she did, throwing all your belongings away like that. I snuck what I could into this box and hid it for you. All this time I've been hiding it. You should have it."

"I saw that box last night," I tell him.

"And you don't want none of it?"

"I took a few things."

"What about this?"

He holds up the grocery bag.

"What is that?"

"Your mother's jewelry," he says. "I planned to let Mike go through it first. He's the oldest and all. He might want to give some of it to his wife, Heather. She's my daughter too. But Mike left already, so maybe you want it?"

He hands me the bag, and I pull out a tangled knot of cheap baubles and pot-metal trinkets. Most of it appears broken.

"There's a ring in there somewhere," Dad says. "I bought it for your mother on our anniversary. A beautiful gold ring, real expensive."

Dad's ideas of what things are worth are utterly fantastic. He has tried to tell me the broken grandfather clock with the cracked and peeling veneer that sits in the corner of the damp basement is worth fifty-thousand dollars. But I did some research online and found a working sample of the same model for under fifty bucks. He says he remembers buying Mom's Baldwin organ, also broken, for close to a hundred grand at a time when he says he earned a dollar a day as a janitor at a mental hospital. The missing ring isn't worth much.

I pick at the sparkling knot of baubles as if searching for something of value in a magpie's nest.

"I don't see a ring, Dad."

"Maybe Mike took it. I wanted him to look through it all before I gave it to you. I thought Heather might want something. You ain't got no one to hand it down to like she does. Then again Alexander is a retard, so what is he going to do with it."

"Dad, watch your language." But whom does he even have around to offend at this point? I can't help thinking of Dad's notebooks. Not his vision diaries, but the daily planners he fills with notes about his relatives, both living and dead. Birthdays, phone numbers, assorted inconsequential details, his own magpie's nest. Life in shards. He even wrote Eric's birthdate in one of them. On the first page, he always draws a family tree, branching back as far as he can remember. Unsteady lines fan out in all directions like ink blown by a straw. Year after year, at the dead-end of a crooked branch hangs the name Rachel—an unfulfilled promise.

"We have to get going."

"What about the rest of it? You don't want your report cards? Your yearbook?"

I put on my coat and nudge Eric to do the same. The dogs scramble to their feet.

"If you need help or get lonely, you can always call me," I say. "Anytime, it doesn't have to be a Saturday. And don't forget Maggie and Jack are right next door."

"I'm already lonely," Dad says, his eyes becoming glassy. He clasps his hands and looks heavenward in his usual way. "You're all I got now, Rachel. You and Mike."

I give him a final hug and a promise to be back soon. My chest feels tight, and I can hardly breathe. It's difficult to leave him this way. How will he survive? At the same time, I am desperate to get away. I need to lie alone in my own bedroom's quiet darkness and process everything.

As we drive away, Dad stands by the side of the road, waving and weeping.

I cry, too, finally.

For miles.

"WONDER HOW LONG HE'LL LAST," I say, half to myself, as we merge onto the Interstate. Eric has learned the way and we've managed to make no mistakes getting out of town.

"Who, your dad?" he says.

"Yes. I give him a year, tops."

"Maybe. But people can be surprisingly resilient. You never know, he might live to be a hundred."

"Don't say that."

I recline the seat and close my eyes, hoping to sleep, but images from the past couple of days race through my head. "You should do a painting of him," I say.

"His face is so turbulent," Eric says. "It's like a Cubist painting as it is. I wouldn't know where to start."

"In heaven, riding a golden lawnmower."

We laugh.

"I'm not sure one painting could contain him."

"He can be your muse," I say.

I'm about to turn the radio on when my phone rings. It's Mike calling, but I don't answer. Not the first time. When he calls again, however, I fear something may have happened.

"Are you still with Dad?" Mike asks.

"Just left."

"We can't leave him alone."

"I had a talk with Jack and Maggie before I left. They'll watch out for him."

He grunts. "It figures Mom would die first," he says. "Thought that bitch would outlast us all."

"Is that why you called? To call Mom a bitch?"

"C'mon Rachel, you're the only person I can speak freely to. You're the one person who gets it. When I ran out of the house yesterday, it wasn't because of Dad's story, you know that, right? I mean, sure, that was part of it—okay, a big part—but it was more than that. Being home—the house—the corner of the kitchen where Mom would scatter hard grains of uncooked rice and make us kneel on it for hours until our knees bled. I was having flashbacks. Kept thinking: Was that really my life? Did that shit actually happen? I had to bolt."

By not responding, I hope he'll understand I don't want to talk about what our lives had been or what *really* happened. I want to remember the woman who recently started to feel like a mother on the phone—the one who'd been talking about birds, sharing recipes, telling funny stories about Dad.

"You're not crying, are you?" he says. "Seriously? Okay, never mind, listen, the main reason I'm calling has nothing to do with any of that."

"What, then?"

"I was telling Heather about the funeral—about you and about your boyfriend. She got curious and went digging—you know how she is. She found Eric's website. We saw the nudes, Rachel. What are you thinking? You need to get that garbage off the internet. What if the Army gets wind of that shit?"

"The Army? What are you talking about?"

"You know exactly what I'm talking about. Eric—his website —the pictures of you. We saw them."

"Big deal."

"Ever consider how it might reflect on me?"

"You?"

"I have a lot of people under my command, Rachel. I need their respect."

"What's that got to do with me?"

"You don't have a clue what it's like to have responsibilities, do you? There's a world beyond your little fantasyland, you know. A real world. But what would you know about it? You don't have a family. Do you even have a job?"

"Give me a break. I've seen how seriously you take your responsibilities."

"Who's the one who stood at Mom's bedside when she died?"

"Stop making me feel bad about that."

"How you feel is up to you. All I'm saying is, check your own shit before you come after me."

"I can't believe you're my brother. I can't believe we're related."

"We aren't related, Rachel. Remember that. I'm not related to Dad, and I'm not related to you!"

"Whatever."

"Yeah, whatever. Just get that shit off the internet."

ANNA'S JOURNAL
Friday, August 4, 1961

Nearly two months now, and things continue to go well here at home. True, when Mother told me to get ready for church, we had our usual spat, but in the end, I went along and managed to stay until it was over.

The only real trouble I've had is with the employment agency. I'm still furious about it. They say they can't place me until I am formally released from the hospital.

But I *have* been released! Clearly, I was sitting right in front of the woman, wasn't I? I couldn't have been any more released.

No, she said, I will need signed paperwork from a doctor.

The only way for me to get such documentation is to go back to Oakville for an interview. If I do that, I'm convinced the doctors will try to keep me there to continue their crazed experiments. They will give me more so-called x-rays and funnel more medicine down my gullet. I've finally finished the bottles they sent me home with. Taking my last pill was a milestone. Fully recovered, at last! Released! And I don't need papers to prove it.

Frederick has turned thirty-three. He says Jesus started a whole religion by that age, so he has set himself the goal of finding a place of his own before his next birthday. A wife, too, Mother prays—though I'm not sure she means it. I often overhear her begging Frederick not to leave her, saying she is afraid to be alone. It's as if I'm nothing more than a forgotten old mug gathering dust in the cupboard. If Mother were to pull that mug down from the shelf and dust it off, she'd see it's not useless.

What difference will it make if Frederick moves out, anyway? He's never home.

Mother wonders where he goes when he's out all night or is gone for days at a time. What does he do? Frederick never tells her, and he gets angry when she asks. "Leave me alone!" he says to her. "I don't ask where you go, do I?"

(But he doesn't need to ask. When Mother goes out at night, it can only be to one place: Bingo. The Demskis pay Mother eighty-eight dollars a month in rent, and it all goes to the game.)

I wish they'd both leave. I'd have a quiet home to myself with a reliable place to sleep. I could do what I want to do, call whomever I like, go wherever I choose. Or if I prefer to stay inside for days on end, I could do that too.

Unfortunately, the placement agency is standing in the way of achieving any such independence. I can't live on my own without a job.

To that end, despite the employment agency turning me

away, I've enrolled in a night class at Charleroi High School to brush up on my clerical skills. Having learned from my mistakes, I'm ready to try again. Dreadfully dull, yes, but not without a glimmer of promise. With luck, the school will place me in a good-paying situation. In Pittsburgh, perhaps. Even The Magic City would do for a while. Anywhere but Washington! We'll see.

I find that while sitting, again, in the same classroom I did during high school, my mind wanders the way it always has. How discouraging to be relearning all the things I would be an expert at by now if I'd had the chance to do more secretarial work these past few years. Not that it is my calling. I mustn't forget: I am an artist!

Sadly, when I took out my paints recently, I discovered all the tubes had gone hard. The caps are crusty and impossible to unscrew. My brushes are in a sorry state as well. I called Esther —my ever-faithful patron—and she promised to take me to the art supply shop in Charleroi. Walter got another promotion at the Pyrex plant, she said. She told me she and Walter might be moving to the Magic City. How wonderful for them. And how I envy their forward momentum.

MONDAY, AUGUST 7, 1961

Esther and Walter came over with little Judy and Walter Jr. the other day. Judy seems to have grown so suddenly. Five years old! I remember when she lived inside Esther's strained belly. What must it be like to live inside someone else? I should know, of course. After all, I lived inside of Mother once upon a time. Or so I'm told—it's hard to believe, as are most of the facts of my life these days. What's it like to have a baby living inside of you? I'm not sure I'll ever know. Or that I want to know. I often feel there are too many people inside of me as it is. The writer, the secretary, the model, the actress, the muse, the dinner date, the daughter, the sister, the seamstress, the patient, the artist...

Little Judy asked me to sit with her at the kitchen table and draw pictures with her crayons. It turns out Judy is quite talented. She scribbled an excellent portrait of me—a long oval head with a dull, flat, numb expression, crookedly balanced atop an angular body with spindly limbs. A frightened bird. Awkward, but accurate. In the distance, a building with a big red cross sat on top of a hill.

"Your hospital," Judy said.

Once again, I start, in horror and shame, at the idea of what Judy may or may not know about me. *What other people think of you is none of your business.* But how in the world can I not care? "I see, yes," I say. "I'm walking away from it."

Judy asked me to draw a portrait of her in return, which I did. But I'm not comfortable drawing people, so I added a few flowers around the face and concentrated on them instead. I spent quite a while carefully rendering the petals, and Judy was fascinated at how I was able to so easily pull them from memory.

"It's because I've been seeing Mother's roses all my life," I said.

Inspired to draw flowers, too, Judy suddenly darted outside and returned with a bushel of voluptuous roses she had plucked from Mother's prized rose bush. She placed the flowers in the middle of the kitchen table and began to draw. Mother was busy cooking, but it didn't take long for her to catch sight of the sacrificial flowers. When she did, her face bloomed like a rose itself—a deep-red scowl of densely clustered petals, undulating with wrath. As Mother snatched the roses from the table and shook them at Judy's face. In doing so, Judy's soft cheek was grazed by a razor-sharp thorn. Walter and Esther heard Judy's cries and rushed in from the living room. Walter screamed at Mother, and Mother screamed at Walter, which caused Walter Jr. to cry. Judy wailed, too, of course, and threw herself into Esther's arms. A line of red pinholes oozed tiny blood drops from Judy's cheek into Esther's sleeve.

I was reminded of how Walter defended me when I was young—when he was still around to catch Mother scolding me for one thing or another. It made me wish Walter still lived in the house with us.

All the noise overwhelmed me, and I locked myself in my room. Or, rather, I would have if Father hadn't removed the lock from my door so long ago.

The house shook from the noise. Despite a pillow over my head, the screams echoed in my ears and shook me, as well.

After what seemed like hours, I heard Walter's car drive off.

I didn't get my paints.

The next day, Frederick came home. He grew bored nearly as soon as he walked through the door and, in the afternoon, said he was going out for a while. Nothing unusual about it, except that this time he invited me to go along with him. I said, no.

"What are you going to do," he said, pointing to the wall, "stay here and bang your head?"

"I'm going to read."

"Come on, I'll buy you a sundae."

He took me to a diner in Charleroi, where we ran into a few of his friends. They were surprised when he introduced me— none of them seemed to know Frederick had a sister. I was glad for it, to be honest—happy to know Frederick hasn't been telling stories about me the way he did with that man, whatever his name is. Peter? Or the way Mother does with everyone. I know I make Frederick uncomfortable sometimes—his face gets the same cold expression Father's often did. But I shouldn't be too hard on him. He mostly treats me like what I am: his little sister.

He bought me lunch—a Reuben sandwich and a mountain of French fries. And a sundae for dessert, as promised.

While we ate, he told me about a girl he met named Twilight. It's not her real name, he said, it's the name of the town where she lives. Twilight Township is a few miles south of The Magic City, but everyone calls the girl Twilight, and now she calls herself that, too.

After telling me about Twilight, Frederick wanted to know if there was anyone I liked. Any men.

He knows all about Stewart, but he didn't want to hear about him. He only wanted to see if I was interested in anyone from the area.

"I saw our friend Peter last week," he said. "He asked about you. He was wondering if you'd been seeing anyone. He'd like to take you out again. Would you like me to arrange a date?"

I said no.

"Spending so much time with Mother isn't good for you," he said, "It's not good for anyone. Her drinking has been getting worse, have you noticed?"

I had noticed. But the more she drinks, the more she sleeps, which is fine by me. And anyway, a local man like Peter will only distract me from my ultimate goal of leaving Pennsylvania for good. I intend to stay focused.

On our way home, Frederick took me to the art supply store and bought me what he could afford. Thank goodness for Frederick.

REUNION

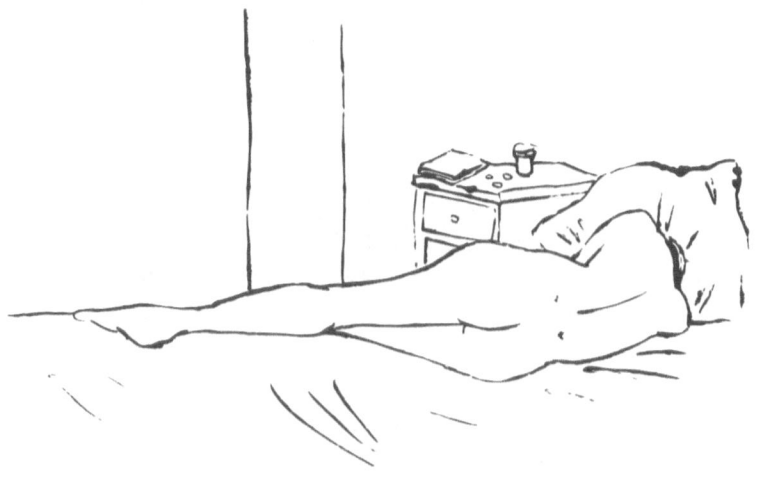

Eric phones regularly—every three days—but I don't pick up or listen to the messages he leaves. His calls are only a way to mark time, like a calendar, or an alarm clock.

Dad's calls are more erratic, yet persistent, and guilt paws at me like the dogs. He has abandoned our Saturday at five o'clock rule altogether. When I finally answer, Dad is already mid-sentence by the time I say hello.

"...may be none of my business but it's not right. We didn't raise you to—"

"What?"

"Mike said you're making *pornography*!"

"Well, Mike's a liar."

Trying to describe Eric's semi-nude art photos, which wouldn't even make the grade for soft-core, isn't worth the effort. Explaining that I am not exactly recognizable nor mentioned by name in the pictures is also moot.

"I shouldn't have given you that ring," Dad says. "Your mother's beautiful gold ring."

"There is no ring."

"I can hear your mother's voice telling me it was a mistake to let you have all her beautiful things. She was a decent woman."

Infuriated to realize Mom is still judging me from beyond the grave, I hang up on Dad and throw my phone across the room. It lands beside the plastic bag of tangled junk on the floor. Next to the jewelry is the paperwork from my adoption, and suddenly I want nothing to do with Dad, or Mom, or my plastic inheritance.

I shake out a wrinkled shirt and a pair of pants and get dressed.

After stuffing the bag of jewelry into a manila envelope, I carry it to the end of the street and drop it into a corner mailbox. Not sure I gave it enough postage, but I don't care.

A slight breeze catches a few dry leaves, and they scrape the asphalt. The autumn sun is low but bright, filling the street with exaggerated shadows. A few people sit on a bench outside the local coffee shop, planning out their day. I want to sit outside in the warm sun, too, but I'm barely dressed and head home to change.

Upon re-entering my gloomy sublet, I'm struck by the mess —the stale smell, the crushed cans of Guinness, the crumpled bags of chips. The sheets are filthy, and the bed is covered with wads of tear-stained tissues. An empty blister pack of grey-market Xanax sits next to my pillow. My suitcase isn't even unpacked.

If I'm not careful, I'll wind up like Dad: crazy, broke, and alone. Much as I hate to admit it, nurture counts as much as nature and, no matter what Mike says, we *are* related.

———

WITH ERIC'S loan quickly spent and next month's rent bill looming, I call a few fellow bartenders to see if I can dig up any work. It's all I know how to do. I once had a job in a realtor's office I lasted maybe six months before I put in my two-weeks' notice. They laughed and fired me on the spot.

"You can't do that." I'd said.

"We just did."

I haven't bothered with a desk job since.

Although he doesn't come highly recommended, I get the number of a guy named Rocco, who owns several dive bars in Williamsburg. When he answers the phone, his Flatbush accent is so thick I assume he's putting it on. I laugh a little, but he doesn't seem to notice.

"Perfect timing," he says. "One of my girls just quit."

From what I'd been told, it happens a lot.

I can't afford to be choosy, so I arrange to meet him at a bar he owns near the Lorimer L stop—only three stops from my place. He shows up in matching sweats and a cauliflower ear, the kind you can only get from a direct blow that stops just short of killing you. He takes one look at me—granted, in dim light—and I know that I am a "yes," which feels gratifying. After a rhetorical "What, you live around here?" he asks me exactly nothing about myself. He tells me about the storied history of the bar—"They say Lucky Luciano used to whack people in here, which I don't want to brag about, exactly, but still..."—clearly trying to instill the premises, and himself by association, with legend. The bar occupies about a thousand rundown square feet off Metropolitan Avenue, and is a far cry from Spark's Steak House. There are still a couple of old-school Italian "social clubs" nearby, though, so who knows what secrets the place might hold. But I'm not looking for stories, I'm looking to make money and, for that, it doesn't instill confidence.

It reminds me of walking into the Sapphire Club for the first time. Still new to New York, I'd come across a want ad in the back of the Village Voice looking for bartenders. I remember the lighted sign hanging above the club's entrance. It featured a line drawing of a top hat, a cane, and what looked like a sparkling diamond, though I assume it was meant to be a sapphire. So-called Gentlemen's Club's had been cropping up everywhere back then and it was hard to keep them straight. Diamond, Gold, Silver, Platinum—I remember triple checking the address to be certain I was at the right place. My roommate at the time convinced me that strip clubs were money machines but, when I pulled open the heavy chrome door and waited for my eyes to adjust to the darkness, all I saw was two listless dancers, each wearing a florescent G-string and a pair of clear plastic platform mules, languishing onstage. One of them spun on a pole—practice as much as performance since there were only two customers, neither of whom were paying much attention. At the opposite end of the stage, the other dancer was inspecting her own reflection in a wall-sized mirror, chewing gum and twirling her hair. I think I saw her pop a zit. Music was playing, but barely. All in all, the so-called money machine was on the fritz. I only lasted a couple of months. And the club itself didn't last much longer.

We'll see how it goes here at Rocco's place. If nothing else, it's convenient—a luxury for a shift worker—so, for now, it's perfect.

WHILE I WIPE down the tap, one of the regulars, who has been here since I arrived and has probably been here for hours, orders a Pabst. I pull a can from a bucket of ice, place it on the bar, and continue what I'm doing.

He picks it up, looks at it, and calls out. "You're s'pposed to open it."

Rinsing the filthy bar rag, I pretend not to hear him.

"You need a lesson in how to bartend," he says. "You open the can, that's proper bartending. Ask Kimmy, she opens them."

"Kimmy's not here."

I assume that's the end of it, but when Rocco arrives later in the night, the customer stops him and says, "Your girl here sucks." He grumbles about the unopened can of beer and my unprofessional attitude.

When Rocco pulls me aside, I try not to stare at his cauliflower ear. His cauliflower face.

"Listen," Rocco says, "serving an unopened can or bottle in a bar is against the law. As a bartender, you should know that."

I want to tell him it's illegal for him to water down the liquor, too, but I need the job, so I stay quiet.

"More important," he says, "this is a neighborhood bar, and these are my regular customers. You need to show some respect. Either treat them right or take a walk. I won't tell you again."

Rocco owns a couple of other bars—better places where I can earn more money—so I collect myself and apologize to him. Apologize to the customer too, who chooses not to make eye contact with me for the moment.

After Rocco leaves, a woman comes in and sits down next to the guy who complained. She gives the guy a peck on the cheek and takes off her jacket. The light is weak, but I recognize her as another regular who never tips.

"Hey sweetheart," the guy calls from down the bar like a big shot. "Yo, sweetheart."

"I'm not your sweetheart," I say.

"What do you want him to call you?" the woman says, "Bitch?"

They both laugh.

I ignore them. If these two want a drink, they'll have to find another bar.

"To hell with you," the guy says. "This is my bar, and Rocco is my pal. Next time I see him, I'm getting your ass fired."

"Go for it. This is my last night at this dump anyway."

Accepting my fate, I break the seal on a yet-to-be diluted bottle of Johnnie Walker Black, the best this bar has to offer, and pour myself a shot.

"Cheers," I say, mimicking the smug smile the guy had given me.

After gulping it down, I pour myself another. Since there's no point in putting off the inevitable, I find the bar back and tell him to watch the place while I head out into the night to continue my drinking someplace else.

SETTLING into my usual seat at Kings County, my local, I'm about to order a drink when a young guy from the neighborhood walks over and introduces himself.

"I've seen you around," he says. "You live in my building."

He's familiar, twenty-something, skinny jeans and a beard, but it doesn't mean much—all the guys around here look exactly like him.

"I'm Devon," he says, and holds out his hand.

It hangs mid-air for an awkward moment before I finally shake it.

He flutters around me like a moth. Probably weighs less than I do, which, after living off Guinness and cheese curls all month —and vomiting up most of it—isn't much. I ask how old he is.

"Old enough to be here, if that's what you mean."

"Barely."

"Twenty-three," he says, proving my point. "How about you?"

"Never mind."

It looks as though the implied age gap might scare him off. But after stammering a bit, he sits and says, "My sister is thirty."

"And?"

"I get along with older women."

He's hopeless, grasping at the edge of a sinkhole. I can either lend him a hand or tap the crown of his head with my boot heel. Before I have a chance to decide, his phone buzzes with a text message, and he turns away to read it. I figure that's the end of it and flag down the bartender to order a drink, but no, Devon swivels back toward me.

"My friend Todd just invited me to a burlesque art party. Want to come?"

I'm not sure what a burlesque art party is, but it's hard to muster up an interest.

"Where is it?" I say.

"Curious 24. Know it? It's a few blocks from here. We can walk. I'll text my friend Todd and let him know we're coming. He'll get us in for free."

AFTER A TEN-MINUTE WALK to the middle of an industrial complex, the only clue to the existence of a party is a small gaggle of art school flunkies smoking outside a warehouse door, which is not that rare a sight outside any of the illegally converted factory buildings in East Williamsburg. As we approach, Devon texts Todd to let him know we're outside, and, soon after, Todd emerges to wave us in like a crossing guard.

The gallery is filled with elaborately costumed performers. Aerialists swinging from the ceiling, dancers teetering atop wobbly pedestals. An acting troupe performs experimental scenes on the floor, circled by a drunk and raucous crowd. It is impossible to tell the spectators from the performers, which I suppose is the whole idea. Todd ushers us across the floor to keep us from being assimilated, raising his arm like the leader of a tour group, leading us toward the bar in the backroom. Along the way, a performer in a blindfold bumps between us, causing Todd to stop abruptly.

"Wait," he says.

The performer struggles blindly onto a nearby pedestal.

"You have to see this dude," Todd says. "He's amazing."

Pitching this way and that, the performer begins a slow-motion striptease down to his saggy briefs. Todd and Devon are transfixed, but I've seen plenty of boney guys in saggy under-wear, so I continue to the bar, alone.

It's more like a lemonade stand—a folding table cluttered with plastic cups and cheap bottles of wine. A handwritten sign reads 'Suggested Donation.' Behind the table, two girls stop dancing long enough to slosh a serving into a plastic cup and hand it to me. I throw a dollar onto the bar. The girl holds up her hand.

"It's five," she says.

I point to the sign.

"It says suggested donation. I'm suggesting a dollar."

"It's a fundraiser," the girl says. "Five dollars a cup."

I put the drink on the table and tell her I'm not paying five dollars for a small plastic cup half-filled with crappy wine. She throws back the wine, herself, and resumes dancing.

Without a drink, the party devolves from absurd to unbear-able. I slip into an adjacent room, which is quiet and nearly empty, to decide if there's any reason not to leave and get drunk at home instead.

A grainy black and white video projection flickers against the wall—it features a dozen nude dancers frolicking in a park. As I pause to make sense of it, someone comes up behind me and puts a hand on my shoulder. I'm about to elbow the creep in the gut when I turn to see it's Eric.

"Surprised to see you here," he says.

"It's my neighborhood," I say. "What's your excuse?"

"Zack invited me. He's a local gallerist I met through work. Zack wants to show my paintings here. I came to check it out."

Despite calling itself a gallery, it seems a strange place to show paintings. Although a couple of canvasses are hanging on the walls, it's not clear if they are meant to be art. They look more like party decorations. Either way, they are nothing like Eric's work.

Eric explains he won't be showing in the main space but the one we're standing in.

I struggle to picture it.

"Trust me," he says, doing a little dance to mimic the wall projection. "It'll work."

"What happened to all that *I'm done with art* stuff?"

"You know better than to believe me when I go off like that," he says. "To tell you the truth, I've been painting a lot since I saw you last. Our trip to Daisytown inspired me."

"What a coincidence, it inspired me too. Inspired me to want to kill myself."

He gives me a concerned look.

"I'm joking."

The place is loud, and he leans in to my ear.

"How have you been doing?" he says. "You never return my calls."

"I know, sorry. It's been a lot to digest. I'm better now." I gesture toward his cup of wine. "Can I have a sip?"

"Finish it. It's terrible."

It's gone in one gulp.

"I can't stay here any longer," I say. "Want to go somewhere else?"

Without a word, he takes my hand and pushes through the crowd.

Performers claw for attention. Devon notices me and calls out as we pass.

"Hey," Devon says, and repeats it, louder. "Hey!"

I'm relieved I never told him my name. I hold Eric's hand tighter, and, with a final push through the gallery door, we burst out of the vortex and onto the quiet street.

"Ah, fresh air," says Eric.

He must be joking—the air is filled with diesel fumes and cement dust. Then again, compared to the boozy musk of sweaty hipsters, the breeze does feel somewhat crisp and clean.

The closest bar is the one I just came from, but I don't dare suggest it. I don't want to be seen in my default pick-up spot with Eric. Or maybe I don't want Eric to be seen there with me. Perhaps both. All I know is I don't want to go back to where I've already been. I want to push forward with the night, with my life, go somewhere I've never been before—somewhere new.

"Did you drive?" I ask.

WE HEAD to Greenpoint and find quiet place near Eric's apartment.

"Is it safe to buy you a drink?" he asks, appearing to suddenly have second thoughts.

"Yes," I say, not sure that it's true.

Eric looks me over as if to do some sort of calculation.

It's a waste of time. No workable formula exists for figuring out whether I'll have a beer or two and call it a night, or continue until I'm tossing barstools. Let him take his best guess.

Eventually, he heads to the bar to order us each a Guinness while I settle into a back booth. The Guinness takes time to pour and, as Eric waits, I catch my sorry reflection in the mirror behind the taps. The lighting is dim, but not dim enough. I dig out my lip balm.

"Here we go," Eric says, returning with the drinks. "Cheers."

He looks me in the eye, almost staring.

"Why are you looking at me like that?" I say.

"You're supposed to look a person in the eye when you toast, that's all." He takes a sip. "I'm glad I ran into you. I've been worried."

I rotate my glass, draw a line through the condensation, stick my finger in the foam and taste it, resisting the urge to guzzle. Do I tell him I've been worried about me, too?

"Tell me about your paintings," I say. "If you can get past the craziness, Daisytown is a beautiful place, isn't it? What have you been painting? Stink bugs?"

"Ha, no, but that's a great idea. I'll have to work some in. How's your old man doing? I've been thinking about him."

"He's fine. I mean, he tells me he wants to die every time I talk to him, but otherwise, he's fine."

"Seriously?"

"He'd never do it. Suicide is a sin. He wants God to take him."

"Do you?"

"Do I what? Want God to take him? Or to take me?"

"Either."

Although I spent a broad swath of childhood wishing my parents were dead—both of them—it's been a long time since I thought about it in such stark terms. If I still feel that way now, I'd rather not admit it.

"Can't we talk about something else?"

The bar crowd ebbs and flows, getting loud at times, other times still and quiet. Vampire Weekend comes over the sound system and I nod along to the song while nursing my drink. If Eric wasn't here, I'd be drinking my second round already, probably bum a cigarette from someone, too. Instead, I play with my coaster, spinning it, scraping it, peeling it apart. Another song comes on—Yeah Yeah Yeahs—and I sing along to the few words I know. *"Heads will roll, heads will roll..."* The way this is all going is precisely why I've been avoiding him.

A wall-mounted television is showing an old black and white movie with the sound off. The female lead is taking long, deliberate, drags from a cigarette before delivering smoke-covered lines with relaxed confidence. I wish that were me.

Eric asks a question, but I have to ask him to repeat it.

"Did you find anything out about your birth mother?" he says.

The table is covered with torn pieces of coaster by now, and I blow them to the floor.

"Didn't you find some papers with your birth mother's name on them? Figured you might have started digging around."

Despite trying to pace myself, I've finished my drink, and I suggest we get another. If we're going to talk about this, I need to relax.

Eric leans back and sizes me up, trying to see how close I am to that invisible line. I give him a look in return, intended to let him know I'm insulted by his lack of faith.

"Just one more," I say.

ANNA'S JOURNAL
Sunday, May 6, 1962

The grandfather clock ticks hard and sharp from the next room. Like a sculptor's chisel, chipping away at my life. Tick-tock, insistent, relentless. But still not loud enough to obscure the memory, still as vivid as if it were yesterday, of Stewart's voice burrowing through the pillow that I press tightly to my ears. What have I done?

Why did I allow Frederick to talk me into seeing his friend

Peter again? And how on earth did Stewart find out that I'd been allowing Peter to kiss me? Now, Stewart's voice echoes all day and into the night, saying things I never imagined I'd hear him say. Awful things. But what did he expect from me? Especially with Mother and Frederick continually pressuring me to meet people while Stewart himself remained so silent. He couldn't expect me to wait forever.

Peter phoned a few days after our interlude, and Mother scolded me for refusing to talk to him. Frederick scolded me, too. "Peter told me you two had a nice time," said Frederick, not knowing the details. "What's wrong with you?"

What's wrong, indeed.

"You're too picky," Mother said when I told her I didn't like Peter and that I didn't want to see him again. "If this fellow is interested in you, you should spend time with him," she said. "You're lucky to find someone. If you wait any longer, you'll never find a man."

Perhaps it was Mother who snitched to Stewart—told him what I'd done as a way to sabotage my frail hopes. Mother sees me as a burden and is eager for someone—anyone but Stewart, that is—to take me off her hands. But I'd rather be alone in my room than to share a bed, a home, a life, with a local man like Peter. He reminds me too much of Frederick. Worse, he reminds me of Father. Could I rely on a man like that to stand up for me? To rescue me the way Stewart was meant to do? Hardly.

I might feel differently if kissing Peter had made me feel pretty and filled me with self-assurance, but it didn't. And now that I've ruined things with Stewart, I have blown my opportunity to ever feel that way.

Or maybe it was Frederick who sabotaged my relationship with Stewart? Or, perhaps, Peter himself? But, no, surely Peter knows nothing about my true love, much less how to reach him. I'm afraid it was I who vandalized my life through my own behavior and gave away my secrets through my own demeanor. Sins waft from my pores.

I'm like the porcelain figurine Mother won playing bingo—the shepherd who is forever trudging across the mantle, burdened with a lamb across his shoulders. Except my burden is not a lamb but a sopping bag of guilt. It's become impossible for me to stand upright under the weight of it. Thus, one more voice is added to the growing choir—that of Miss Keeble, my teacher in modeling school. I hear her talk of being elegant, of being a lady, while scolding my posture. "You must stand up straight!" Impossible.

There's no one to blame for this mess but myself. Peter didn't force himself on me—I wanted to be loved. Willed it, in fact. Not that I have feelings for him. It was a lifeless act. Like watching *Walt Disney's Wonderful World of Color* on my black and white TV set.

Peter didn't seem so well dressed this time. And his car appeared to be rusting in front of my eyes. He wanted to take me dancing at Park Casino—a well-known passion pit. I suggested a movie, instead. We went to the State Theater and saw *Tender is the Night*. I didn't know anything about it other than it starred Jason Robards who I thought was so wonderful in *The Ice Man Cometh* a couple of years ago. If I'd known *Tender is the Night* involved a woman who married her psychiatrist I never would have suggested it. I tried to imagine me marrying Dr. Abrams, and it turned my stomach. Maybe it's why I turned so wooden toward Peter. When Peter squeezed my hand in the theater, I didn't squeeze back. But when he kissed my neck, and petted my breast through my sweater, I didn't protest. He held my chin and turned my face towards his and we made out for maybe fifteen minutes before I excused myself to use the bathroom.

Whatever it was, the kiss is worthless to me now. Worse than worthless, because Frederick says that Peter wants to be my boyfriend! I'll never see him that way, and I must be direct in telling him so. "But what about the kisses?" he's sure to ask. Do I admit to him that I just wanted to see what a kiss was like? That I just needed some attention to reassure myself that I exist? Yes, that's all it was—proof that I exist. And now I wish I didn't.

This feeling of guilt is nothing new. I suffer guilt about all my weaknesses, both mental and physical. Guilt about my failures—in school, at work, with my art and my writing. I once wanted to be a reporter, but all I have succeeded in reporting on are my own inadequacies. I am useless.

And I'm not just saddled with guilt, but filled with anger, too. Anger at Frederick for introducing me to his friends. At Mother for putting me in the hospital. Anger at the world for expecting too much from me. And at myself for expecting too much from the world.

It's tempting to write to Stewart and explain why I did what I did, but I'm too ashamed. He'll never forgive me. I'll never be pure again. If ever I was.

HOSPITAL

H ushed voices, the ring of an office phone, a muffled intercom—I begin to wake. The curtain opens with a loud metallic whoosh. A nurse comes in and stands beside me, preparing to check my blood pressure or to fiddle with my IV. I open my eyes and realize it's not a nurse—it's Eric holding my hand. I had been so embarrassed for him to see where I came from, and now I'm mortified for him to see where I wound up—crumpled and broken in an Emergency Room.

I try to pull the thin white sheet over my head, but he stops me.

"I'm sorry," I say. I'm not sure why I'm apologizing, but I repeat it. "I'm sorry."

Maybe I'm apologizing to myself—that nothing has changed in all these years. Or perhaps I'm apologizing for not being a better girlfriend, assuming that that's what he wants me to be.

Seeing his face brings back snippets from last night, but nothing more. I remember drinking with him and talking about my adoption. I remember going back to his place, not being able to sleep, and slipping back to the bar. After that, nothing. Paved over like a parking lot, hard, lifeless, and black.

"I'm such a loser," I say.

Eric runs his hand across my face.

"What happened to your cheek?" he asks.

"I don't know. Why?"

"It's a little red, bruised, maybe."

"How did I get here? Did you bring me?"

"No. The last time I saw you, you were in bed next to me. By the time the cops called to let me know you were here, the sun was up. They said they bought you in for your own protection. That's all I know. I feel responsible. I shouldn't have bought you those drinks."

I shake my head, no, and the room spins.

"You can't go on like this," he says. "It's not healthy. It's dangerous."

The impending lecture is cut short when the doctor walks in.

"Are you her...?" the doctor asks Eric, trying not to make any assumptions.

"A friend," Eric replies hastily, hanging his head a bit.

Yes, I weakly nod, just a friend.

"The test results came back. Everything is satisfactory. We gave her activated charcoal and put her on a drip to regulate her blood sugar levels. Her vitals look good. If you're here to escort her home, we can release her. Her alcohol poisoning is a relatively mild case, as these things go. Nevertheless, she wound up here, and that's not good."

They huddle together and speak in muffled voices for a moment before the doctor turns to me.

"I don't see any reason to keep you," he says. "But you need to take this seriously. We don't want to see you here again, do we?"

His kindness is matter-of-fact and it brings tears to my eyes. As if it's that simple.

The doctor says a nurse will be by shortly with paperwork to sign. He wishes me well and walks out.

A hospital worker enters carrying a clear plastic bag filled with clothing. She lifts a pair of glasses to her eyes and double-checks its label before tossing the bag onto the bed.

"Make sure this stuff is yours," she says. "Be sure you got everything."

The hospital staff shows less sympathy toward me as a woman pushing forty who has so many mistakes behind her than they did to me as a teenage waif with so many of them still ahead. It can only get worse as time churns forward. Eventually, I'll be old and crazy like Dad, with everyone's patience having long run out.

When I was nineteen, the doctor had said that my gallbladder condition was likely congenital, always a tricky thing to say to an adoptee. I remember regarding the sharp pangs like a tug toward some vague history. An unknown mother or father standing at the far end of a long rope, yanking at the hook in my gut. It had given me the idea to use the condition as an excuse to petition the courts for access to my adoption information. A need to know my medical history. "A matter of life and death!" I would say. It's so long ago, but I remember sending a letter to a judge who denied the request. Pennsylvania's privacy laws concerning adoption were among the strictest in the country, I was told. Like my gallbladder, I now wonder if my drinking is congenital, too. They say it often is. Questions about my birth parents—my birth mother in particular—keep gurgling to the surface, slushing around in my head. I sit up and try to puke, but I'm spent.

The clothes in the bag are cold. Everything in the hospital is. The clothes are mine, but they feel as if they belong to someone else—someone with other plans. I put on my shirt and pants. I slip on my socks and pull on my boots. The movement gives me a head rush, and I sit against the edge of the bed to regain my equilibrium.

"Where's your coat?" Eric asks.

"Did I have one? I don't remember."

"Here," he says, handing me his jacket. "It's cold outside."

I struggle to get my arms in the sleeves.

"Take your time. We still have to wait for someone to come by with the paperwork."

I want to lie down, but I'm afraid I'll never get up again, so I remain half-perched while we wait. When a woman finally arrives, she hands me a clipboard and gives Eric a few pamphlets. After I sign what I need to sign, the attendant notices me struggling to remove my hospital ID bracelet. She pulls a pair of scissors from her pocket and cuts it from my wrist. I toss the bracelet toward a nearby bin, and it lands on the floor.

Eric picks it up. "You don't want this?" he says.

Why would I?

With the attendant on one side and Eric on the other, they help me stand.

"Go slow," the woman says.

Once in the car, I mess with the controls attempting to open the window but only succeed in locking and unlocking the door a couple of times. Eric works a button from his side and opens the window.

"A little more," I say.

He reaches over and helps me with my seat belt. The pamphlets fall to the floor.

"What is that stuff?"

He picks them up and flips through them—an explanation of alcohol poisoning, a list of rehab facilities, a phone number for AA. He places them on my lap.

"You'll stay with me for a couple of days," he says firmly.

I close my eyes and lean into the headrest. Let him drive me into the East River for all I care.

As we pull away, the literature falls to the floor again.

"Hang onto that stuff," he says. He's saying it more to himself than me at this point.

ANNA'S JOURNAL
Thursday July 18, 1963

I 've been smothered by a dense cloud, again. The weight of
so much guilt pushed me into a deep hole, which tunneled
back to Oakville. Building 5, Jamison cottage.

Nurse Winthrop scolded me for hoarding a stack of magazines I took from the day ward. She would only let me to keep

one so I chose a copy of *Life*, saying, "Choose life, that both thou and thy seed may live."

I laughed, and a second later, she laughed, too.

The magazine is four years old already—July 9. 1959—but the world it contains is so alien to me, it may as well have been printed in the future. A future I once felt destined to join but now, especially back at Oakville, seems beyond an impenetrable pane of glass.

I remember riding with Mother and Father to West Penn Hospital in Pittsburgh for the first time. A station wagon passed us, sun glinting from its chrome. Inside the car was a perfect family. A sharply-dressed man behind the wheel, his beautiful wife beside him. Two young children—not much younger than I was—bouncing with laughter in the back seat. They caught me staring and began to pull faces at me. I turned away and held my breath until they passed. That's how the future feels. Time is moving too fast for me to keep up, mocking me as I trail behind in an old jalopy under someone else's control, mocked by my peers. Holding my breath until things get better. Will they?

I only have to glance around this hospital to see what lies ahead—ultimate disaster. Doomed to years of suffering before my bones finally collapse in plumes of dust like broken light bulbs. I will wake up tomorrow and be old. Or am I already old? Have I already died? How would I know? Is it too late to pray for a fairy godmother to come to my rescue? Frederick is gone. When will I disappear too?

When I met with Dr. Abrams this morning, he tried to tell me the machine and the pills are designed to help me cast aside such gloomy thoughts and feelings. But what if dark thoughts and feelings are all I have, what if my flaws are who I am? What if erasing them will leave me with nothing? What's the point of life in that case? Do I even have a choice?

Gardner McKay is on the cover of the magazine I chose to keep. I've watched him in *Adventures in Paradise* on television.

He's handsome, like Stewart. The article says he is an artist, too, like me. But a sculptor. I've inhaled the pages so many times already, waiting for something to wash over me, but nothing ever comes. No twisting, no shuddering, no legs like noodles. I seem incapable of any such feelings or sensations now.

The other day, Olive asked me if I would rather be happy and stupid like Henrietta in her rocking chair, or smart, yet extremely sad. Like me, she didn't have to add. I don't think she wanted to know my answer as much as tell me her own because, without hesitation, she said: "I want to be like Henrietta."

The grass is always greener, I guess. Henrietta has been here longer than any of us and she can barely speak. She had an operation years ago that scrambled her brain.

"I want to have an operation like that," Olive said. "I've even asked for one, I don't know why they won't do it. It would be best for everyone."

I feel like an idiot as it is, and being one doesn't lessen my suffering so, no, I do not want such an operation.

DESPERATE FOR SOMETHING TO occupy my time, I went to the crafts room to look for clay. I've seen people do simple things with it. Ashtrays, mostly. But, after reading of Gardner McKay's sculptures, I was inspired to try something more elaborate. The magazine features a picture of Gardner McKay sculpting a bust. A self-portrait? I'm not sure, but it's what I wanted to do—to sculpt a life-sized self-portrait which I could then mold into the face of someone new. I felt inspired to start on it right away. But, they wouldn't allow me as much clay as I needed. "We have to save some for the others," they said. Why? So that they can make more ashtrays? Apparently, yes. The little mound of clay they gave to me was barely enough to craft even the tiniest shrunken head, so, in the end, I made an ashtray, too. Just like everyone else. I'll offer it to Frederick as an apology for what-ever I've done. If I ever see him again.

GREENPOINT

My things gradually migrate from my apartment to Eric's—my toothbrush, clothes, choice unguents and toiletries, finally my favorite pillow—until, before I know it, I've moved in completely.

Eric lives on the first floor of a vinyl-sided row house on a tree-lined street in Greenpoint. It feels like a real neighborhood. As Eric and I carry the last of my things into Eric's apartment, we run into the landlord, and Eric introduces me to him.

"Wait," says the landlord, before ducking into his own apartment. He returns a moment later with a housewarming gift for me—a bottle of wine he made from the grapes growing in the backyard. "Welcome," he says in a heavy Polish accent.

I can't help but be reminded of Papa, and I like the landlord instantly.

I place the bottle on the kitchen counter and begin to unpack my things while Eric complains to the landlord about the broken door buzzer. Once the man is gone, Eric heads straight for the bottle, opens it, and unceremoniously pours it into the sink.

"Don't trust me?" I say.

"It's not you," he says. "I'd pour this wine in my car's oil tank before I'd let *anyone* drink it."

I don't believe him. "Why?"

"Because we're sitting less than a block away from the epicenter of a decades-old underground oil spill bigger than the Exxon Valdez." As he rinses the bottle, he tells me more. "Up the road lies Newtown Creek—an industrial dumping ground for the past hundred years. Everything from smelting waste to animal fats. Not to mention overflow from the sewage treatment plant. It's a superfund site." To hear him tell it, the house's backyard garden floats above a cesspool for the circles of hell. "Seriously," he says.

It's disappointing to hear. After living in the middle of an industrial park, I was looking forward to trees, flowers, birds, and squirrels, if not a little homemade wine. It seems everything is tainted if you dig deep enough.

Eric shakes the last few drops into the sink and rinses the bottle.

"Have you thought any more about what I suggested?" he says, drying his hands on his pants.

I'd actually been making a concerted effort not to think about it.

"I just think you should try it, that's all. It seems to help people."

I slam my mug down hard on the table—harder than I mean to. The spoons jump.

"I tried it for two fucking years, okay? It's not for me. Praying to a higher power, thanking God—it reminds me too much of my childhood. You met my dad. You can understand, can't you?"

He stares dumbly. I don't think he can.

I bump him out of the way so I can wash out the coffee pot and make some coffee. He says nothing further, not wanting to upset me.

The coffee is bitter. I dump an extra spoonful of sugar into my mug—a little more milk, too—as I consider sharing more with Eric. I want him to understand.

But, no. He knows too much as it is. And, I am continually finding out, I don't know enough, or at least not enough to keep me out of trouble.

THE NEXT DAY, Eric is up and out early for his day job at an art warehouse. Usually, the job entails getting things in and out of storage, but sometimes he gets to smash things. The way he explains it, galleries don't like to pay warehouse storage fees for pieces that aren't likely to sell and, since they can't just toss art in a dumpster, these artworks have to be destroyed. If it's something big, it can be an ordeal. Once a gallery complained that the art hadn't been destroyed to their satisfaction and, ever since then, the warehouse has gone above and beyond. Eric loves it—jokes about it being his superpower and threatens to take the warehouse sledgehammer—the *Kunsthammer* he calls it —outside the warehouse to the galleries and studios beyond. He'll even smash his own studio, he says. *Especially* his own studio.

Eric is always so controlled, I have a hard time picturing him wielding the hammer with the level of abandon he describes. He's nothing like me, the way I cry, scream, spill, and break things—phones, dishes, lamps. I'm surprised I haven't already pulverized every piece of pottery I've ever made. Then again, I haven't made much. Or at least, once again, not enough.

With another small loan to cover the rental fee and supplies, Eric helps me get my workspace back. He's stopped pushing AA but wants me to stay on track and wonders whether I can't plug up my alcohol cravings with clay. I'm curious to know the answer, too. And as soon as I get back into the swing of it, I'm determined to make him the long-overdue bowls I promised. A small first step toward settling the score between the two of us.

"What's your plan for the day?" Eric says, as he finishes his coffee. "Why not use my laptop to poke around online and see what you can find out about your birth mother."

It's not the first time he's suggested it. He's full of suggestions.

"Should be easy now that you have her name," he says.

I gently clink a teaspoon against my coffee mug. What if it turns out she's still alive? Do I want a second chance at being rejected? I won't be able to take it.

Eric stands up, pats me on the back, and kisses the top of my head. "Up to you," he says.

───────────

ONCE ERIC IS GONE, I open his laptop and get as far as typing, "Anna Rubik," into a search engine, but I can't bring myself to hit SEARCH.

Twenty minutes go by, maybe more, before I shut the laptop and pull out my phone to do a little job hunting instead. That's how desperate I am for a distraction.

One of my bartender friends knows of a coffee shop looking

for a bookkeeper and offers to recommend me. It's only two days a week, and the job doesn't pay much, but it's a start.

Hunting through rows of transactions in search of a few missing pennies is something I learned to do while working late nights in restaurants. I hate doing it, but it comes fairly easily. So easily, I sometimes worry that I've inherited Dad's obsessive-compulsive tendencies. Inherited isn't the right word, of course, but whatever the case, it's a good sober job, and if Dad has anything to do with my march forward into a worthwhile, meaningful, possibly even solvent life, so be it. He would be proud to know it.

I worry what Mother may have told Frederick about recent events. Hopefully, his knowledge of Mother will serve as an explanation for my return to Oakville after what seemed to be a successful visit home.

He's well aware Mother can be quite impossible. Any real conversation with her begins with her attempting to change the subject and inevitably ends with harsh words, if not shouting, and, on this last occasion, Mother running away from me in feigned horror. (Mother loves to put on a grand show.)

She told me Frederick moved away because of something I'd done. I called her a liar. She said he is afraid of me in the way Father used to be. (She came close to outright accusing me of causing Father's heart attack.) It made me furious. I won't deny that I grabbed Mother by the arm. Gently, until she started struggling against me, violently. I let go, and she lost her balance, like a rubber band once you pull it taut—it springs out. Her head slammed hard against the wooden floorboards. (She claims she needed stitches, but did she?)

She is dramatic, and I waited for her to get up on her own. Once I realized she wasn't just pretending, I helped her off the floor, sat her on the davenport, and went to the kitchen for ice.

As I did, she ran out the door, shouting for Mr. Demski. Meaning that she clearly wasn't hurt at all.

Convinced that she would try to have me sent back here, I followed her outside in a panic to stop her lies.

During the commotion, Mr. Demski must have called the police because, soon, the Matron of Washington County arrived. She's not much older than me, and I told her she looked like the girl behind one of the counters in Rach's Department Store. She smiled and said, yes, she used to work there. "Are you arresting me?" I asked.

"No, I'm escorting you to the hospital."

Although she looked stern in her crisp uniform, she was surprised me by being warm and soft spoken. I offered no struggle.

I don't know whether Frederick arrived at the house later that day, but Mother wrote to tell me that he won't be coming home anymore because of me, and that he won't be visiting me here at Oakville, either. She said that everyone is fearful of me. I must find a way to contact Frederick. I have to know it isn't true.

COMING BACK to Oakville is like reliving a dream I'd been trying to forget I ever had: the raised beds of the flower garden as we pulled up the drive; the heavy wooden doors to the administration building; the rocking chair, card tables, and piano in the day ward; the same old expressions; the same tired questions.

I gave the same answers, too, while looking at the floor, trying to become as small and invisible as possible so as not to be seen. As if I could sneak in and assume my old routine without all the fuss. I didn't want to go back to that routine, but I also didn't have any other answers to give.

A student nurse came by—a new one. I don't remember her name, and she may as well have had a stocking over her head for as much as I remember her face. She handed me a small paper cup containing three pills. Two blue tablets and a one bright green capsule.

"What about the orange ones? I asked.

"You get the blue ones now."

It doesn't matter, this new combination makes me just as stupid as the others. I get them multiple times a day. "Time for your pills, Anna, time for your pills."

They ask me why I don't eat, but who needs food when I feast on medicine morning, noon, and night? Last night they even woke me to give me more. Or maybe it was a dream. Perhaps it's all a dream. I dream I'm in a hospital. I dream I'm writing this down. Last night I dreamt I was dreaming. And when I awoke, I was awake.

I'm exhausted from so much dreaming.

THE STAFF HELD a meeting to celebrate my return. I sat alongside Dr. Abrams, who went through my history as if he were reading an old familiar bedtime story to a kindergarten class full of doctors, nurses, and students. A priest, too. Once upon a time there was a rabbit stuck in a briar patch. Said rabbit couldn't get out of the briar patch. Said rabbit learned to love the briar patch, because it was where he was born and raised. I hate this briar patch.

Dr. Abrams told stories about me for several minutes as if I were invisible before he finally spoke to me directly.

What else could I do but laugh when Stewart's name came up again after all this time?

Everyone at home, at the hospital, and everywhere else, has spent years conspiring to crush the only true love I've ever known. I should have been the one to ask the doctor about Stewart—ask him the one question that's never been answered: Why?

When it became clear I didn't want to talk about Stewart, the doctor asked about God.

"Does God still talk to you?"

"Why not ask the priest," I wanted to say. "Does God talk to him?"

"You said they tell you not to eat," asked the doctor. "Who do you mean? Who are they?"

Isn't that what I'm here to find out? If I came to the hospital because my heart stopped working, would I sit in front of a panel to be interrogated about why?

I didn't say any of this, of course. Let the mad scientists hook me up to their machines if that's what they're so desperate to do.

Mother once told me I was getting x-rays. She said I would be here in this hospital for only one day. And I believed it, too. I'm embarrassed to recall mentioning the x-rays to Nurse Winthrop. She laughed.

"Why do you keep calling it that? You're not getting x-rays, you're getting ECT."

I stared dumbly.

"Shock treatment," she said.

That alone shocked me. Nurse Winthrop saw my reaction, and didn't say any more. She didn't need to. When I asked Dr. Abrams about it, he asked me who I'd been speaking to, assured me my treatments were perfectly safe, and told me not to believe everything I heard. In other words, I should be a good girl and not worry my pretty little head about it.

But Olive, who hasn't been getting the treatments herself, told me all about ECT. "Like a fork in a toaster," she said.

She just wanted to scare me, though, because it isn't anything like a fork in a toaster at all—though my memory of it is no more vivid than my memories of anything else. One more experience tossed into the landfill. The only reason I fear the treatment, whatever it is, is because it continues to erode my crumbling banks. It drops me inch by inch into the acid bath of the Monongahela River, dissolving me away like the Army plane.

They used to call Pittsburgh The Smokey City. The air and everything it touched was sooty and black. But, by the time Frederick was driving me to painting classes at the Arts Center, we could often see the sun. And by the time I went to West Penn for my first so-called x-rays, the air had become even purer still. I remember how warm the sun felt on my face as I walked from the car. Well, I believe the doctors here at Oakville must feel inspired by the cleanup of Pittsburgh. If the air of an entire city can be cleaned, how simple to do the same for my little head—"Let us blow out the black smoke, shine a light into the deep wrinkles, shake out the carpets one by one." But there is a limit, no? They didn't blow out *all* the air in Pittsburgh, did they? If they had, there would be nothing left to breathe.

They're going to give me treatments twice a week starting next week. I'm like a stubborn spot that they keep trying to clean. Eventually, I will disintegrate like the printed dresses in the laundry room after too much bleach.

Not that things were going any better at home, as recent events have shown. During my interview, the doctor seemed to ask more about Mother than he did about me. If I only knew what to tell him. Something that would lead him to bring her here and hook her up to the dreaded machine. I'd like to watch them funnel fistfuls of pills down Mother's gullet until she chokes. I wouldn't be here if it weren't for her—my executioner.

Mother has been sending me notes through the ward physician. I don't understand why. And the physician doesn't understand why, either. "You mother can send them to you directly," he says. "Please be sure she understands that."

As if Mother listens to anything I have to say.

In her most recent letter, she told me she had spoken to a woman who came to the house asking the same questions they ask when Mother comes here to the hospital. She's worried she might have signed something she shouldn't have. She didn't explain what it was, or why she felt she shouldn't have signed it, but I can't help wondering about it. What questions? About me? About herself? Are the body snatchers finally closing in, burrowing into her husk?

Whether or not they are, she needs to know she has nothing to fear from me. (If she is actually afraid, that is—not just feeling sorry for herself and looking for sympathy.) And Frederick must be made to understand he has nothing to fear from me, either. He needs to visit me soon. And tell me the truth, that he still loves me as much as he always has. I miss him.

WORD PROBLEMS

Eric and I settle into a state of relative domestic bliss. Or a drama-free routine, in any case—helped by the fact that we don't see each other much. Eric works his day job at the gallery and spends many nights and weekends at his painting studio. Meanwhile, I work two days a week at the bookkeeping gig and spend most of my free days at the ceramic studio. The cupboard is growing cluttered with my mismatched experiments. I grab one, fill it with coffee, and sit at the kitchen table beside Eric, who is clicking through a website on his laptop.

"Getting ready for another day of smashing artist's dreams?"
I say.

"It's never-ending," he says. "Like stink bugs."

I sit next to him, and he swivels the laptop toward me. It shows what appears to be an old newspaper page scanned from microfilm. Dropouts on a few of the letters and others clogged with ink make it challenging to read. "What's this?"

"Read it."

I realize it's a page of old obituaries. Among them, one for someone named Joseph Rubik. I slide my coffee mug out of the way and pull the laptop closer.

Joseph Rubik of North Charleroi died in the Charleroi-Monessen Hospital, January 16, 1958, at 2:25 a.m.

He was born in Poland, August 14, 1897, the son of Aleksander and Florentyna Rubik and came to North Charleroi thirty-four years ago. He was retired from the cold draw department of the Allenport Works plant of Pittsburgh Steel Company. He was a member of Mother of Sorrows church.

He is survived by his wife Frances Rubik, two sons, Frederick of North Charleroi, Walter of Coal Center, one daughter, Anna, at home, and two grandchildren.

It takes a moment for me to realize what I'm looking at, but when I do, I'm motionless, astonished.

"Found this, too," he says, clicking to an article about a local Pittsburgh art show mentioning Anna by name. "Your mom won a ribbon at an arts and crafts fair in Pittsburgh. Didn't you say you won a ribbon there, too?"

I should be mad that Eric took it upon himself to find this when I expressly asked him not to. What is it with him and my family? He had pressured me to reconnect with Mom and Dad, and I'm still not convinced anything good came of it. Why this new obsession? My hands tremble. My body shakes—my entire world does.

"Somebody must still be alive," he says. "Not your grandmother—she'd have to be a hundred years old by now—but maybe one of these uncles. Or a cousin. Who knows, maybe even your mother."

"Mom and Dad told me she died."

"They aren't exactly reliable. Maybe she did, I have no idea, but somebody must still be around. Someone to confirm it and hopefully fill in the gaps."

Some gaps are too big to fill. Still, I can't help reading.

It says Joseph died in Charleroi-Monessen Hospital. It's called Monongahela Valley Hospital now, but it's where Mom died—a twenty-minute drive from Daisytown. Two neighboring towns in the middle of nowhere—who knows whose paths may have crossed over the years? Maybe I even crossed paths with Anna beyond the moment I slipped from her womb.

The sun creeps around a building next door and throws a beam of light through the kitchen window. It streams across the computer screen. I angle the laptop to avoid the glare. It's a short obituary, the basic facts, but I read it again and again. My coffee is cold by the time I stand up. The room feels cockeyed.

"I guess I'm going to the studio," I say, tugging my jacket from the coat rack. I'm not completely certain that this statement is true.

"Go tomorrow."

"If I don't go now, I'll have to give up my slot. I won't be able to schedule kiln time again for a week or more." Now I'm lying.

"Sorry. I should have waited to show you this stuff. I couldn't help it. I was too excited."

"It's fine," I say. Also a lie.

"I won't do anything more unless you ask me to, I promise. In the meantime, I'll print these pages, so you have them."

"Thanks." I wish I meant it.

MY PIECES LINE the shelf above my table, and I inspect them to be sure they are dry enough for firing. I knock one, and it shatters onto my workbench in a tiny explosion of dust. Who needs a *Kunsthammer* when there's gravity? What pulls us to each other can pull us apart, too. I stop thinking about force fields. I sweep the fragments into a bucket of scrap for reclamation. They whisper when they touch the water, like a release of tiny spirits, as the bone-dry shards succumb to the mud.

I place the remaining greenware on a tray and carry them to the firing room, where a studio tech is busy loading one of the kilns. When the tech says hello and asks me what's new, it's tempting to spew my entire life story. But the thought of how Dad answers simple questions like, *How are you?*—and how people react when he does—causes me to choke back the urge.

"Nothing much," is all I manage to say.

"Everything marked?"

I'm distracted and don't answer.

"Your pieces—are they marked?"

"I think so."

The tech turns each one over to be sure that I've scribed my name onto them before she carefully stacks them into the kiln.

"Tomorrow afternoon," she says. "Look for them on the shelf."

With the kiln loaded, I can't decide whether to sit at the wheel and throw some clay or head back to Eric's place. It's my place now, too, I suppose, but I can't get used to calling it that. If I stay at the studio, I'm not sure I can focus. Not that the wheel takes concentration. It requires the exact opposite of concentration—meditation. Stray thoughts too easily transfer to my fingertips. For anything to turn out well, I need a quiet mind. But it's hard to say which comes first—the lullaby of spinning clay, or a clear head. Maybe doing some work will tune out the static and calm me.

A milk crate under my table hides a set of dusty work

clothes. After a quick look around, I strip naked behind a storage cabinet and change into them.

Seated at the wheel, I kick off my shoes and gently press the pedal with my bare toes—the mound spins, the wheel hums. I push a damp thumb into the middle of the centered hump. Rather than providing calming hypnosis, however, the twirling motion makes me dizzy. Sick. What a terrible idea.

Abandoning the wheel, I carry the clay and tools back to my table to wait out my nausea, mindlessly squeezing a lump of clay until my knuckles turn white. I put the clay down and shake out my hands before picking it up again and absentmindedly molding it into abstract shapes.

Some studio mates create things this way—pinching, rolling, pounding, building. I see why. The formless, muddy earth squeezing through my fingers is therapeutic. I can't stop.

MY KEY barely touches the lock before the door swings open, and Eric pulls me inside.

"Pretty sure I found some relatives," he says. "*Living* relatives."

I shimmy out of my jacket, sit on the couch, and tug off my boots. The couch swallows me with a hiss.

"I'm sorry," he says. "I know I promised, but I couldn't help myself."

"Tell me."

"I think I discovered the email address of a woman who is married to your cousin. It's hard to keep the connections straight. It seems Anna's brothers were ten years older than her, and their kids—your cousins—must be at least that much older than you. On top of that, Anna's brother, Walter, had a son named Walter Junior, and Walter Junior is married to a woman named Cathy. The two of them live in Delaware—but before that, they lived in western Pennsylvania. I forget the town. Anyway, Cathy has a website where she posts her photography."

It feels like a word problem in math class, and I wrestle for the relevant information.

"I'm pretty sure Cathy is married to Anna's nephew, Walter Jr.—your cousin. There's an email address on Cathy's webpage. I think you should send her a message."

It's as though he just woke up and is trying to describe his dreams while I'm still half-asleep.

"Trust me," he says, "there's a connection here. I know it."

Who is who, I'm still confused, but I don't want him to explain it again.

"I think it will help you," he says.

"Help me how?"

He looks confused.

"Do you think there's something wrong with me?"

Gently, he closes the lid to his laptop. We both endure a full minute of silence.

"Stop pressuring me, okay?"

He gets up and leans against the kitchen counter, pouting with his arms folded.

"I need time to think about this," I say. "To absorb it all. It's *my* life."

I CAN'T SLEEP and spend the night trying to compose an email in my head. It's not working, so I get out of bed and try writing something on the laptop. I write, delete, write, delete, obsessing over each word, making the message unnecessarily complicated. When I think I have something, I bring it into the bedroom and read it to Eric, but he's barely awake.

"Just tell her you're the daughter of Anna Rubik," he says. "She'll either know what you're talking about or not."

I read it to myself one last time.

Your message has been sent.

DAYS PASS WITH NO ANSWER. Maybe my message got filtered into Cathy's junk folder? Or, worse, perhaps she read it and moved it to the trash, thinking it was an internet con job—*Six Degrees of Separation* and all that. Did she even know I exist? Did anyone? If they believe my story, they still might imagine I'm creeping from the ether looking for money. I can't blame them. What *am* I looking for?

"Should I re-send the message? Rewrite it and then send?"

"It hasn't even been a week," Eric assures me. "She might be away. Or maybe she doesn't check her email often. Who knows, it could be anything."

If Eric hadn't gone digging, I might have spent the rest of my life paralyzed in an amber nugget of ambivalence. But now that I've taken the first step toward uncovering the truth, the waiting is torture.

A week goes by, then a week and a half. I pester Eric for more leads, other ideas, until, after two weeks, I finally get a reply—a long message with a phone number listed at the end of it.

Yes, Cathy is married to my cousin, Walter. And I have another cousin, his sister, Judy. Walter and Judy have fond memories of their aunt Anna, they say. They knew Anna gave birth, and the baby had been adopted out, but that's all they ever knew. Until now, they didn't even know if I was a boy or a girl. They often wondered—Judy, especially. They seem as curious and excited as I am—a long-standing family mystery finally solved.

"Call us," they say.

ANNA'S JOURNAL
Saturday, August 17, 1965

This morning, I woke in a panic again, crying out like a newborn baby, smacked on the bottom and suddenly alive. Looking around, I didn't recognize where I was —or even who I was. Gradually, visions of my life emerged— faces, names—but when I tried to make sense of them, they dissolved away like grains of sugar in a cup of tea.

I finally understand why no one explained electroshock to me when I was still so young, that first time that I went to get my "x-ray". If that had been the only time I received treatment, I might have forgotten all about the Frankenstein machine by now. The subsequent treatments since then might have dissolved into a murky soup, too, if not for what they did to me last week. I should have believed Olive when she told me what was really going on.

I've heard that surgeons sometimes absentmindedly leave sponges and things inside their patient's belly after an operation. Or one of them might accidentally amputate a patient's healthy leg instead of their rotten one. In the past, when I've heard these stories, I've wondered whether they were real. After last week, I have no doubt that they are. During my treatment, something went wrong. Someone must have missed a step. To make it worse, as I recovered in the room next door, no one believed me when I told them about it. Nurse Winthrop accused me of making up stories—of having an overactive imagination. She said, "Whatever you think you remember was just a dream."

Maybe it was, but since my whole life is a dream, this was as real as anything.

Other than a vague déjà vu as I was helped onto the ECT table and then strapped in, I didn't remember any of my previous treatments. The "x-rays." And I wasn't expecting to remember this one, either. The procedure has become routine. I've had scores of them—maybe hundreds. Even while living at home with Mother, I'll still go to the hospital two days a week. "Maintenance treatment," they call it. Like mowing the lawn or pulling up weeds. (Why would anyone need an x-ray two days a week? I don't know why I didn't question this sooner. Maybe I didn't want to know.) Mother drives me to the hospital on Tuesday mornings. I'm interviewed, given treatment, allowed to recover in bed for a night and, then, after some porridge and a glass of orange juice the following morning, Mother arrives to drive me home.

It's always silent in the car with Mother regardless of where we go, but it's especially quiet after treatment. Then again, it's silent on the occasions Frederick drives me home from the hospital, as well. Even when Esther volunteers as my escort, she stares ahead at the road while I sit beside her in utter silence. There's a warmth between Esther and me, however, and I like it best when she's the one who picks me up. She might ask me how I'm feeling, but when I don't respond, she holds my hand and says, "You don't have to answer, I understand."

It's not that I don't want to talk about it, it's that I can't. Even if my mouth could form words, how could I possibly explain something so foggy and mysterious?

Generally, the treatments are like the interrupted melody of a skipping record. One moment, I lie down on the table, and the next moment I wake up in a different room entirely with no idea of how I got there. Sometimes, I don't become aware of the world again until I'm in the car, on my way home—occasionally, it takes days. It's like when I wake up in the middle of the night, having fallen asleep on the davenport, and think, "Where am I?"

At least that is how it usually is, and I've grown used to not knowing where I am, not to mention who I am. But last time was different, and like a nightmare, it has haunted me since.

When I close my eyes, I can see myself led into the ECT room. Usually at this point in the procedure, I am already groggy from the pills they give me whenever I set foot in Oakville. They keep changing them—round orange shiny ones, chalky blue tablets, bright green capsules–but the effects are all the same. On top of all that, before treatment, they give me multiple injections.

"Sodium Pentothal," Olive told me. "You know what that is, don't you? Truth serum! Like the CIA uses. They want your deepest sins to rise to the surface so they can burn them off like Cherries Jubilee."

The combination of serums leaves me lifeless, and I usually remember nothing after entering the "x-ray" room. (I've never been x-rayed before. How was I to know what an x-ray machine looked like? But why didn't I ever ask to see the x-ray photos they were supposedly taking? Why did no one tell me what was going on? Why didn't I ask? Why doesn't it help?) This time, I am still lifeless, unable to move—but this time, they must not have used the right anesthetic, so I am aware. Paralyzed. And wide awake. I see the doctor holding what looks like a set of ice tongs—or forceps, or car battery clamps—as if they were prepared to grab my head and pull me through a birth canal. The tongs are wired into something resembling a military radio —or a control panel for a rocket to Mars—cluttered with knobs, and dials, and switches.

The nurse helps me lie down on the table as Dr. Candler stands at the ready with a strap with which to hold my head. My body, too, is strapped down, so that I can't move—but I can't move, anyway, because of the injection. Or the pills. Nothing is certain, except that they have been lying to me about something, I just don't know what. I am under the total control of people who may not have my best interests at heart. I struggle to cry out, but it's like poking at a dead dog with a stick. Or night palsy. My body is no longer my own.

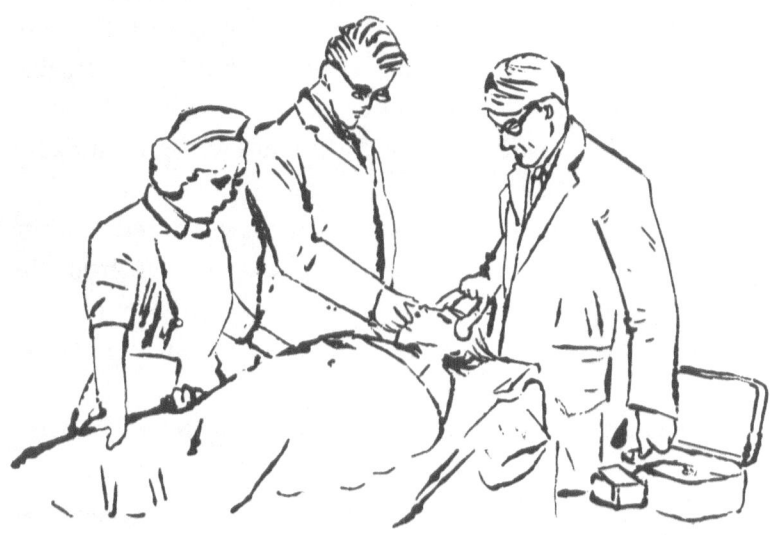

After massaging my temples with a greasy salve, Dr. Candler places the contraption around my head and tightens the tongs. The pads are pressed snug against my temples. I can't see him, but I sense the doctor fiddling with the knobs and toggles on the radio as if trying to tune in instructions from a far-off civilization spinning around a distant star.

I remember a *Tom and Jerry* cartoon I watched on television once, where an orange cat and a blue dog sat side by side with colanders on their heads. The colanders were wired to a machine operated by a mad scientist. When the scientist flipped a switch, the colanders surged with electricity, and the cat and dog shook violently. When the power ceased, the two animals had switched minds—the dog had the mind of a cat, and a cat had the mind of a dog. They had each other's voices, too. The contraption my doctor clamps to my temples is wired to a machine like the one the cartoon scientist uses. Except no one is strapped down beside me—no other person to switch personalities with. I realize I am about to swap my mind with empty space. Whatever feeble thoughts or feelings I have will waft into the air of the quiet room and dissipate like a plume of smoke from Father's pipe. In exchange, my head will be filled with nothing. My voice will be the voice of oblivion. I imagine flinging a penny into the vacuum that will soon exist between my temples, then losing count of the seconds while listening for a faint splash. Make a wish.

Without warning, Dr. Candler flips a switch and a white light explodes across my eyes. His forceps pull me from the warm safety of the womb through space and time into the stark loneliness of existence. I dance on the table from the pain of being born.

The next morning, I wake up anxious. Sweat creeps from my temples, where the grease had been applied. I shiver in fear.

"What's wrong?" Nurse Winthrop asks, noticing me gasping.

It's difficult to speak.

"What is it?" she says.

"The machine," I mutter. "The shock—"

Her face hardens. "You don't remember that," she insists. "It was just a dream."

My boat isn't rowing merrily but my life is (nothing) but a dream. My next treatment is in a few days, I am sure. When Mother arrived to drive me home, she refused to talk about it and we lapsed into the same cold silence we always have in the car. I asked Frederick about it in a letter but he didn't respond. No one else will talk to me about it. Stewart is mum and has been ever since he found out about Peter. I feel so alone. My soul and my dreams were all I ever had and now I'm watching even them swirl down a drain.

Only a faint memory exists of a time before the machine—

before the glimmer of a happy future exploded into the void of a white-hot flash. It's impossible to imagine the positivity I once enjoyed will ever return. I have succumbed to a state of numbness. Maybe it's a safer place to be, where the world can't touch me. But buried under these clouds I feel myself fall apart, decay, rot. Is this God's revenge? The sludge of my sins is eating my insides away.

I'll hardly have time to catch my breath before I'm back next week to do it again. I feel like the Greek king we learned about in school. The one who pushes the rock up the hill only to have it roll down whenever it nears the top. I must convince someone of the horror. Frederick? Esther? Someone has to believe me. I don't want to come back. There has to be another way.

COUSINS

Skyscrapers disappear behind me as New Jersey's shipping docks and refineries give way to suburban backyards. The train to Wilmington follows the bank of the misty Delaware River. Needles of rain angle across the windows. I stare blankly, hypnotized by the lull. The rain eases, and the ragged haze breaks apart as if torn by cat claws. Damp weeds shimmer beside the tracks, buffeted in waves. The rhythm slows, the wheels whine, the conductor announces my stop. Brakes hiss in a long sigh as if they've been holding their breath the same way I have.

Stepping off the train, I realize I don't know what Judy looks like. Each woman I pass might be her—I have a slight familial resemblance to all of them in one way or another. This one has my body type, that one has my nose. When I see a woman looking equally as lost as I am, I approach her, and she starts back. "Sorry, I thought you were my cousin." Which sounded absurd out loud and did nothing to make me look less creepy.

Finally, a woman looking at me and also looking a little less like me than any of the others calls my name. "Oh my gosh," says Judy, rushing toward me, her sensible, rubber-soled shoes squeaking against the station floor. "I can't believe you're here. I can't believe you found us."

I can't believe it, either. We look each other up and down with frank curiosity and laugh. Judy is shorter than I am, twelve years older, too, but she's familiar. Like an old high school friend whom you don't recognize at first, but then you do.

"Just the one bag?" she asks.

The conversation is stilted, small talk feels inadequate, and my legs unsteady as I follow her to the parking lot. How was the ride, she asks, when did you leave, looks like a beautiful day after all and so on. Judy is a schoolteacher and tells me about her grammar school class as if I am a friend she hasn't seen in a couple of days, and we have no other catching up to do, since the only person we have in common has been long unknown to both of us. She rarely leaves her little neighborhood of Wood-dale, she says, buckling her seat belt. Even the twenty-minute car ride to the Wilmington train station is further than she usually travels. "A two-hour train ride all the way to New York City would be such an exciting adventure for me."

On a bad day, it could take nearly two hours on the subway just to get from my old apartment in Bushwick to Eric's place in Greenpoint, but this particular ride is different. "It's an exciting adventure for me, too," I say.

"Of course it is, dear," she says, in a soothing schoolteacher voice. "Of course."

TURNING DOWN A WELL-MANICURED SUBURBAN STREET, we pass a neighbor jogging with a dog. Judy waves to the woman before pulling into the driveway of a pristine little house. The grass is a flawless blanket of green. At its edge grow shrubs trimmed with perfect geometry. Flower boxes overflow with chrysanthemums. I never had this life.

Waiting by the door is Judy's husband, Jim. He walks to the car, ready with a friendly hug as soon as I step out. "Judy has been talking about you all week," he says. "You have no idea."

Judy prepares coffee, while Jim gives me a tour of the house and tells me about some minor renovations they're planning to do. He points out a framed high school graduation picture. "This is our daughter, Anna," he says. "She's away at college."

Judy chimes in from the kitchen, "We named her after your mother. "

"Oh, that's right," says Jim, as if he's only just realizing the fact. "I guess we did."

"I always loved that name," says Judy.

I tell them about my Brooklyn neighborhood, my job as a bookkeeper, my ceramics—attempting to present the best version of who I am.

It turns out that, although Jim has been living in Delaware for a couple of decades, he grew up in Coal Center—a speck of land set between Daisytown and the Monongahela River. It's where Mike tells people he's from when he's too embarrassed to admit he comes from a place called Daisytown. "Couldn't wait to leave," Jim says. "Joined the Marines, and never looked back."

Soon, Walter and Cathy arrive. Walter gives me the kind of hug reserved for long lost relatives before introducing me to his wife, Cathy, whose website is the reunion's lynchpin. He then introduces me to his mother, Esther—my aunt.

Married to Anna's brother, Esther had known Anna better than any of them, but no one had told me about Esther.

"You're so beautiful," Esther says. I've heard it a few times in my life, but never from a family member. "You look exactly like your mother."

"Doesn't she?" says Judy.

It begs a million questions, but I'm too shell-shocked to ask any of them.

Walter stands outside, under an awning, tending to an outdoor grill. Cathy makes a potato salad, and Judy brings out a homemade apple pie. I should help, but no one lets me, so I sit and chat with Esther.

"Are you a model?" she asks.

"Hardly," I say, though I admit to her I'd modeled briefly in my twenties. "It's a tough business," I say, without getting into what a misadventure it had been.

"Your mother went to modeling school, you know."

"I didn't know that. I really don't know anything about her at all. I'm hoping you'll fill me in."

"Time to eat," says Walter, coming inside, carrying a plate of burgers.

As we prepare to dig in, Walter says grace. It's short and straightforward, only veering from a few rote lines to add thanks for the reunion. Touching, sweet, and easy to follow. A relief.

Not much is said during the meal aside from, "We can't believe you're here." And me replying, "I can't believe it, either." It's a companionable silence. But, as the pie gets sliced and served, Judy runs into another room, and returns with a box of old family photos.

"Let her finish eating," Walter says.

Thankfully, Judy ignores him and begins laying the pictures in front of me one by one. "Those are your grandparents, Joe and Frances... That's my mom and dad... This one is me, can you believe it?" She shows me four or five pictures before finally laying one down with the flourish of a winning poker hand. "And this—*this* is your mother."

I see a young woman posing in a white graduation gown on the front lawn of a modest two-family house beside a set of railroad tracks. The photo is grainy and out of focus. I hold it close and squint. "Here's a better one," she says—a hand-colored senior portrait, class of 1953. Esther is right—Anna Rubik looks exactly like me. Even has the same hair I had at that age, the same awkward teenage smile. More photos follow —school portraits, grainy snapshots. After a lifetime of never seeing a single picture of my mother, dozens flutter around me as if blown by the October wind. "Can I get copies of these?"

"The ones of your mother are yours," she says. "Keep them."

I'm stunned. The photographs seem too valuable to stuff in my bag. But what else can I do?

As I gather them together, Esther tells Walter to fetch the shopping bag she brought with her. "It's by the door," she says. Walter gets the bag and gives it to Esther, but Esther says, "No, give it to Rachel."

Inside is an oil painting, beautifully framed, featuring a lonely cottage nestled on a hillside surrounded by towering evergreens—all of it blanketed with snow. The sky is deep blue and dotted with a few pale clouds. At first, I'm not sure why Esther is giving it to me, but then I see the signature in the lower-left corner, almost too small to read: Anna Rubik 1953. The painting is well composed and skillfully rendered. But of course, I would love it no matter what it looked like. The back is neatly sealed with Kraft paper, very slightly worn at the edges, with a yellowing label stuck to it: ANNA RUBIK, PITTSBURGH ARTS AND CRAFTS FAIR, 1953. It feels a bit heavier than it should for a stretched canvas of this size, but then everything I'm taking in feels a bit heavier than anyone could expect, and I don't question it.

"It has been hanging on my wall for ages," Esther says. "I've been taking care of it, but it has always belonged to you."

Judy hands me a paper napkin to blot my cheeks and blow my nose.

NO ONE HAS SAID the one thing I've been dying to know for sure. It seems obvious, but I need to ask. "Is she dead?"

It seems to catch them unprepared. They are visibly uncomfortable with how little they can tell me.

"I've always heard she died in childbirth," I say.

"We don't really know," they all say. But that's not the same as saying no one knows at all. What I thought had been a family mystery starts to feel more like a family secret, and I work at getting everyone to let me in on it.

"She was home with Grandma when it happened," says Judy. "But Grandma never had anything to say about it. Never had much to say about Anna at all once she died, did she, Mom?"

Esther tuts and shakes her head.

"Grandma was a piece of work," says Walter, flatly.

Esther is getting old and might be having trouble remembering all the details, but she must know more than she's letting on. When I look at her, she says one word: "Oakville."

"What's that?"

"Your mother had been sick for a long time," says Judy.

"I don't understand."

"It's a hospital."

"Why was she there?"

"We wanted to adopt you," Esther says. For reasons she never understood and can't explain, Anna's mother refused to allow it. "We wanted to adopt you," Esther says again, softer this time, almost to herself. "Your mother is buried in Mother of Sorrows Cemetery in Charleroi," she says.

If Esther has any more info, she doesn't share it. Or maybe I don't hear it.

"What about my father?" I say, my voice cracking with nerves. "Who was he? Is he still alive?"

"Anna never spoke about him to anyone," Esther says. "No one knows."

———

AFTER COFFEE and promises made to keep in touch, I carry my pictures and my painting on a return train to New York. I wouldn't have thought it possible, but I'm more dazed now than I had been during the trip down. Instead of staring out the window this time, I stare into the photos, scanning the details, searching for secret meanings hidden in the grain. I hold them gingerly, afraid they will crumble and disintegrate in my hands, or blow away with the tiniest breath.

ANNA'S JOURNAL
Wednesday, October 13, 1965

S till no word from Frederick. I don't even know how to reach him anymore. I send my letters home, but does Mother deliver them? I've been here a month or more without a visit from him. Mother, too. Funny I should find myself aching for a visit from Mother, who has done so much to harm me. I begin to wonder if I'll ever see her again, either. I wonder whether she has thrown away the rest of my belongings the way she threw away my movie magazines. The way she has thrown away her daughter. I worry I no longer have a home.

But then, just as I had lost hope of having any contact with the world beyond Oakville, Esther came to see me. Thank God for Esther! I have been doing so little talking that when she came, it was hard for my mouth to form words. My face kept twitching, too, the way it always seems to, now. Esther told me not to worry, but I still felt ashamed for being so dull. I wouldn't visit me again in this state.

She bought me a pullover for the cold weather that's coming. Thinking I was shivering from the cold, she had me put it on. But I wasn't cold—I shake all the time.

Esther bought me a new journal, as well. Even though my old notebook is only half-filled, the entries are so disjointed and hard to decipher I'll be happy to begin again with the one Esther gave me. I like its bright green cover, which somehow feels fresh like spring. It has ruled pages, too, which will help me keep my writing straight and legible despite my trembling hand. It will help if I ever use these entries for my memoirs.

A memoir seems less and less likely though. When Esther bought me my first journal from the stationery shop in Charleroi, I promised myself to write every day. I wanted to be a reporter, work at a newspaper, or a movie magazine. To "only write what I know to be true." Eventually, I planned to write my life story. Before that, I planned to live the kind of life worth writing about. To live a life at all. That's impossible now. I don't have a life to write about. I've always tried to keep copies of the letters I write, in case they are intercepted by Mother, but even those seem to be written by a stranger. It's no wonder I get so few replies. My mind is like a shoebox full of random mementos found in a secondhand shop, snippets of memories that aren't even my own.

Or don't seem to be.

Journals full of fiction.

Esther tells me Walter sends his love, but I wonder if he

does. He has never been here to see me, after all. He is our Father's son. Walter and Father both objected to keeping me here at Oakville, and I appreciate their faith in me. Still, neither of them did anything to stop it. And, other than the one time Father drove me here—the very first time—neither he nor Walter ever set foot in this wretched place. Fine for Father. He and I grew suspicious of each other, and I never wanted him to come. He preferred to die rather than to see his daughter committed to this life. And so, he did. Walter, on the other hand, I would like to see. The children, too. When I ask Esther about them, she says this hospital is no place for children, but Oakville seems to be full of them. A new patient, Eleanor, even sucks her thumb.

So, I am left with a longing for a visit from Mother. I asked Esther where Mother is, where she has been, but Esther is not much help in that regard. Why is everyone so good at not telling me things? Did they all take an extension course at Charleroi High on Keeping (Relevant Life) Information from Anna?

"She'll be here next weekend," Esther promised me.

We'll see.

It's impossible to hide my anger toward Mother over what she has done—and continues to do—to me. I told Esther how I wish I could once and for all wrestle my life from Mother's sturdy hands—hands so calloused she can pull potatoes from a pot of boiling water. My own frail and twitchy hands are no match. They barely afford me the strength to push a pencil. Mother looks down on my weaknesses and shames me for them. If I have headaches or feel ill, she considers me lazy. Well, if I am, she has sent me to the wrong place to learn how not to be! Even a simple visit with Esther is exhausting.

Esther agrees I have reason to be mad at Mother. "It's every daughter's right," she said and shared that she and her own mother don't get along well, either. I had nothing to say about that. I don't know her mother; but I do know that Esther is free to come and go without comment or persecution.

Before Esther left, I handed her a letter to Frederick, which she agreed to deliver for me.

Hopefully, Esther will come again soon. I become untethered without visitors.

GHOSTS OF OAKVILLE

I spend my days monopolizing Eric's laptop, scouring the internet for information about the place Esther mentioned during my visit. The only place I know of with the name Oakville is the state mental hospital where Dad used to work. I hate to think that's where Anna was, but looking back to how cagey my relatives had been when talking about her, it makes sense. Perhaps she suffered from depression, as I do.

Turns out the hospital is still in use. Part of it anyway. What was once home to over three thousand patients barely houses three hundred now, and most of the original property got sold off along the way. Nothing has been repurposed or demolished, however, and many, if not all, the old buildings still exist as abandoned shells. An image search reveals photos of once state-of-the-art facilities, now crumbling and vandalized. Some images are striking, taken by skilled photographers: low-angled streams of sunlight speckled by window grates; walls of broken tiles and crumbling plaster; floors covered in moss. Crumbling walls surround rooms small enough to be jail cells, and I shudder to think of what might have taken place in them. To my closest kin. Other photos are blurry snapshots furtively captured by amateur ghost hunters trespassing on private property.

The hospital appears to be a magnet for thrill-seekers, as there exist dozens of websites describing Oakville's old compound as the most haunted place in Pennsylvania. Some say in the whole country. I try to skip over the most sensationalized nonsense, but the stories are hard to miss.

Anna isn't haunting anyone, I catch myself saying. Other than her daughter, that is. I become obsessed and feel compelled to visit the place.

While I read one of the articles for the third or fourth time, Dad calls, and my life feels suddenly split in two. I don't pick up the phone.

The last time Dad and I spoke, he sounded better—less upset about Eric's pictures of me, which he's never seen, anyway—but, even at his best, his nervous energy is hard to deflect. A day goes by before I muster up the courage to listen to the message he leaves. He's inviting me home for Christmas—offers to pick me up from the airport if need be.

No way. Not even if I had a license and could rent a car.

Not now. Or...the more I think about it, not alone.

LATER, I agree to meet Eric at an Irish pub near the art warehouse.

The hostess leads us to a small booth for two. We take off our coats and sit as she lays down silverware and hands us menus.

"Can I start you off with drinks?" she says.

"Have a Guinness if you want one," I say to Eric. "It won't bother me."

It's a lie, of course, but it bothers me more if he can't enjoy a drink after work because of me. My drinking is not his problem. It's me that's his problem, though for some reason he seems to see me as a solution.

"Water will do," he says.

"My dad wants me to visit," I say. "It's his first Christmas without Mom."

"You should go."

Eric's own father has been dead a couple of years now, and he always worries about his mom during the holidays. He tells me he had been planning to visit her in Michigan, but it turns out she won't be home.

"She'll be with a friend," Eric says. "A special man friend."

Now a footloose widow with a disposable income, his mother is planning a Christmas cruise in the Caribbean. He's upset about it, I can tell, but he tries to play it off like it's nothing.

"A holiday cruise sounds like a total nightmare to me," he says, "but if it makes her happy, good for her. Anyway, it frees me up to get more painting done. I'm still struggling with my *masterpiece*."

He chuckles with self-conscious sarcasm as he uses his fork to trace a flourish in the air.

It's been two months since our trip and I still haven't seen any of Eric's Daisytown paintings. He rarely speaks about them. More landscapes, I assume. Horse barns and cow pastures. Stink bugs? The only thing he has told me is that Zach took a minor collector to Eric's studio for a private preview. The collector seems interested in buying a painting—the one Eric has been struggling with the most. It's meant to be the centerpiece of his show, the key to the whole exhibit. I hear the stress in his voice.

"Maybe it would help to pay a visit to your muse," I say.

He uses his spoon to trace the silhouette of my face in the air. *"C'est toi qui est ma muse,"* he says, using his best high-school French.

I swat the spoon away. "What the hell does that mean?"

"You are my muse."

"No, I mean, my dad. Didn't you say he was your twisted muse?"

"Did I?"

"You don't want to be alone on Christmas, do you? What if we drive to Daisytown and visit my dad? We don't have to stay long—a couple of days max. Cook him Christmas dinner or something. What do you say? Maybe it will re-inspire you."

Eric puts his spoon on the table and gives it a spin. I won't blame him if he's apprehensive about another deep dive into Dad's bizarre universe. Instead, he surprises me with an odd question: "Do you think he would let me take his photo?"

"What? Why? Don't tell me you're painting my dad. He's not *really* your muse, is he?"

"I just want to know if he's capable of holding still while I take a picture."

"Your guess is as good as mine. But is that a yes? We can stay at the Holiday Inn this time."

"No, the King's Inn!" he says, picking up the spoon again and banging it against the table like he's at a medieval feast.

Is he serious? I remind him The King's Inn isn't any cheaper.

"Research," he explains. "I want more pictures of the place."

The clean, quiet comfort of a modern motel would be better, but I don't have any leverage. Especially after confessing that I have other reasons for the trip aside from checking on Dad.

"I'd like to find Anna's gravesite," I say. "Maybe drive to Oakville Hospital, too."

"Do you think that's a good idea? It's pretty grim."

"I need to see it, that's all—to make a connection, somehow. Anna is still such a mystery."

"We can pass by, sure. Could be interesting."

By the time our food comes, I'm too excited to eat.

Walter, Esther, and the two kids came to the house for Thanksgiving dinner. I think the kids are afraid of me. They are fearful of Mother, that's certain. As well they should be. Frederick came, too, with his girlfriend, Twilight. Mother doesn't like Twilight and seemed upset she was there, which makes me like Twilight more than I otherwise might.

Frederick gave Walter a belated birthday present—an engraved lighter—and I realized Walter recently turned forty-one. Frederick is not far behind. The two of them joked about me having been a mistake. I feel like one. Mother insisted it isn't true, but she is a proven liar. The way Father hardly spoke to me, the way Mother blames me for all her troubles, I'm surprised it took the two of them as long as it did to hide away their "mistake.".

After dinner, Frederick drove Mother to bingo. Walter drove Esther and the kids home, while Twilight stayed behind with me.

"Don't worry," Twilight said to everyone as they left. "I'll keep an eye on Anna."

No one believes I can care for myself or that I can be trusted to be left alone. But no one watches me when Mother goes to the market or church. Where is Frederick when Mother goes to bingo? I'm alone all the time. And I prefer it that way.

Twilight took a beer from the refrigerator and pulled up a chair beside me.

"Did you want one?" she asked.

I didn't answer. Twilight asked a few more questions, and I didn't answer them, either, preferring to sit wordlessly with my arms folded.

Twilight gave up talking for a little while. But after so much activity, the house felt like it was stuffed with cotton and the dead-silence became too much for her to bear. She stood up and began pacing the room the way I sometimes do.

"You have the doldrums, is what you have," she said.

I began to feel self-conscious about being so dull—about my twitchy appearance, and my inability to carry on a conversation. I've come to realize that what's doing it is the Haldol. Before that, it was the Thorazine. It makes it impossible to think, or speak, or behave in the way a person is expected to behave. In the hospital, I have no choice but to swallow what they give me. It doesn't matter what I say or do there, so who cares—but, at home, I prefer to feel some tingle of life, so I skip the pills whenever I can, toss them into the yard, the trash, the toilet. Mother gets upset whenever she finds them, but who is she to judge? It can take days or weeks for the effects of my pills to wear off, however, so I continued to sit quietly while Twilight talked.

"I used to suffer from the doldrums, too," she said. "But since meeting Freddie, I'm a new person. He snapped me out of it. That's what you need, too. A man would do you a world of good."

It's something Mother often says, Father before her, and the words send me deeper into my chair. Being allowed to speak to Stewart would have done me a world of good, but what good did they let it do me back then? Maybe it just wasn't meant to be. Maybe I just wasn't meant to be.

"I read a book not too long ago called *I Never Promised You a Rose Garden*," said Twilight. "Heard of it? It's about a girl like you. Crazy stuff was going on in her head, so it was hard to follow. Not all of it, but the crazy parts."

As she told me about the main character's visions, Twilight seemed to be speaking in code. As if she were secretly trying to tell me something or to read my mind. Did Twilight know I planned to write a book? Had she gotten into my journals? Did Frederick show her my letters? Much of what I've written is hard to follow, too—the crazy parts. Still, it was nice to chat about anything with someone I'm not either related to or incarcerated alongside, as though I had friends and a social life. I wish what Twilight thought of me actually were my business.

"Freddy says they shocked your brain. Is that true?"

She was trying to suppress me. To hypnotize me into giving her more information to steal for a book. She doesn't realize how much practice I've had at resisting techniques of interrogation like this. I clammed up, but she redoubled her efforts and spoke rapidly in an attempt to confuse me.

"They wanted to try that stuff on me, too," she said. "The doctor thought he could shock me out of my doldrums. Never went through with it, though. Don't need it no more, anyhow, since I met Freddie. He saved me. I bet that once you meet the right man, you'll get better, too."

Any man, as long as it isn't Stewart, I expected her to say.

"How old are you now? Have you ever had a boyfriend? I don't know why Freddie thought Peter would be a good match for you. Freddie told me about that."

It seems Frederick has told her a lot of things. And I will never know what she knows, that much I realize. Does she know about Stewart? If so, she should know that no one can compare to him. Not even a handsome actor like Gardner McKay, so how in the world does Twilight think anyone within a thousand miles of Lock 4 ever could? Peter is everybody, and everybody is Peter. Only Stewart is Stewart.

When Frederick returned, Twilight suggested we all go to the beer garden. Frederick was grumpy and wanted to stay home, drinking the beer he had just bought at the liquor store. But Twilight used her hypnotic powers on him, too, and, soon, he was excited to go. When Twilight turned her skills toward me, again, I became all the more resistant toward going out than I already was. But Frederick didn't want to leave me home by myself, so he worked on persuading me, too.

"Why not take advantage of Mother being away for the night?" he said.

But that's what I had been hoping to do—be home without Mother. Then again, being out without Mother was also appealing.

"I'll buy you a pack of cigarettes," he said.

I don't recall when I first started sneaking cigarettes, but it clears my head and brings me to life. Mother doesn't know I smoke, and wouldn't allow me to smoke in the house even if she did. The persuasion took hold, and the beer garden began to sound like a fabulous idea. I'd never been there before.

FREDERICK BOUGHT ME A BEER, then another, and the bartender bought me one more. As we watched the beers pour from the tap, Frederick did his best Ray Milland impression: *"C'mon I need that liquor, I want it and I'm gonna get it, understand? I'm gonna walk out of here with a quart of rye one way or another."*

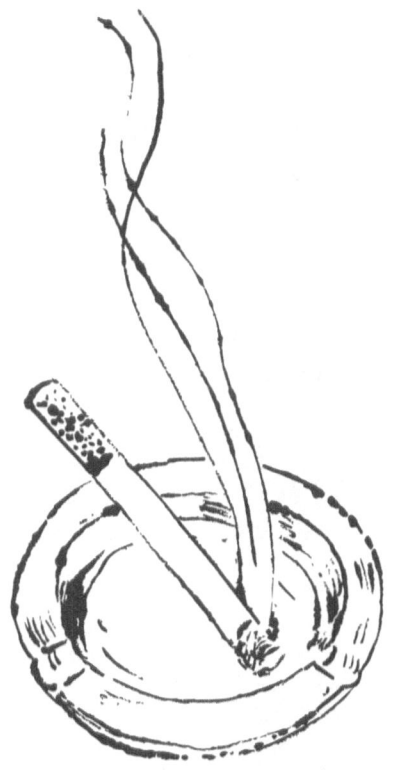

Twilight didn't know what movie it was from.
"The Lost Weekend!" I said.
Then Frederick became Jack Lemmon: *"Look at me, I'm a bum. Look at you, you're a bum."* Frederick put his arm over

Twilight's shoulder and pointed to their reflection in the mirror behind the bar. *"Look at us, see? A couple of bums."*

"Days of Wine and Roses!" I said, enjoying the game.

With each round, we clinked our glasses. The liquid warmed my insides while Frederick and Twilight began to sing "Who's Afraid of Virginia Woolf" over and over, stopping now and then to laugh manically. The song is from the film with Elizabeth Taylor. They'd just seen it last weekend. I love Elizabeth Taylor and was jealous they hadn't invited me.

We were there for several hours, and I smoked most of my cigarettes.

The rest of the night is fuzzy, but I remember Frederick crashed the car on our way home. It wasn't bad. In fact, Twilight found it funny. She continued to sing while Frederick somehow managed to back his car out of the gully. *"Who's afraid of Virginia Woolf?"*

We made it home okay, and they were right; it was nice to be out of the house for a while.

TWISTED MUSE

As we approach Dad's house, rain turns to snow. It falls in heavy wet flakes that melt as soon as they hit the windshield. Before stopping, I suggest we drive a little further down the road to an old barn I always loved. I want to show Eric there's more to Daisytown than the surreal universe Dad represents. Remind myself, too.

"There used to be a couple of horses," I say. "I don't know if they're still around—or if the horses will be out in this weather —but it's worth a look."

We find the barn and the horses—two angular old beasts. Each slumped in the middle. They watch as we approach the fence, keeping perfectly still while snowflakes melt on their backs, and steam escapes their nostrils. One of them snorts. Eric takes a few pictures, zooms in, and takes a few more. An expanse of patchy snow slopes up a field toward a distant white house perched at the top. The horses are white, too, save a few black spots on each of them. It's a painting, it's a pastoral, it's a cover of *The Saturday Evening Post.*

The cold leeches into my bones, but I'm still not ready to see Dad. I face the silvery sky and let the flakes melt on my face— the beautiful silence only snow affords—before I'm being buried alive under Dad's endless avalanche of gibberish.

"Just a few more," says Eric, between clicks of his camera's shutter.

"Take your time," I say. Tired but grateful, I seem to find more patience for him by the day.

I GRAB Eric's arm so as not to slip as we shuffle along the snowy wet grass of Dad's half-mowed lawn. We stomp our boots against the cement stoop, kicking off the snow, while the dogs announce our arrival with a discordant fanfare of whimpers and barks.

Dad greets us at the door. His T-shirt is spotted and stained, and his blue jeans aren't blue at all but rather a grayish-green. No laces on his well-worn boots. A piece of clothesline serves as a belt. Like a cartoon hillbilly.

Even though Dad's ragged appearance is the first thing I notice, I don't want it to be the first thing I mention—if I mention it at all.

"You have a goatee," I say.

He looks sinister as he smiles and scratches the scruff with his crooked fingers.

"What made you decide to grow it?"

"I always wanted to," he says, "but your mother never let me have hair on my face. I need to dye it, though."

"No, Dad," I say, hoping to save him from looking any more like a beatnik hobo than he already does. "You don't need to dye it. Why would you?"

He gives a coy smile.

"Have you met someone?" I ask.

"No! Who would want to be with me, what with my…issues and all? Besides, I still love Dorothy."

By issues, I'm guessing he means the paper towels he stuffs into his underpants. Maybe the penis clamp he's been using in the years since his prostate surgery. But these things barely scuff the surface.

As we take off our coats, Eric points out a puddle of dog piss near the door.

Dad doesn't flinch. "Cheng has been doing that," he says.

Dad hobbles into the kitchen and gets a paper towel. As he bends to mop the urine, he lets out a small wince. When he stands, he lets out a bigger one. He twists his face and cradles his abdomen as if someone unexpectedly tossed him a newborn baby.

"My hernia," he says.

"You never had that taken care of, Dad? I remember hearing you complain about your hernia at least twenty years ago."

"I need to lie down," he says. "It'll be okay once I take a pill and lie down."

"What kind of pill?"

If it's anything good, I'll steal a few for myself.

"They're on my dresser."

I follow behind as he staggers into his bedroom.

Shaking the pill bottle releases a tiny speck almost too small to see. Using a penknife, Dad attempts to shave it in two, but it crumbles into a powdery grit. Using a moistened fingertip, he lifts some into his mouth.

"That's what you're taking?"

"It's all I got."

I read the label: Percocet. Good thing they're gone.

"Are these for your hernia? Can you get a refill?"

"No, I got them for my knee. I hurt my knee mulching the leaves, but it's better now."

"Lucky that's all you hurt."

"Well, I hit my head on a tree branch, too. That's why I fell. Everything around me got small, and I turned into a giant. I had giant hands and feet. Angels flew over me. Maybe my guardian angels, I don't know. Everyone has one. They were pointing down, saying, That's him!"

"Wait, this was *before* you had the pills, right? You probably had a concussion."

"That's what the doctor said."

"Come spring, I'm going to find someone to cut your grass for you."

"I don't have money for that."

"I'll pay for it, Dad. I can hire a high school kid to do it."

"You think I can't do nothing for myself? How do you think I've been doing all this time? How do you think I do?"

"You don't, Dad, you don't *do*! Look at you. You're falling apart. Your clothes are filthy."

"Everything's clean. I bleach my underwear in a bucket downstairs."

I've seen the bucket he's talking about. I thought they were cleaning rags.

"What about the rest of your clothes?" I say. "Why not ask Maggie to wash them?"

"She steals things, that's why."

"What has she stolen?"

"Some of your mother's plates. Nice plates with birds on them. Your mother had a set of four but one of them is gone."

"Maybe it broke?"

"I'm telling you Rachel, Maggie stole it."

He opens a drawer filled with baggy old socks and pulls out a piece of cardboard.

"That's why I made these signs. I put these in all my drawers."

Written in black marker, it merely says: DO NOT STEAL MY THINGS!

"Maggie is not going to steal your socks, Dad."

"She might take my towels."

"You'll be lucky if she touches your towels. Go to the laundromat if you're so worried. There's got to be one around here somewhere."

He eases onto his bed and tries to stretch out but remains stiff and forked, tensely crossed out like a medieval pieta. Through clenched teeth, he asks me to turn out the light. But as I leave, he calls me back.

"Can you send Ernie in here a minute? I want to show him something."

I retrieve Eric, who looks suitably perplexed.

"I have no idea," I say. "But when the muse calls, you must answer."

I follow Eric to the door to eavesdrop, but they talk too softly for me to hear.

When Eric comes out, his face is ashen.

"What was that all about?"

"He wanted to show me his hernia," he says. "It's a big hairy bulb like a kiwi fruit straining at his pubic line. But I saw more than that. He pulled down his pants, his underwear, his paper towels. His junk, the clamp, I saw it all. I wish I hadn't."

"Why did he show it to you?"

"Too embarrassed to show you, I guess. He asked for my opinion. I told him he needed to get it checked out. He does. There's a lot going on down there."

"Was that the pose you wanted to photograph?"

"Very funny. I don't need a photo to remember that mess. If anything, I need something to help me forget it."

"I know where you can find a few dusty flecks of Percocet."

WALMART IS the last place I want to be on Christmas Eve, but as Dad rests, it's where Eric and I go. The crowd is ferocious, and the "Gifts for Dad" department has been pretty well picked over by the time we arrive.

It takes some digging, but we manage to find the basics—T-shirts, jeans, sheets, and so on. I splurge for a box of adult diapers, too.

As we wait to check out, I remember Dad's clothesline and tell Eric to hold our place in line while I run to find a belt.

Mom was worse than Dad ever was. He only whipped us when Mom told him to—and his heart was never in it—but I still cringe to recall the sound of Dad's belt whipping through his belt loops. As I look for Dad's size, I tell myself over and over: It's just a belt. I wear one myself sometimes.

THE DOGS AREN'T TETHERED, but when we return, neither of them makes a run for it. One of them can barely walk.

Dad shuffles out of the bathroom, cinching his pants, knotting his clothesline.

"Feeling better, Dad?"

"I'm doing okay."

I start cooking and ask Dad to clear the table. Among the newspapers and junk mail, there are rows of holiday greeting cards. He collects them from the table and neatly arranges them atop the old Baldwin organ. The organ is older than I am, but it's still the newest piece of furniture in the house. "First, we got Mike, then we got the organ, and then we got Rachel," Dad likes to say. He seems to give the same significance to the purchase of the organ as to the adoption of two living human beings. The organ short-circuited years ago. With no money to fix it, it has been relegated to nothing more than a place to display greeting cards and old photographs.

"Twenty-seven cards," Dad says, as he struggles to find room for them all. "I sent out thirty-one, but I only got Twenty-seven back."

"Twenty-seven? Do you even know twenty-seven people?"

"Sure I do—from church."

He goes into his office to fetch his notebook so he can give me an accurate total of the money that came with the cards.

"Five-hundred and twenty dollars," he says.

He points to a few names underlined in red.

"These people here, they didn't give me no cards back."

"What are you going to do with all that money?" says Eric.

"I already spent it on clothes."

"Why aren't you wearing them?" I say.

"They're for church."

He dashes into Mike's old bedroom again.

Dad calls it his office, but he didn't convert it with the same definitive flourish as Mom did with mine. The bed has been replaced by a desk, but otherwise, the room still looks like a high-school boy's bedroom. Sports trophies line the shelves, a model airplane hangs from the ceiling, and the closet is filled with Polo shirts and sports jerseys that haven't been worn in decades.

Dad returns with a gray suit, a white dress shirt, a blue dress shirt, and three purple ties. The shirts are still wrapped in plastic.

"Look here," he says, holding up a tie that looks exactly like the others. "It looked purple in the store, but when I got it home, I saw it was pink. I can't wear a pink tie—pink isn't a man's color. So, I prayed and prayed that it would change and, look, overnight, it turned this beautiful shade of purple."

"You prayed to turn your tie purple? Really, Dad?"

He holds it under the weak yellow light of the dusty chandelier.

"Don't it look purple to you?"

When I don't answer, he turns to Eric. "Don't it look purple to you?"

Eric agrees it looks purple.

"How much did all of this cost, anyway? The suit and the ties?"

"And two shirts," he says.

"How much?"

"Five-hundred dollars. Five-hundred and twenty dollars, something like that. Five-hundred and fifteen, maybe. Something right around that. I didn't have no good church clothes."

"Why didn't you buy yourself a belt while you were at it?" I ask.

"But I did!"

Despite his hernia, he darts into his office and returns with the exact belt I just bought for him.

CHRISTMAS MORNING, after breakfast, we give Dad his gifts—a couple of pairs of jeans, the belt, a pair of slippers, T-shirts, diapers, sheets, and a winter coat. As much as I could afford. More than I could afford—Eric paid for the coat. He insisted.

Dad sits in his easy chair with the dogs at his feet. He carefully slips a long, bony finger under the cellophane tape. It's cheap wrapping paper and tears easily. When it does, Dad grimaces as though someone jammed a sharp fork into his back.

He tries the slippers first. They fit okay, but they aren't perfect. He tugs off his socks, straightens his legs, and holds his bare feet side by side to show Eric how they are two different sizes.

"Rachel knows the story," Dad says. "I ran barefoot over a big piece of glass, and my foot went flat. It's why they sent me home from the Army. This one here is a size eleven, and this other one is a size twelve. I couldn't march right."

So many possibilities for why Dad was discharged from the Army, but it's better not to speculate—especially after his confessions about the gay magazines, Grandpa in the bath, etc. Best to believe it was merely his feet.

After Dad opens his final gift, he molds his face into a pout. The clothes are beautiful, he says, and practical, but he had been hoping for a new brown suit.

He has the outfit he wore to Mom's funeral—the black one that fits like a pillowcase over a broom handle—and a new gray suit he got with his Christmas card money. "But what I need is a brown one. With an orange tie like what I saw the preacher wearing on TV. A brown suit and an orange tie. It looked so sharp. I wish you told me you were going to buy all these things. I don't mean to say I don't appreciate what you done, but—"

"Maybe you can pray for one of your extra purple ties to turn orange," I say.

He looks at me like it's the most ridiculous thing he's ever heard.

Dad gives Eric and me each a present in return: a calendar from Dad's church.

I regret spending all my money on these stupid gifts. Not only is Dad not happy with any of them but, to make matters worse, unwrapping them hasn't consumed nearly as much time as I hoped it would. It's only eleven AM—we still have an entire day left to kill, when all I can think about is Oakville.

I ask Dad if he'd like to visit the cemetery. I haven't been to Mom's grave since the funeral—before they installed the headstone—and I'm curious to find out if seeing Mom's name engraved in granite brings any closure.

"I visited Dorothy a few days ago," Dad says. "I don't need to go again. Unless you want to go. I don't mean to say you can't go. It's your mother and all. It's snowing now, but if you want to go…"

I pull back the picture window's fraying white curtain and see the snow is accumulating.

"Maybe tomorrow," I say. "I'm going to visit my birth mother's grave then, too."

I explain to Dad how I'd used my adoption papers to find some relatives. Without going into detail, I tell him about visiting them in Delaware.

"Oh, did you? That's good. I hoped you might do that."

It's hard to know if he's telling the truth, but I choose to believe him.

"My birth mother is buried at a Catholic cemetery somewhere in Charleroi," I say. "Mother of Sorrows."

"I know where that be. We used to take your grandmother to that cemetery."

"Are you sure?"

"Your grandmother knew people buried at that cemetery. We would drive her there once in a while. She knew people at that church."

I don't want it to be true—I want Anna's world to be totally separate from Dad's. Turns out there are a lot of things I don't want to be true. Can't do a thing about any of them.

THE MEAL GOES MUCH the same as my previous dinner with Dad. Except for this time, we have pumpkin pie—Dad's favorite. As I hunt around for a plate to serve it on, I come across one with a bluebird on it. "Is this the bird plate you said was missing?" I ask.

"Where'd you find that?"

"It was in the cupboard."

Dad squints, looking confused and suspicious. "Well don't put no punkin pie on it," he says. "It belongs in the display cabinet. Put it up in there with the others, behind the sign I made."

After we eat, Eric offers to do the dishes, but Dad won't allow it. The house's plumbing is a mess. A plumber once came to the house to snake a clog and, in the process, shattered the pipes.

"You should have told me you had clay pipes," the plumber said before packing his equipment and walking out the door.

Dad had paid the plumber for destroying the pipes but subsequently, in fact consequently, hadn't been able to afford to get them fixed. They have been broken ever since. As a result, Dad has developed a technique for doing the dishes that won't overwhelm the dysfunctional plumbing. He doesn't trust anyone else to be as careful about it as he is. Nothing is allowed down the drain, not the tiniest scrap of food. "Nothing," he repeats again and again.

It's only five o'clock, but I'm already desperate to retreat into a cocoon of bedcovers—sleep if I can, or escape into a book or the television if I can't—so once the dishes are done I announce it's time to go. Dad wants us to stay longer, of course.

"You told me you were going to stay the whole day."

"We don't want to get stuck in the snow," I say.

"Or have an accident," says Eric.

Sensing what may be his last chance, Eric asks Dad to pose for a quick photo before we go. Dad agrees, but only if I get in the picture, too. I haven't posed with Dad in years.

Dad asks Eric if he knows about my "modeling career."

"I have a postcard in my office with some of her modeling pictures on it," he says. "I'll get it."

"Stand still, Dad. Let Eric finish."

I've told Eric a little about my modeling days, but I don't remember how much—I can't keep track of what he knows about anything anymore. Either way, it's funny to hear Dad speak so enthusiastically about my so-called modeling career. When he first learned of it, he and Mom both thought I was making it all up to impress them. As proof, I remember showing them a magazine layout shot on location in the Austrian Alps. When they saw it, they accused me of having posed in front of a backdrop at a Sears portrait studio.

"Them mountains don't look real," Dad had said.

It's hard to blame him—the mountains didn't look real to me, either, not even as I posed in their midst. Until then, the only mountain I'd ever seen was the little hill behind our house. Beautiful in its way, but not nearly as majestic. The Alps were real, though, and, for some reason, Dad finally seems to believe it.

In his wallet, Dad carries a shampoo ad he clipped from a magazine featuring a model he thinks is me. Eric can tell right away it isn't, but Dad is convinced. It's nice to see him proud of me for a change, but I would prefer the stories to be more firmly grounded in reality. It's a lot to ask.

After Eric pops off a few more shots, he hands me his camera so I can scroll through them.

"Pretty good," I say, and angle the camera to let Dad have a look. "What do you think?"

"Is that me?" he says. He squints at the camera's scratched display before finding his reading glasses and looking closer. "I look so old."

"You are old. You ought to think about moving into the Bentleyville Apartments."

Ten miles or so down the road is an assisted living complex. It's the first time I've mentioned it—the first time I've thought of it—but it's a good idea. I prepare for a fight, but Dad is too busy staring at his image to respond. If I ever talk to Mike again, I'll see what he thinks about the idea. I don't know how either of us would pay for it; I don't know what kind of an income Dad has at this point either. It can't be much.

"I'll mail you a print," Eric says, putting his camera away. "Can I see Rachel's postcard?"

As Dad shuffles into his office to find the card, I struggle to remember what it looks like. When he returns with it in his hand, I snatch it away to be sure it's not embarrassing.

I'm astonished by how young I look. Maybe not twenty, as stated on the card, but young. The next time some hotel clerk tells me I look twenty-four, I'll know she is full of shit. *That's* what twenty-four looks like—a baby.

ERIC PUTS the car in gear and attempts to pull out of the driveway, but we only get halfway up the hill before losing traction and spinning the wheels. Dad's world is going to be even more difficult to escape than I hoped—as if he creates a force field all his own. I hold my breath and think of Anna. "We'll get there," I say to myself. We have to. Eric tries again. The tires spin through the snow and gravel, into the mud below.

"Maybe you better start from where the ground is flat," I say.

But a line of hedges at the top of the driveway blocks the view, and Eric is worried a running start will jettison us into the street, risking a fiery collision with one of the cars or trucks that whiz along the narrow country road doing twice the legal limit.

Chugging slowly up the grade isn't working, either, though.

Dad, who has been standing beside us mumbling suggestions, shuffles behind the car and prepares to push.

I roll down my window.

"Get away from the car. You're going to get run over."

I roll the window up and grumble to Eric.

"His hernia, his bum knee—the idiot thinks he's going to push?"

I collect myself and roll the window down again.

"I know how you can help, Dad. Why don't you stand at the top of the driveway and let us know when the coast is clear? That way, we can get some momentum."

Eric eases the car to the flat end of the driveway, floors it, and powers up the grade. The tires spin again before managing enough traction to roll us onto the street.

We pause at the side of the road as Dad comes to the window to thank us for coming one last time. He acknowledges the gifts we gave him, thanks Eric for bringing me home. Snowflakes melt on his cheeks. I melt, too.

When we finally pull away, I turn and watch through the rear window as Dad stands at the curb and waves goodbye.

He's wearing his new winter coat.

———

SNOW CONTINUES to fall through the night, stranding us at the motel. Eric is anxious about the uncertainty of it, wondering when the roads will be clear. I'd be perfectly content with an excuse to have nothing to do and nowhere to go—away from New York, away from Dad—but the snow leaves me distressed, too. An unexpected roadblock on the way to Anna's grave.

After too much TV, a brief snowball fight in the parking lot, and an early meal at the diner, it's back to the room to lounge some more. Eric massages my neck and shoulders, moving to my lower back and legs. It must be like wedging a cold slab of clay. I begin to warm up and tell him it feels nice. Encouraged, he tugs my underwear down and begins to massage my ass.

I stiffen.

As he leans down to kiss my neck, I see where this is going and shuffle him off. It feels too…transactional.

"I can't," I say, pulling my panties up. "Not here. Not now."

Eric pats my ass and stands up.

"I get it," he says.

He puts on his boots and coat and picks up his camera.

"Don't be that way," I say.

He pauses at the door, his hand on the door handle.

"You have to understand how preoccupied I am," I say.

"It's not just here, Rachel. It's not just now. If you're not interested in me anymore, you need to tell me."

"I can't talk about this. I'm going through a lot."

As he walks out the door, I imagine him leaving for good. Still interested? I must be. But I'm numb to him lately. Numb to everything. I tell myself it's a phase. Hormones, biorhythms, sunspots, the moon.

I peer at him through the curtains, his silhouette descending the hill, casting a long thin shadow like a man on the moon. Snowflakes flicker in the motel lights as if they are passing stars. I think of space missions and how the calculations need to be so precise to make connections—lunar landings, journeys to Mars. A misplaced decimal point and my little one-woman space capsule will deflect off the atmosphere and go hurtling into the void once and for all.

Alone.

ANNA'S JOURNAL
Saturday, September 30, 1967

I want to write to Stewart, but I feel so estranged. Nevertheless, I need to put these thoughts on paper, regardless of whether they make it into his hands:

Oh, Stewart, where are you, my love? I will finally tell you where I am. After some time at home, The Matron of Washington County has once again escorted me to Oakville. Where is Oakville? I'll get to that.

Am I alive? Am I meant to be? Once again, I'm waking as if passing through the spinning center of a hypnotist's wheel—like The Time Tunnel on TV. Anything left over from what went before—including my alternate life with you—belongs to a different Anna from a different era, impossible to reach.

I'm so ashamed of what's become of me, I won't blame you if you've chosen to stay behind in that previous world. Even if you have forgiven me, I will never forgive myself.

Forget whatever you may have heard from Mother, or Frederick, or anyone else who claims to know me. No one can be trusted to tell my story. Let me try to get to the five W's.

You know me as Anna Rubik, of Lock 4, Pennsylvania, born in 1934. You spoke to me for the first time in 1952 and when we fell in love at first sight, it changed my life. Un coup de foudre. I've never told you this, but I was diagnosed with a mental disease in May of 1953 and hospitalized for the first time at age twenty after a traumatic event in Washington, DC. At the time, I had everything to live for. I was on my own with a good-paying job and was planning to move to California, where you and I would be married. But everything changed. The world folded in on itself, and I panicked. I can't tell you everything because so much of my life and its memories have disintegrated like the fine ash of burnt silk. And much of what I do recall must remain secret for other reasons. I hope you understand. I will, however, tell you what it is safe for you to know.

I began to hear voices when I was sixteen. I missed a year of school because of it. I gave up singing in the choir, which I loved. I couldn't cope with the competing chorus in my head and lost interest in everything. Mother and Father took me to a doctor in the Magic City of Charleroi, and then to a hospital in Pittsburgh, where I received my first treatment. I was told that it was an x-ray, though I realize now it was something more sinister. The treatments muffled my mind. The voices became hard to decipher, like hearing the sound of Mother and Father through my bedroom wall whispering in Polish.

You might not realize this but I would not have made it through those early years without you. To this day, you are the only consistent thing in my life. As such, you are the thing they've tried hardest to have me forget. But their efforts in this regard only make me cling to you all the more. That is why the thought that you have finally given up and abandoned me is so painful. I pray it's not true, though if it is, I understand.

I spent nearly a year lying in bed, struggling to read, listening to the radio or watching television. While watching something like a news broadcast, I believed the newsmen could see me, and they would purposefully direct signals toward me. To this day, along with the belief that everyone knows my thoughts, I still believe the newsmen on TV can see me and attempt to hypnotize me. Sometimes they succeed. For this reason, I prefer my magazines. Their voices are much softer.

In time, the voices came from everywhere. They became vicious and sometimes would tell me to do and say bad things. I thought I might kill myself as a way to silence them. Upon returning home to Pennsylvania from Washington, I was sent to Oakville Hospital for more "x-rays" (I still call them that) as a way to find the voices and root them out. Like roaches in the light, however, they merely scattered into the labyrinth of my brain, where they festered and multiplied.

I'm not sure how much time I spent in Oakville that first time, but I have been in and out ever since. I can't say which is worse. When at home, Mother takes over the chore of feeding me buckets of pills, but I don't always take them. I rather flush them down the toilet or throw them to the birds.

"Have you taken your pills, Anna?" Mother says if I get upset about something the way anyone might.

"Have you taken yours?" I reply.

Mother has pills for her maladies, too, after all.

I get so angry! Why must I be given pills to be understood? Why can't everyone else be given tablets that will make them understand me? You understand me, though, don't you, Stewart?

I know you don't want to hear about what a sinner I have been or how I betrayed you, but believe me when I tell you I became subjugated by that man. He controlled my thoughts like a newsman on TV. When we kissed, my mind and body were not my own.

Recently, when I refused to go to church, Mother, again, said, "Have you been taking your pills?"

Church is where I sometimes hear the cruelest voices, so I often don't go. The priests have abandoned Latin and the services are in English, now, but it doesn't make any difference. They may as well be speaking in tongues. Or in a secret language I'm not pure enough to understand. When I do go, and meet Mother's friends before service, her friends are all cautious with their words. They say things like, "You look well, dear," or "So nice to see you." They are stiff, robotic contraptions with mechanical language like the newsmen on TV. They say these things while I'm looking at them. All of it is directed at me and said purposefully. I can't stand it. I hardly go anymore. God has abandoned me, and so I have abandoned Him.

Everyone makes strange noises, too, as if their throats are tiny radios. Every time a man scratches his chin or touches his temple, it is also directed at me, though he will try to pretend it's just an itch.

The garbled noises in everybody's throats, the fake coughs, the scratching—it tests my nerves. But I have to control my anger so that I can stay out of the hospital. I try not to let it get to me.

You never coughed at me, though, did you, Stewart? Your voice was always clear, calm, and reassuring. It's why I continue to write to you after all these years. There are so few trustworthy people in this world.

The paranoia affects me more than the voices, now. The voices are manageable, dulled by pills. They still haunt me, but not as much as they used to. The main problem is that I don't always know what's real and what's not.

For example, I still believe everyone in America knows my face and knows everything about me. But the doctors insist it's not true. The same doctors who allowed me to believe I was getting x-rays tell me I'm paranoid and delusional. When I was hallucinating, I saw things, and they were altogether real to me. Yet, everyone was telling me there was nothing there, so, again, I didn't know what was real and what wasn't. I still don't.

As a child, the dentist tried to pull all of my teeth.

"No, they didn't, Anna," Mother says.

When I was thirteen, my body trembled violently as the wrath of God rained down upon me and left me paralyzed.

"But look, you're not paralyzed, are you, Anna?" say the doctors.

While at home, I tried to start painting again but got nowhere. Writing, as well, is so much more of a struggle than it used to be. Once upon a time, I had wanted to be a writer, to work for a newspaper, or a magazine. I wanted to live in Hollywood with you. I still do. If you've moved to Malibu by now, that's fine too, Stewart. But writing is next to impossible. It's too hard to organize my thoughts. I think I am making sense, but when I read back something I wrote previously, it's just a random mess of words. I say the same things over and over in an attempt to make myself understood. It's always a miserable failure. Like this letter. That's why I might not mail it.

Sometimes, when I try to write in my journal, I draw pictures on the pages instead. It's sometimes easier to draw or paint because I don't have to think. But drawing doesn't come easy anymore, either. Whenever I see an old painting of mine, I wonder who made it—another Anna, from another time.

The doctors here at Oakville were allowing me to go home with Mother on the weekends and for holidays, which was good as I was able to take classes at night school. I still hope to get a job and live on my own. Or live with you if you'll yet have me after my humiliating night with that man. I shouldn't mention it again, but I am so ashamed. There is so much that I want you to know.

Whatever the case, I feel I have nothing to lose anymore. I don't want to be embarrassed to tell you things because being judged and embarrassed is what led me here in the first place. Losing you has caused me to feel even more alone than I ever did. When I think about you, all I can do is imagine the world you are in and wish I was there with you. It's all I've ever wanted.

I feel I must let go of any hope for a normal life. When I am feeling better, I can do things, go places, write letters. When I feel nothing, I am nothing.

During my most recent visit home, I barely left my room for two months. Mother burst through the door, holding the container of my medicine in her fist.

"I counted them," she screamed. "You have not been taking your pills!"

When she threw the canister at me, I unscrewed the lid and dumped the contents of the entire bottle into my mouth.

I don't remember much after that. Mother continued to scream, but because I thought I would never have to hear her again, it didn't bother me. I may have even laughed.

So, now I must ask, did I die? Am I now waking into a new world? A better world? Tell me, does a better one exist?

The clock in the day ward creaks more than it ticks, and I feel as though I've been back in the hospital forever, once again a prisoner of my limitations. I was wandering the ward, the halls, pacing, crawling, when something suddenly crashed over me in a breaking wave, like the breeched dam of the Johnstown flood. I had barely enough time to yelp, let alone time to stand out of its way. Its gushing momentum carried me a few feet down the hall until I lost balance. My head cracked against the tile floor in an explosion of blue and yellow stars. I floated in a great white void as my hair became warm and sticky with an ooze of blood. Above me, I saw a ghostly apparition like a haloed angel.

"What happened?"

It was Nurse Winthrop's voice. She cradled my head and stroked my hair with a calming caress. I tried to answer, but I discovered my jaw was frozen with pain.

Soon, I heard the approaching tap of Dr. Abrams' shoes as he ran down the hall. He knelt and groped at my face as if he were Gardner McKay sculpting a bust. Eventually, with a click, like a key in a lock, my jawbone snapped into place. They led me to a room with a private bed and let me rest. My jaw is still terribly sore, and I can't chew to eat. It is impossible to speak, too, but I don't have anything to say that can't be conveyed with a simple nod or shake.

Despite my discomfort, I'm happy to have a private room—especially with so much activity in the ward. It's been busy for weeks.

They tell me it's because we will all be moving soon.

"Leaving the cottages," they say as if we've all been away at summer camp.

I've watched the new building going up. Every time I come back after being away, it is further along. Clean and modern, but so small. How will everyone fit?

But not everyone will be going, they tell me. Some will be going elsewhere. Some will be going home.

"And me?" I ask.

"We'll always have a nice place for you, Anna, don't worry." Nurse Winthrop says.

Whether it is reassuring or disappointing, I can't decide, but I'm wary. No one has ever truly had a place for me.

For now, I'm in Jamison Cottage with Olive and Nancy. Will there always be a place for them, too?

Poor Olive would probably be content to find a place away from me. A few weeks ago, I kicked her in her head and loosened two of her teeth. I'm embarrassed to say, I would have done worse if they hadn't pulled me off. The doctor wanted to know why.

"What were you hearing," he asked. "Is it God?"

Maybe.

What does God sound like? The entire universe chattering like an infinite field of chickens? Is it God I hear when the clouds skulk across the sky? When I hear the earth groan and the planets spin, is that God? Or is it his entire panoply of creation I hear jabbering, sneering, crying, calling. Olive happened to be the loudest at the time, so I grabbed her by the hair, threw her to the ground, and made her shut up.

Condemned as I am to a radius of activity as tight a potted plant, I am suddenly aware that I don't know any of the people in this hospital. Not even my friend, Olive, it seems. Despite having lived amongst many of these women for years. I've eaten with them, have occasionally shared exchanges while watching television, or eating our meals, but I have not truly known a single one of them. Nor have they known me. I am as distant from them as I was from the girls in high school or my coworkers in Washington, DC. Even if I made the effort, most of them would hardly speak to me out of sheer force of habit. And it's not likely I will ever try due to habits of my own. Soon it will be goodbye to many of them.

I often feel like a mouse with two separate cages. When I've exhausted myself on the exercise wheel at home, I move to the cottages and exhaust myself here. I imagine that once they've finished construction on the new wheel in the new building, I will drain myself there, too. Since I have given up hope for a decent life, what difference does it make?

When I'm asked, "Would you like to go home for a visit?"

I can reply with either a nod or a shake.

When I'm asked, "Would you like to return to the hospital?"

Nod or shake. Maybe a shrug.

It's all the same to me.

I'm looking forward to my night sedatives, when my head will merge with the pillow beneath it, full of feathers and empty of thoughts. If I ever mail this letter, and if you receive it, please respond with words of love and encouragement. I'd rather die all over again than to hear from you what you have every right to say.

Eternally yours,

Anna

FINDING OAKVILLE

Patches of ice lay hidden under wisps of dry snow as we rise and fall through the frozen hills. Eric drives slowly, carefully, following Dad's directions, until we spot a roadside sign. Its faded white letters are challenging to read, so the cross gives us our hint, though the snow is so deep, there isn't a tombstone in sight.

Below the cross, a pale blue arrow points to a narrow, unplowed road snaking up a treacherous hill. Does interring people at vertiginous heights make the final journey shorter? Why can't people just UberPool to heaven?

"The car won't make it," he says, flatly.

I beg him to try.

Beyond the first bend, the tires lose traction, and the car slips backward. Looking over his shoulder, Eric strains to steer, but the car is like a king-size bed on castors. The tires finally clutch the road an inch shy of us toppling into a ditch.

Gingerly turning the wheel, Eric points the car downhill, and we inch back to the main road.

He parks on the shoulder.

"We can try to walk," he says.

Again, we don't get far. I slip on some ice, and when I break my fall, an iced-over piece of gravel rips a hole in my glove. Looking up and realizing how much further we have to go, I lose confidence.

"Next time," Eric promises.

He takes my hand and we skate back to the car.

"When the weather gets warm, we'll come back," he says. "We'll bring flowers and everything. I promise. We won't even tell your Dad we're here."

I stare up the hill for what must be a full minute. "We can still try to find Oakville, right?"

Not reaching Anna's grave makes a trip to Oakville essential. I'm determined to connect, somehow.

CALCULATING THE DATES, I learn that Anna was a patient at Oakville during a period of transition. According to my online research, nearly all the old buildings were abandoned by 1968, which means Anna would have spent her last couple of years in one of the current hospital buildings. I'm more interested in the older, abandoned ones, however, because it's where Anna would have spent the majority of her time. Although I found the paranormal websites distasteful, they provide detailed instructions for how to locate them.

I read aloud from directions I printed before we left—straight, left, left again—until we come upon a gated road marked: NO TRESPASSING. Pay dirt.

Looking around, I realize a similar sign marks nearly every tree. The websites cautioned about state cops who patrol the area and warned of hefty fines and possible arrest if you get caught. I haven't mentioned any of this to Eric. Not until we're at the gate.

"My car is so conspicuous against the snow," he says, shaking his head, searching for a hidden place to park. "I better stay here and act as a lookout while you do some reconnaissance. How's the battery on your phone? Reception?"

It's an imperfect plan. What if a cop does roll up? Assuming Eric is lucky enough to avoid arrest, he'll still be told to move along, leaving me stranded. Not a seasoned ghost hunter, I haven't thought this through.

I step out of the car and trek about a hundred yards to the nearest building, red brick overgrown with black, leafless vines. Although I don't know what the building was used for, or whether Anna ever set foot inside, it beckons me to enter.

Cement stairs lead to an archway and, beyond it, a doorway with no door. Gaining entry is as simple as crossing the threshold.

Inside is a vision of post-apocalyptic devastation. Graffiti covers the walls, some fresh, some peeling away with the coats of old paint and thick layers of plaster. I imagine kids drinking here, telling stories, hearing ghosts, hallucinating spectral shadows the way the patients might have done.

I kick at the loose tiles strewn about the floor. I pick one up and dust it off, put it in my pocket.

Partway down a hall, there's an open door into a room with a broken old metal bed frame. Pale green water-stained paint covers the walls. From inside the room, I stare out to the hall through the door's small window pane, which is reinforced with wire and still intact. I try to imagine whether Anna might have looked through this window before me. If so, what did she see? What did she think? What did she feel?

A gust of wind whistles through the hall, and I think I hear someone coming.

I pull off a glove and send Eric a text: "Come find me!"

"No time," he texts back. "Security heading this way."

I double back and spot a security vehicle idling on the nearby access road. It will be impossible to slip into Eric's car unnoticed—too late to pretend I have been sitting there all along.

As casually as I can, I get into the car. Eric and I scramble to agree on a story: I'd merely been urinating behind a tree.

Before long, a uniformed woman emerges from the cruiser, walks the few yards to Eric's window, and taps the glass with her radio.

"Everything okay here?" the woman asks as Eric rolls down his window.

"Yes, fine," Eric tells her. "We're a little lost, that's all."

He's a terrible liar, and I doubt she believes him. She doesn't appear to be a cop, however, so maybe there's nothing she can do other than shoo us away or call the State Police. Perhaps she already has.

Soon, we are boxed in by three more cruisers.

"Let's see some ID." The woman says.

Eric digs out his license and hands it to her.

"I was taking a pee," I say, trying to salvage our story. "Honestly, I was too embarrassed to tell you."

"Who are you?" she says, leaning down, peering at me through the open window.

I've been close to tears since we arrived, and I can't contain myself any longer.

"I might have been born here," I say, before breaking into a full-blown sob.

The stark possibility hadn't occurred to me, but now that it has, I'm overwhelmed.

The rent-a-cop looks at me skeptically, being as our story has changed thrice in three minutes. Eric hands me a tissue from his coat pocket.

"I doubt it," she says.

"My mother died in 1973," I add, though I'm not exactly sure why. I'm having trouble controlling what comes from my mouth, as if ventriloquist ghosts have taken control. "She was an inmate—I mean a patient—here. I was adopted."

She sends two of the guards away with a jerk of her head and passes Eric's ID to the one remaining who takes the ID to his cruiser. Just the three of us now, the woman leans down to talk to us more intimately, recrimination lingering in her voice.

"Some of the patients on this premises are being criminally detained—sexual offenders and so on. We can't allow anyone to wander around unescorted, no matter who they are."

"Understood," says Eric.

"And this here," she says, pointing to the land behind us with a sweep of her radio's antennae, "this is all private property."

The woman steps away for a moment, scans the desolate surroundings. Kicks at some ice.

"If your mother was a patient here, as you say,"—she peers at me closely—"then why don't I escort you to the front desk so you can go through the proper channels. I can't promise they'll have specific information regarding your mother, but they might."

The male guard returns with Eric's ID, and he speaks with the woman for a minute before getting back into his cruiser and pulling away. The woman hands Eric his ID and says, "Follow me."

Is she merely escorting us to the front desk, or is there a problem? She clearly does not trust us to go either forward or backward alone. Either way, we feel obliged to go along.

Other than the barred windows of the upper floors, the

current hospital building looks like the mid-century public high school of a mid-sized city. It's hard not to picture the rows of windows having construction paper snowflakes taped to each of them. The place feels innocuous and small against the vast expanse of virgin snow.

Our escort nods hello to a guard sitting inside the main entrance, who has us sign our names in a book. She then leads us to the front desk and hands us off to the receptionist.

"I'll leave you here," the woman says. "But understand: if we catch you wandering the premises again, you *will* be arrested. Got it?"

When the receptionist gets off the phone, and she takes her time, I tell her what I know about Anna. It's a lot more than I ever used to know, but it's still not much.

"I'm desperate for any information you might have," I say, and I immediately regret using the word desperate, regardless of how true it is. "Do you have records dating back that far?"

"Believe it or not, we do," the receptionist says. "But I'm afraid I can't give out any information here."

I am on the verge of tears again, and the receptionist's gaze turns glassy.

"What you can do is have your doctor send a formal records request. The clerks will sort through the microfiche and send whatever they find. No promises. And it will take time—a few weeks at least."

She taps her keyboard, causing the printer beside her to whiz, sputter and shake.

I've never had a doctor. Not one that I would call my doctor. Not even as a child. Mom and Dad took the dogs to the vet more often than they ever took me to a doctor. No dentists, either, for that matter. But, after my recent hospital stay, I was given the name of someone to see for a routine checkup. Blood test, pap smear, all that. I'm sure she'll give me a hard time for not yet scheduling the mammogram she ordered, but maybe I can get her to help me out with this paperwork.

The receptionist pulls the paper from the printer and hands it to me: *Authorization for Use or Disclosure of Personal Information.*

"Fill this out and send it back with a letter from your doctor. If anything turns up, we'll let you know."

ANNA'S JOURNAL
Tuesday, August 13, 1968

Why do I persist in writing to Stewart when he no longer responds? Letters to him are a force of habit as I desperately cling to the idea of a better world with a better me. Still, I don't know where to seek help anymore. The criminals here have conspired with Mother to steal my life and use their powers to commit all manner of atrocities. I don't know how to protect myself any longer. Even if Stewart were to rescue me, I'm afraid the culprits will follow me to Hollywood, too, and corrupt my life there as well. They've done so much already to stand in my way. They keep me tethered to this so-called mental hospital, feeding me a twisted rainbow of pills, injecting me with who-knows-what. Every time they attach me to the wires, my brain becomes soggy mush like a boiled potato. I need protection. Won't someone come for me? Finally?

People do escape sometimes. It *is* possible. I heard about one man who escaped thirteen times in the span of only two years. Nancy is gone. They have replaced her with a girl whose name I haven't had time to learn—and may never learn before she, too, is replaced. Or maybe the new girl is the girl who has always been here, and Nancy was merely a specter from an alternate world. The world of the previous second. Every moment is an eternity, and every second contains an entire universe. One second, it's a world with Nancy, the next, it's one with the new girl. One second I'm home in my familiar bed, the next I'm here in Oakville. There's no way to predict. And it's not only my surroundings. I, too, am constantly changing. And yet, I am always the same.

The girl who replaced Nancy is young—just eighteen. She says she's only here for the summer and believes she's different from those of us who have been here for years. Until I saw her, I'd been fooling myself into thinking I was still young, too. And, like her, that a life outside was waiting for me. I can't fool myself any longer. When they gather us together and I stand alongside the new girl, I realize I am nothing but an odd collection of dry bones rattling inside a withered bag of skin.

The new girl sees me that way, too, and has already shown herself to be as spiteful and taunting as the others. I caught her scheming in the hallway with another girl, conjuring malicious taunts. When I told them to shut up, they smirked at my hair.

I can no longer contain my reactions to these slights. In a violent froth, I hurtled into the two women like a bowling ball picking up a spare. Yes, I did it on purpose! And yes, I'll do it again next time I catch them chirping about me.

They were laughing at my hair because, earlier, I had grabbed a dull pair of scissors in the crafts room and cut it.

"Anna, what did you do?" Nurse Winthrop said, clucking her teeth.

"I cut my hair."

"But why, Anna, why did you do it?"

I didn't answer—a person shouldn't need a reason for a haircut—but the truth is this: I'd been instructed to do it. I don't always do what they say to do. Sometimes I bang my head against the wall until the voices disperse like a plume of dust from a beaten rug. But often it's easier to do as they say and be done with it. So, I cut my hair. I was angry at them for telling me do it, but angrier at myself for listening. Most of all, I was angry at Nurse Winthrop for her reaction.

It was on my way back to the day ward when I caught the

girls snickering. After knocking them down, I stood over them, flailing and screaming, "Shut up! Shut up! Shut up!" Yelling with everything I had. At the girls, at the voices, at the universe.

A male attendant with arms of stone grabbed me from behind and lifted me off the ground and suddenly I was bounding through the air like Peter Pan as he carried me to Seclusion—a small green room with only a mattress and bare walls. The place where time ceases to exist. Neverland.

The only window is in the door facing the hall. A small square of glass, reinforced with chicken wire. Strapped into bed, I was given an injection that turned my blood to kerosene and put me to sleep. Perhaps it's what I wanted all along.

I don't know how long I slept in Seclusion—days, it seemed. The staff wasn't taking any chances with me this time. Not after what I'd done to Olive. And Olive was my friend!

They put me to bed then, too, and, again, I woke up quiet. Nurse Winthrop has threatened to move me upstairs to the Disturbed ward. I believe I am disturbed, and it's where I belong. But then, isn't the entire world disturbed?

If the doctor asks me more questions, I'll have nothing to say to him. I have nothing to say to anyone anymore and am beginning to understand the joy in Henrietta's rocking. The back and forth is comforting—as long as no one creeps up and slaps my head with a shoe. They all would love to do it. I can tell—a morbid band of miscreants, all of them. But when I quietly rock back and forth, I'm like a pencil eraser across the page. Everything disappears.

Mother came to visit yesterday. She was insistent about bringing me home.

"Our birthdays are next month," Mother said to Dr. Abrams.

Was it true? I'm not sure I have a birthday anymore.

Mother told Dr. Abrams she understood now what I needed and promised him she would watch after me.

Dr. Abrams told us both, "No, not now."

He was braced for me to explode—eager for an excuse to send me to Disturbed—and kept repeating himself: "Not advisable. Not right now."

But I was okay with it.

I said a quiet goodbye to Mother and shuffled back to the day ward, back to Henrietta's rocking chair.

My dear Stewart, my one true love, my heart, my hope. If you've abandoned me because of what I've told you, so be it. I will never stop writing to you. And as a reporter, I will remain truthful. I need you to understand how important you are to me. I beg of you, please save me once and for all. I can't wait any longer.

CLAY

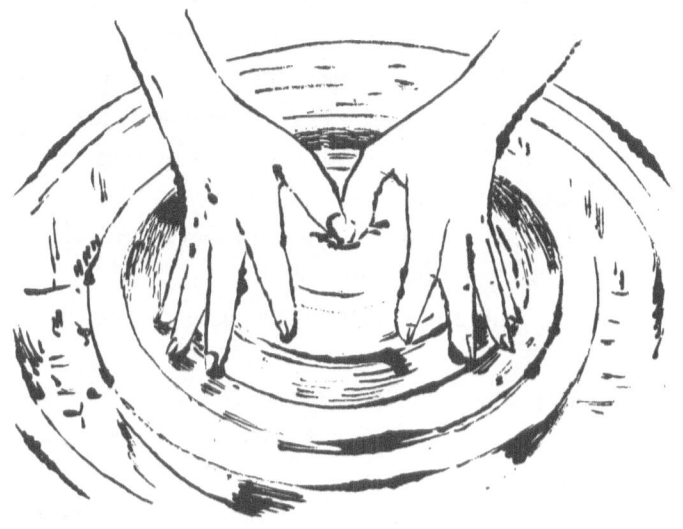

I mages arrive fully formed in a series of semi-conscious dreams. Visions, you could say. And I furiously scramble to capture them in a bedside sketchbook before they evaporate with the morning light. The ideas aren't for vases and bowls—I do still intend to make those—but for what I can only describe as miniature sculptures inspired by the beautiful, elusive woman who gave birth to me.

An open studio is scheduled for next month, and I've been hoping to have some pieces to sell. Not masterpieces—just simple clay pots. If that's what I hope to do, however, there's little time to experiment. But my focus on the sale has been eclipsed by an essential need for expression.

I sketch through the night and into the morning, fiendishly, uncontrollably.

The way an artist might. Or a madwoman.

PERFECTIONISM GENERALLY FIGHTS against such playfulness in my work. I get frustrated when things don't turn out precisely as I plan, which in the messy world of clay—not to mention the messy world of my life—is often. For each semi-successful ceramic piece currently cluttering Eric's cupboard, dozens more have been smushed or smashed and relegated to the slimy bucket of reclaimed slop beneath my bench.

Why do I admire lopsided beauty in other's work while I so often struggle to erase it from my own?

"Love it," the studio tech says as she passes my bench on her way to the kiln.

She's talking about a small piece drying on my shelf. A simple one copied from my sketchbook. Not abstract, exactly, but not purely figurative, either.

"It's different from your usual work," she says, pointing at the recently fired mugs neatly aligned on my shelf.

"I'm just playing around," I say. "I'll get back on the wheel, eventually. My mind is too spastic for it right now."

"No, keep it up," she says. "I like it."

Nice to hear, but it's unlikely to sell. And isn't that the point?

The prospect of working for myself, making my own hours, creating with my hands—that's always been the hope. There's a woman at the studio making hundreds of pieces for a popular restaurant. Many other people sell their work at flea markets and craft fairs. Some earn a few hundred bucks a week—as much as I make bookkeeping at the coffee shop. It's possible. But not if I tumble too far down the rabbit hole of Art for Art's sake. It's better to stick with making functional items. There's an art to them, as well, isn't there? Plus, they have a purpose. Making them gives *me* a purpose. But, for now, I have no choice. I lack focus and have no control over what I create. I can only aimlessly work the clay with impressionistic gestures until something emerges. A face, a feeling, a figurine, made manifest like baby animals from a womb. It doesn't always work, of course, and the bucket beneath my table is brimming with these mushy failures, too. But I'm not as frustrated by these mistakes as I am by a disaster at the wheel.

The main advantage of modeling this way is that there's no need to corral my thoughts. If I get frustrated with Dad, and my thumb pushes too hard, or if I get angry at Mom and my fingers squeeze too tightly, there's no fear of skewing the symmetry of a spinning vase. Perhaps I can build something for Eric this way. I know I promised him bowls, but maybe he'll appreciate a tiny sculpture instead. Either way, I need to make him something, and soon—to finally get out from under that annoying obligation and move on.

I plug a pair of headphones into my phone, wrap the phone in plastic to keep it clean, and put on some music. On the wheel, my music choices are limited. Anything too emotional or dynamic will upset my focus. On the bench, however, I can listen to whatever I want—including many of the same tunes that I've been listening to for years, like those on the mixtape that Lorelei gave me in high school.

I used to keep a scrapbook back then, too—pictures of Duran Duran, mostly. I'd spend hours staring at Andy Taylor, imagining him next to me, whispering sweet nothings. I even dreamed of moving to England to find him and fantasized that he would fall in love with me. Funny what fangirls imagine.

Mom found the scrapbook during one of her regular Saturday afternoon bedroom raids. I can't remember where I'd been hiding it, but it didn't matter—nowhere was safe.

She jerked me by the arm and dragged me into the living room. She threw the scrapbook into the fireplace, and gave me a match. *Sinful, sinful things.*

Maybe I shouldn't give my thoughts free rein after all. The

little sculpture I'm working on now is a mess, crushed by bad memories. I mash it and start again, rolling, wedging, pinching.

I made an appointment to see my new doctor, but it's still a week away. I'd tried to explain everything over the phone, but she asked to see me. Hopefully, she'll be willing to sign the records request. Even if she does, I shouldn't get my hopes up. Oakville might not have any information. Might turn out to be like the pages from the orphanage—height, weight. It will be nice to have a diagnosis, however. Depression, I'm sure, since I've suffered from it myself for so many years.

I remember bearing the worst of it, sitting in my teenage bedroom with a sticky tar pit of despair deep in my gut. I don't know why I was upset. Could have been anything. Everything. More likely nothing. I vaguely remember slamming my bedroom door, but I couldn't have—by then, my room no longer had a door to slam. Dad had taken it off the hinges. *Privacy is earned,* he'd said.

I can still feel the bitter, lime-ey, chalky paste in my throat that formed from the full bottle of aspirin, impossible to force down my throat without full protest from my gag reflex. I spat it out immediately and vomited into the toilet.

"What's wrong with you this time?" Mom called from the living room.

"Nothing, Mom, nothing."

Somewhere deep inside must have been a fleck of hope. Still there, I suppose. Tiny, about the size of a pepper flake, but enough to keep me going. Going where, is the eternal question.

The sculpture shows more promise now. It goes nicely with the one from the other day, and I'm feeling a rhythm. Finding the pulse. If I can keep it up, I might collect enough of these new pieces for the open studio. What's the date again? Pretty sure I wrote it down in the church calendar Dad gave me.

DR. YOUNG WRAPS a blood pressure cuff around my arm and begins to pump it with air.

"I've struggled with mental health issues my entire life," I say. "Depression, anxiety, substance abuse. I told you about all that last time I saw you."

How much I had told her, I can't recall. I know I had been drenched in a feverish sweat of memories, but it's been that way since Mom died. How many of those stories had been formed into words and spoken to Dr. Young?

"Yes," she says, jotting down my blood pressure, skimming her notes. "Have you thought about what I suggested?"

Anti-depressants? I forgot she had suggested it. I've taken them before—when a restaurant I'd been working in disappeared under a poisonous cloud of dust from the Twin Tower collapse. I'd been heading to work and got trapped in a subway tunnel for hours. The whole city was depressed then. A social worker had set me up with a prescribing doctor, and I started taking Zoloft.

After the dust settled and I decided I didn't want to take it anymore, it was nearly impossible to stop. It took a year of swallowing progressively smaller shavings before my brain stopped buzzing and I was finally free. I'm not sure I want to make that commitment again.

"Maybe, eventually," I say. "Not right now."

She scribbles something into my record.

"I told you I was adopted, right? And that I don't know my family's medical history?" She hardly seems to be listening. "Since the last time I was here, I've learned my birth mother had been a patient in a mental hospital. She's dead now, but I'd like to get her records in case they reveal something about my own problems."

Dr. Young closes the folder and looks at me, interested at last.

"I've contacted the hospital," I say, "but they tell me I need a doctor to write a formal request."

The name Dr. Young might have been fitting once upon a time, but she's not young anymore. She's been around and is probably used to patients asking her to write letters—to avoid work, maybe, or skip jury duty. It takes a minute, but her curiosity wins out.

"We might need a release form—" she begins.

I hop off the examination table and dig through my bag joyfully. "I have one!"

ANNA'S JOURNAL
Sunday, July 20, 1969

T he voices come like a marching band in a distant parade strutting slowly toward me, horns and drums making their way closer and closer until I am filled with their havoc.

I've learned not to talk about them, the way I've learned not to speak about Stewart.

"None of it is real," the doctors say.

"It's all in your head," says Mother.

But the doctors and nurses, Mother and Frederick, aren't they all in my head, as well?

The other evening, I found the new girl (Lilly is her name) in the day ward, where she was babbling about a man on the Moon. Now that's the craziest idea I've heard yet in here. I felt foolish, but couldn't help from getting out of the rocking chair to look out the window.

A thin shaving of Moon hung low in the sky, surrounded by stars sizzling like pin-sized bubbles in the haze. How could a man be perched on that sliver of green cheese, so far away, all alone in the dark? Who could believe it?

"It's all in Lilly's head," I said to one of the student nurses who stood beside me at the window.

"No, really," the nurse said, "Men are walking on the moon right now."

I tapped a steady rhythm against the pane. It's so hard to know what to believe anymore. If anything.

When I first met Twilight, she told me she lived on the Moon. "I'm from Twilight, and I live on the Moon," she said. Frederick corrected her, telling me Twilight lived in Moon Township, but Twilight thinks it's funny to insist she lives on the Moon. And why not? Esther says she lives in Daisytown, while she really lives in Coal Center. I've given up on sticking to the truth, too. I now tell people I live in The Magic City. Even while I spend half my time in Lock 4 and the other half in Building 5.

There was a crowd around the television in the day ward. Patients, nurses, attendants, everyone. Even Dr. Abrams and Nurse Winthrop. They all watched in rapt silence as a man bounced on a carpet of dust.

I returned to the rocking chair.

"You're right, you know," Dolores said to me from the couch as I began to rock. "It ain't real."

I closed my eyes and found myself on the moon, making snow angels in the silvery talc while men in white spacesuits danced around me.

The newsmen tell me that in a few days the Moon-men will return to Earth. They will land in the middle of the ocean—a place no better suited for a man than the Moon. As the newsmen continue to chatter, I find myself at a Malibu bunga-low, in a beach chair at the shoreline of the vast Pacific Ocean. Stewart relaxes in the chair beside me. He's dressed in white, sipping a cocktail. He puts down his drink and holds my hand. "You're so beautiful, Anna," he says, gazing into my eyes. "I love you. Look," he says, turning reluctantly from me and pointing to the horizon. A flare arcs through the sky and lands in the ocean with the sound of a flaming match head into a glass of water. In time, three men raft toward us. When they reach the shore, they walk to where we are sitting. One of them removes his helmet and shakes my hand.

"Believe me now?" he says.

I turn to Stewart with a beatific smile, but Stewart is gone. The bungalow behind me becomes the crooked yellow house in Lock 4, between the railroad tracks and the Monongahela River. Above me I see the Charleroi-Monessen Bridge—the bridge that leads me back and forth between my two lives. Its multiple metal trusses look like the bars crossing the windows on the top floor of the new building. (Where the criminals live.) On the far side of the bridge, Mother is alone at the house—a quiet place to herself. As she prunes her roses, I call to her from across the river, but she doesn't respond. "Mother!" I yell. "Mother! Why have you forsaken me? I'm still here! I'm still alive!" But she ignores me, enjoying the quiet house all to herself.

The house wasn't always so quiet. From the time I was a baby in a crib I can remember Walter's cries as his fragile young arms flailed in defense of Mother's switch. The sound of Frederick choking back tears, his face pressed against the kitchen wall, a bar of soap in his mouth. As I grew, I tried to block out the world around me with a box of crayons. "You're making a mess!" Mother would say. "Anna! Anna! Do you hear me?"

Suddenly I am back on the day-ward couch. "Anna," Nurse Winthrop says, gently tapping my shoulder, "don't you want to watch?"

CASE HISTORY

Dr. Young's office is teeming with patients. I tell the receptionist I'm there to pick up records, and she has me take a seat.

I fidget in the only empty chair for a few minutes before returning to the receptionist's desk.

"Excuse me," I say, trying my luck with a different woman at the other end of the long reception counter.

She doesn't appear to be busy, but she ignores me, too.

A few other women are milling behind the counter, talking and joking. I can't get anyone's attention. Eventually, the first woman looks up.

"All these people are here ahead of you," she says.

"I understand," I say. "But I'm just here to pick up an enve-lope. Dr. Young said she would leave it at the desk. She told me to come by anytime."

"We'll get to you."

I loiter by a vending machine stocked with candy and chips. Funny to offer so much junk in a doctor's office. May as well be filled with mini bottles of booze. Good thing it's not, or I'd be digging through my pockets for change.

The women continue their chit-chat as I pace around the room. Finally, the first woman rolls her eyes and asks for my name.

"Reese," I say. "Rachel Reese."

She has me spell it before shuffling through a mess of papers. After flipping through documents in a tray, she rifles through some folders on the shelf behind her. She doesn't seem to actually be looking for anything. Just a show.

After a minute, she walks through a door and out of sight. When she returns a few minutes later, she appears irritated to find me still waiting.

"I don't see nothing," she says.

I repeat myself: "Doctor Young said I could come for the envelope anytime. Is she here? It's important."

The receptionist has the look of someone who has seen it all —or at least thinks she has. I'm sure she is used to things being urgent and important; it will take a lot more than this to move her, but I don't know what else to say.

Finally, one of the other women exits through the back door and returns with a young guy in blue scrubs. A nurse prac-titioner.

"What can I do for you?" he says.

The nurse practitioner listens but, like the receptionists, tells me to have a seat.

Did Dr. Young forget? She's getting old. Perhaps her

memory is failing. Or maybe she doesn't trust these people with something marked *Personal and Confidential*. I'm ready to climb over the desk and rummage through the mess of documents myself, kicking and elbowing the receptionists in the process. Before I do, however, the nurse practitioner returns with a large, sealed envelope.

"What's your name again?" He squints at the envelope, struggling to decipher Dr. Young's scrawled cursive. "Rachel—"

"That's me!"

Outside, I tear open the envelope and slide out the pages. I'm not prepared to read anything on the street, but I want to prove to myself it's real.

Doctor Young told me what to expect, but not until I see everything do I realize what a wealth of information it is. Thirty-six pages total, it includes a case history beginning in 1955 when Anna was only twenty-one years old.

At the bottom of one of the pages, I see *Diagnostic Impression —Dementia Praecox*. The words confuse me. Are they even words? I don't know what they mean.

After stuffing the pages back into the envelope, I clutch them to my chest and run toward the subway station. Pacing anxiously on the platform, I peek inside again and remove a random page. I slide it back as if the information might get sucked into the blackness of the subway tunnel, stolen by the rats on the tracks. I grip the envelope tightly, alternately curling it and straightening it out. I put it to my face and smell it. It doesn't smell like anything. Of course not. The records are old, but not the paper they are printed on. It's only a stack of paper. I smell it again, anyway.

THE TEAPOT WHISTLES A MOIST PLUME, and I drown two bags of Kava tea in an extra-large mug. Click on a reading lamp, arrange a couple of pillows—two behind my back, another behind my head—then slip the records from their envelope, rest them against my thighs, and begin to read. Doctor Young told me not to be alone when I did, but Eric won't be home for several hours, and I can't wait. I don't want him here, anyway.

The first few pages are hard to read—literally. They are distorted photocopies of handwritten admission forms that don't seem to contain any compelling information. Sure, it's interesting to know my mother had been an inch taller than me. (No reason for them to lie about it. *Five-eight? We'll say you're five-nine.*) Still, I don't particularly care what her pulse rate or temperature had been on such-and-such a day in such-and-such a year. Anna was marked *clean, no vermin noted,* which is good news—and not necessarily something I could have said about myself at her age while squatting in Pittsburgh. Anna's cardiovascular, gastrointestinal, nervous, and respiratory systems were all *without pathological findings.* Anna's reproductive system, too, was healthy. No surprise, since I wouldn't be sitting in bed reading so many tiny details about this otherwise forgotten story if it hadn't been. I do my best to decipher the notes, but don't linger on them. A lot of it is repeated later, anyway, typewritten and clear among notes that are hard to read in a different way.

Included with various logs, accident reports, and incidental notes, is a case study summarizing most of Anna's hospital stay, and much of her life in general. They reveal that when she was only sixteen years old, she spent five months under evaluation in the psychiatric ward of West Penn Hospital in Pittsburgh. Notes from West Penn state that Anna lived *in a world of her own.* They say she was seclusive and withdrawn and had been refusing to go to church. She had been refusing to leave the house at all—claiming she didn't have any clothes to wear or she didn't like her haircut. It all strikes me as typical teenage girl behavior and could easily be a description of me at that age. If not a description of me now. Nevertheless, combined with apparent delusions—including a belief she was, as the doctor put it, *part of a mysterious scheme in California*—a doctor diagnosed Anna with schizophrenia. Nothing in the records reveal the treatment she received at West Penn, or why they released her, but according to the papers, the doctors believed her well enough to return to school.

After graduating a year behind schedule, Anna left home for a job in Washington, DC. My cousins told me that a lot of young women in the area found jobs in DC at that time, working as secretaries or stenographers in any one of the city's booming post-war offices. Anna took a job as a clerk somewhere, but it says she grew bored and, during her off-hours, attended modeling school. I read this with a start and hope that her modeling days hadn't gone like mine had. I imagine she had the intention, or hope anyway, of getting involved in something more exciting than the ho-hum world of governmental bureaucracy. Reading the file, I fear for her and fret for her, much as I would a child of my own. I analyze her choices, trying to imagine how making them might have felt for her, and think through each detail that I read, weighing out what sounds accurate, what sounds like something I would do.

Anna took a bus home every weekend and seemed to be getting along reasonably well at first. But, it was noted, she *couldn't account for her money, and didn't like to be advised about what she should do*—things that, again, could easily be mistaken for a description of me as a distracted and depressed young girl at community college, taking the bus home every weekend, continually being scolded by my parents for this or that.

As time went on, Anna came to think people were conspiring against her. She complained about the other women in her office, saying they didn't like her and talked about her all the time. But Anna sounds like something of a spitfire, picking battles and pulling no punches. She argued with her coworkers, had an altercation with a waitress in a restaurant, and fought with her landlady. Within a year, she moved back home. Whether she quit or got fired, it doesn't say.

Like me, Anna had trouble sleeping and often stayed awake until four or five in the morning, reading magazines or watching television. After a late-night broadcast of *Caravan* triggered an obsession with its star, Stewart Granger, she ran across his face in a magazine and decided that the picture in print was actually both looking back at her—and speaking to her. She decided that they had fallen in love at first sight—*un coup de foudre,* she called it. (Where did she learn a phrase like that?) She began to make long-distance phone calls to Hollywood in an attempt to contact him. While her parents may have tolerated some of Anna's unusual behaviors, exorbitantly expensive long-distance phone calls to Hollywood were not among them. Because of this, Anna's parents immediately returned her to the hospital. After several weeks and a few electro-shock treatments, they released Anna with little change, other than to be described as more irritable and aggressive than she had been previously. Her anger, it was noted, was directed mainly at her parents, Frances and Joseph.

With shock treatment either not working or its effects wearing off, Frances and Joseph were advised to commit Anna to an extended-stay asylum and recommended Oakville State Mental Hospital.

Quiet and cooperative upon admission, it doesn't appear as though Anna understood why she was there. "I'm just here for the day," the admitting nurse quoted her as saying. "I came to get x-rays." Whatever she may have thought, or whatever they may have told her, she was oblivious to the fact she was about to be committed to an indefinite stay.

Anna's facial expression was marked as *indifferent, though sometimes pleasant and smiling.* She was considered *friendly and cooperative.* Her attention could be *gained and held* despite some *preoccupation and distractibility.* A few long-distance phone calls aside, it's hard to understand what the problem was, or why Anna's behavior warranted a fifteen-year stay.

October 4, 1956

Answers to the questions are coherent and free but not always relevant. Thinking is disordered, circumstantial, and delusional. The patient is seclusive and withdrawn but under some pressure will willingly talk about her delusions. Many utterly fantastic, vague, illogical, false ideas of religious and paranoid nature were presented. The patient believes she has a "mission in California." She says, "I'm expecting a very important telephone call from California tonight from [actor] Stewart Granger." When asked how she was acquainted with this actor, she replied, "I saw a picture of him and his wife, and through it, I received much information about what he wants from me. I wrote my story to a newspaper and intend to send it to him. I am inclined to marry him." When asked how she could marry the actor when he already has a wife, she replied, "God will arrange it."

A lot of the people I grew up with trusted God to take care of all sorts of things—changing the color of a necktie from pink to purple, for instance—so Anna's belief that God would take care of something as common as a Hollywood divorce doesn't strike me as particularly outlandish. Regardless, what bothers me more than anything is learning how Anna's trust in God to arrange things for her went hand in hand with her thinking she didn't deserve it.

Patient believes she is a sinner and that God will never forgive her.

Dad has been saying things like that for as long as I can remember—although not until after Mom died did I begin to understand why—but what about Anna? What could Anna have done at such a young age? The doctors were curious, too, and she told them.

"In my youth, during my grade school period, when I was 13 years of age, something happened to me. My body and legs were in need." When asked to explain, she replied only with a smile but could not describe better her feeling and physical status. During her attack of "twisting," she felt that she was doing something wrong and God would never forgive her for doing it.

Naturally, her legs *twisting*, her body *in need*, were euphemisms for her blossoming and apparently repressed sexuality. I'm sure it was Anna's mother, Frances, who had instilled the notion that such a thing was an unforgivable sin. Not only because Frances was a strict and domineering Catholic, but because of the stories Judy told me about her grandmother—*our* grandmother.

Frances, and her husband Joseph, a Polish immigrant who worked in the steel mills, had been interviewed by Social Services after their neighbors called the cops with allegations of child abuse. Joseph died when Judy and Walter were still quite young, so neither of them had much to say about him, but they both clearly remember Frances and the feelings of abject terror she inspired whenever she was around.

It's a lot to absorb, and I take a break to sip a little tea. What I really want to do is vomit, or punch the wall, or scream, but instead, I lay still, massaging my eyes, hoping the feeling in my head isn't the start of a migraine.

My tea has grown tepid, and I heat more water, unsure if I want to continue reading or leave the rest for later. Pacing around the apartment, waiting for the water to boil, I pick a page off the bed at random:

Patient became irritable when Nurse Winthrop tried to dress her for dinner. She insists on wearing jeans and a blouse, would not put on a dress; does not take part in activities.

Irritable? I'm getting irritable just reading about it. Sure, Anna had issues, but not wanting to wear a dress? Seriously? I guess once someone is diagnosed as psychotic, everything they do becomes suspect. Like Dad—once in a while he says something that makes sense, but it never sounds like it does. Not that anyone committed him to an institution, while his ideas are just as far-fetched as some of Anna's. Judging by Anna's behavior at a staff conference a few months after her admittance, she seemed to have caught on to what was troubling everyone about her behavior at some point, which suggests a degree of self-awareness that should have made them reconsider her diagnosis. A total of twelve doctors, one registered nurse, four student nurses, two attendants, and a priest attended the meeting. The notes from the meeting mentioned Anna's obsession with a certain Hollywood actor, but went on to say, despite some prodding, "She did not want to discuss it."

Tell us the story about the actor, I can hear them all say. "Fuck you all," I imagine saying back to them. "She knows better now."

The teapot whistles and I slide the paper back into the stack.

Eric's apartment is perpetually cold in the winter, but at a particular time of day, the sun hits the perfect angle to filter through the window with an intense whiteness. The apartment glows. At the kitchen table, cradling my mug, I allow the sun to warm my face. I'm glad I hadn't known about Anna's diagnosis when I was younger. I spent enough time wondering about my mental health without knowing my mother was a patient in a psychiatric hospital. Better still, Mom hadn't known the truth. If she had, she would have added it to her torturous repertoire: *No one else wanted you, your mother was crazy, and you're crazy, too.* But, wait, she *had* said those things. Mom even threatened to commit me to a mental ward if I didn't behave. Anna's own mom, Frances, sounds as fearsome, or maybe fearful, as mine. Maybe Mom knew more than she let on. *You belong in a mental hospital*, she would sometimes say. *And if you don't straighten up, I'm going to send you to one.* If I had been born a decade or two earlier, she might have done it, too. And what about Dad? He worked as a janitor in a mental hospital. I never paid attention to the name of it. Oakville?

As the sun's angle changes, the light grows dimmer. When I return to bed and continue reading, something unexpected appears on the next page. It's a letter Anna wrote to her mother. I flush at finding something written by Anna, herself—the closest I'll get to hear my mother's voice.

April 10, 1958

Copy of letter written by the patient to her mother.

Dear Mother

I haven't written to you for two weeks because I didn't need for you to come and visit me, but it is necessary this week, I wonder if you know. Frederick said a doctor called you and said I wanted to go home, but it wasn't my doctor, and I wasn't talking to any doctor. Frederick came for me just the same. Maybe I should say something like that in this letter, and then maybe you'll come and see me. On the 26th of this month, I'll be 24. If you don't come and see me this Sunday before the 26th, you don't have to see me ever again. I'll never write to you. I have everything going for me in the world at this moment, I have a life, but after just a few more weeks in this hospital, I'll have nothing left. I can't have anything without your help. You said that if I told you I want to go home, you would come, well I say that now because I

81626

need to leave this hospital forever, there's no more waiting for me, there's no more time, it's now or never.

I wish I could put it into words in a way that would make it sound as important as it is, if that would make you believe me more than with what I've already written you. You know that this can't go on forever, and you know that if nothing happens now, nothing will happen anymore that is worthwhile. It was on the radio this morning that a patient here committed suicide by jumping out of the window, I think they said he was 64.

When my birthday comes all hope is gone, please come and see me now, I promise you I'll leave this hospital this time, I'll not care about leaving this hospital if I don't leave now.

Please come and see me on Sunday. I wouldn't be here if it weren't for you.

Anna

It couldn't have been easy writing a letter on Thorazine, or Stelazine, or Haldol—or any of the other medications listed in the reports. (Ritalin, Compazine, Proketazine, Tofranil, Artane, Dilantin, and on and on.) But below the transcript, the doctor noted Anna wrote many letters like this. I flip through the pages to see if I can find any more, but there's only the one. I read it several times.

Despite the letter's pleading tone, when Frances arrived at the hospital to take Anna home, Anna changed her mind at the last minute and refused to go.

May 18, 1958

Patient's mother wishes to take her home for a visit, but patient does not wish to go. She feels that her father is ill at ease when she is around. Feels that he is afraid of her; therefore, she prefers to remain at the hospital at present.

Her father's discomfort aside, Anna did go home once in a while. The visits generally lasted anywhere from overnight to a few days—occasionally a little longer for a holiday like Christmas or Easter. Dozens of dated entries record nothing more than these comings and goings. *Patient went home for a visit, Patient returned to the hospital today.* Even when Anna's father died, his death was merely recorded as a visit home. There is no mention of how Anna reacted to the news other than a distinct uptick in her visits home.

November 3, 1958

Patient stated in the past that she heard God telling her to stay in the hospital, but states she hasn't heard God talk to her for a long time. She won't talk about her relationship with Stewart Granger or why she attempted to make long-distance calls to him. She insists she wants to leave the hospital, and that she plans to rest and to do a little painting.

With her husband gone, Frances began to write letters, too. She addressed them to the ward physician, often including a separate message for Anna, which she would ask the doctor to deliver. The doctor noted Frances seemed to be developing paranoid and persecutory ideas of her own. Perhaps Joseph had been keeping Frances in check, the way Mom had done for Dad, but, whatever the cause, Frances seemed to be losing coherence. The doctor thought it okay for Anna to go home for short visits, but he worried Frances would defy the medical staff's advice and keep Anna out of the hospital for good. *"Patient's mother,"* the doctor wrote, *"has very little understanding of the patient."*

Until that point, Anna hadn't left the hospital for more than a week at a time, but in April of 1960, precisely as the doctor had feared, she went home on a weekend pass and didn't return.

The visit went surprisingly well at first. Anna did chores around the house, ate normally, talked about her previous interests in painting, classical music, and the classes she took at the YWCA. Still, over time she lost focus and, gradually, fell into her old pattern of staying up all night and sleeping all day. She often got into arguments with her older brother, Frederick, who also lived at home.

My cousins don't seem to know much about Frederick, who

severed all contact with the family many years ago. The last they heard, he was living in Montana with a girl half his age named Twinkle or something like that. He'd been in multiple car accidents involving drunk driving, which, if they had occurred today, would have likely resulted in significant jail time. No one knows whether he is still alive. If he is, he's over eighty and, considering his lifestyle, it's not likely. The Social History record doesn't have much to say about him either. Just this:

At times, he goes away and stays away for several days and is not willing to discuss his thoughts or behaviors with the family.

Who could blame him?

Fights between Frederick and Anna aren't described in any great detail, but they appeared to have arguments over the living arrangements. After Joseph's death, Frances took Anna's room as her own and gave the larger bedroom to Frederick. When Anna went home, she was expected to share a bed with her mother. Anna refused and, instead, took to sleeping on the floor in the hallway. Frederick wasn't happy about this solution, however, and admitted to the doctors that it caused him to lash out at Anna now and then.

Somehow, despite spending most days asleep on the floor, Anna managed to complete night school classes in clerical work. Afterward, she went to an employment agency to see about finding a job, perhaps with the hope of moving into her own apartment, with her own bed. But because Anna was never formally released from the hospital, the employment agency said they couldn't help her, leaving Anna crushed and resentful. Without the prospect of a job, Anna had few options. She could either continue to sleep in the hallway or return to the hospital. A third alternative existed, of course, and that was to run away. It would have been a fiasco, of course, but it's what I would have done. Had Anna ever thought of it? She must have. If so, she never followed through. Instead, she made the sobering choice to return to the hospital.

Upon re-admittance, Anna presented no paranoid ideation. She was well oriented in all spheres and didn't mention anything about God talking to her, nor did she talk about Stewart Granger. Anna did, however, confess to feelings of hatred toward everyone else. She hated the other patients, hated the nurses, and even hated seeing children play in the street in front of her mother's house. Most of all, she hated her mother. "I would do anything to embarrass her," she said. Frances, however, didn't need any help in this regard and was perfectly capable of embarrassing herself. By this point, Frances had evolved into a full-fledged bingo addict. My cousins told me Frances spent all her money at the church every Tuesday night, stealing Frederick's money whenever she ran out of her own. She had become a heavy drinker, too, and often went to bingo drunk. The church was only a quarter-mile from the house, but it involved a treacherous walk across the railroad tracks, and, on several occasions, a passing train nearly hit her. Anna's decision to return to the hospital was clearly the best option. Still, I can't help thinking: Why not let Anna stay in the house and send Frances to Oakville for a while?

The doctors immediately resumed electro-shock therapy at the hospital, along with an evolving regimen of pills—many still in use today, others long outdated. After each round of shock treatment, the comment was always the same: *Mildly improved.* Why was it so essential to improve mildly upon what had already been such a marked improvement? If anything, after the initial daze of a few hundred volts wore off, the treatments only seemed to make Anna more aggressive. Seems to me, being held captive, drugged up, and periodically zapped in the brain would turn anyone aggressive, wouldn't it? It's noted that Anna *continues to refer to her ECT treatment as "x-rays."* A lie her mother told her when Anna was still quite young, which seemed to have stuck. Apparently, no one was interested in correcting her. Perhaps it made Anna more compliant towards treatment, thus making life easier for everyone. But it's hard to imagine Anna didn't know what was really going on.

Other than occasional visits home, most of the entries that follow are accident reports filled with redacted names. Although "accident" isn't exactly the right word, since it doesn't appear to have been an accident when Anna smacked someone with her shoe or a lunch tray, or when she pulled someone's hair. She sent one woman to the hospital with a cracked skull. "She was laughing at me," Anna said by way of explanation. She bulldozed into a group of nurses, including Nurse Winthrop—a name that keeps cropping up. Two of them were knocked to the floor. Anna said later that she hadn't hurt them as badly as she would have liked. *"Next time, I'll do more than that,"* she said. Nearly all of the accident reports end the same way: *No apparent injuries to Anna.*

"Go, Mom!" I quietly cheer. I'm surprised to hear myself say it. Not from the visceral thrill I feel to read about Anna knocking down the nurses and attendants, but at calling Anna Mom for the first time.

I find only a single account mentioning any injuries to Anna, and it doesn't involve anyone but herself. One day, Anna walked into the hallway, appeared startled, let out a loud cry, and fell backward to the floor. When Nurse Winthrop arrived, Anna lay face up, her head in a pool of blood. She didn't respond for a few minutes and, then, only to make strange oral noises. Anna pointed to her mouth. A dislocated jaw.

After three stitches were sewn into her skull and her jaw was manually adjusted into place, *patient was put to bed for 48-hour observation.*

The seizure was apparently a side effect of something she was taking. As more and more drugs were tried, others were added to counteract their side effects—a pharmacological clusterfuck impossible to untangle.

With only a few pages left to read, I need another break.

Struggling to get comfortable, I undress and throw on a T-shirt and a pair of Eric's boxer shorts. My tea is cold again, and I debate whether to heat more water. But I'm sick of tea. What I want is a drink—a *real* drink—and maybe a cigarette, too. I dig through my purse, my closet, and my drawers, looking for a Xanax, or one of Dad's Lorazepam I had managed to steal. They're long gone. Nevertheless, I continue to look.

I use the bathroom and wash my hands and face, my sweaty armpits, too. It's getting late, and Eric will be home soon. I want to finish reading before he is, so I get back into bed and pick up where I left off.

Skimming through repetitive accident reports and records of Anna's comings and goings gets tedious, and I skim past two seemingly unremarkable entries:

November 26, 1971

Patient went home for a temporary visit.

December 22, 1971

Patient returned to the hospital today.

The entries are the same as so many others, it's only after reading further that I understand their significance.

April 25, 1972

Patient states that she had her last menstrual period in November 1971. Claims she was out for a visit with her mother from November 26 to December 22, 1971, that she did go out with some men. States she was in a beer garden, and she invited these men to go out with her. States there were three men, and two of them had relations with her; that subsequently, one of these men did come to her house, and her mother allowed her to go out with him. States she had relations with him again. She states that she hasn't menstruated since that time. Urine examination for pregnancy done on April 15, 1972, and it is positive. Her mother, Frances, was informed about this. The mother stated that if Anna is pregnant and has a child, that either she or the patient's brother Walter and his wife Esther will take care of it. She was advised to come to the hospital with her son and daughter-in-law to discuss these matters more specifically.

Anna was thirty-seven years old, roughly the same age as I am as I sit here reading about my conception. No one knew the father—presumably not even Anna—and Anna wasn't interested in offering clues. "I hate them," was all she would say, "and I won't have them as the father of my child."

At least I was spared the grim reality of being conceived in a mental hospital.

Returning to Oakville a few days later, Anna was interviewed and said she knew she had given birth to a little girl. She said she remembered seeing the child, but said she hadn't touched or held it. Anna hadn't signed adoption papers and said she wasn't inclined to sign anything. When she felt better, she would see her child and hold it before deciding what to do. Reading about it makes me want to go back in time and adopt the baby myself. But I have to remind myself who it is I'm reading about. Taking care of Anna and her baby would mean taking care of me—something I've never been good at doing.

The doctor didn't consider Anna competent to make any

decisions one way or the other, and there were discussions about what to do with little baby Rubik. It's noted that Anna's oldest brother, Walter, and his wife, Esther, were eager to adopt the baby, just as Esther had said to me when we met. It would have made Judy and Walter my brother and sister—and meant a life with a mother who thought I was beautiful. Raised in a loving household alongside two good-natured and well-adjusted siblings is a lovely fantasy, but it didn't happen that way. After consulting with a priest, Frances stated that Walter and Esther would not be able to take care of the child. "They already have two children and a seven-month-old baby," Frances is quoted as saying. "They have a pile of debts as it is." All lies, judging from what Esther told me. She and Walter didn't have a seven-month-old baby and didn't have any debt. Frances obviously didn't want the family to have anything to do with me. Why did Frances have to fuck up such an elegant solution, barring the gate to my alternate universe? I can't help myself and throw the stack of papers against the wall where they explode in a shuffle as if driven by a leaf blower. I've got to learn to stop throwing things. The papers are still settling as I hold a pillow to my face and scream. I scream again. After a few deep breaths, I stand up, collect the papers, put them in order, and read the final page.

After giving birth, Anna feels people are making remarks about her—they probably are—and, once home, spends most of her time alone in her room. As she begins to feel better, she helps with chores in the dining room. Anna gets into a few fights with her mother but nothing remarkable. She appears to be settling into a quiet routine at Oakville, including a few routine visits home. That is, until Frances brings Anna home and keeps her indefinitely once again. As usual, Anna gets along well enough at first, eating with the family, doing chores around the house, taking her medication as required. At least she claims to be. Either way, Anna's insomnia gradually returns, and she falls into old patterns. She walks into her mother's room every night at four in the morning to complain she can't sleep. After several nights of being disturbed this way, Frances gets a prescription from her own doctor for *large red and black sleeping capsules.* Frances claims she kept the pills hidden, doling them out to Anna only as needed, but she also claims Anna found the bottle and swallowed its entire contents.

May 13, 1973
Died during home visit. Unimproved.

ERIC ARRIVES home to find me burrowed under the covers, Anna's records in a messy pile on the bedside table. He kneels on the floor next to the bed, gently tugs the sheets away from my face, and asks if I'm okay.

"I just need to cry," I say.

"Are these your mother's hospital records? Can I see?"

He lies next to me and reads through everything quickly. Quicker than I did, anyway. But, like me, when he reaches the end, he doesn't know what to say. "So sad."

After such an overload, I fantasize about swallowing a handful of those giant red and black sleeping capsules myself. Not enough to kill me—I don't think so, anyway—but enough to stop the humming jumble of thoughts crisscrossing my throbbing skull. "Am I crazy?" I ask Eric.

"Of course not."

I lean in and study his face, searching for a clue to his sincerity. "Nobody knows it when they're crazy," I say. "Not when they are *truly* crazy. Anna didn't know it. Her mom didn't know it. Dad sure as hell doesn't know it. Maybe I'm crazy, too. I've done so many stupid things in my life."

"Everyone does stupid things. You're doing fine. You're overwhelmed right now, that's all. Who wouldn't be? Maybe you need to find someone to talk to."

A psychiatrist? A therapist? The idea turns my stomach. I'd rather get drunk. But I have a new reason to stay sober now: to add a happy addendum to my mother's story, to prevent it from being a complete and utter tragedy.

If Anna hadn't succeeded in killing herself, would she still be alive? It's possible. Dad is still alive, after all. If Anna were alive, would the two of us get a chance to meet? Would she recognize me? How could she not—we're nearly identical. I want so badly to talk to her, but what would we talk about? Compare notes about each of our fucked-up lives to start.

"Too bad there's isn't more information about your father," Eric says.

"I don't care about those scumbags." Eric appears taken aback. Is he that clueless? "Anna was acting out. She didn't know what she was doing. They took advantage of her."

"They might not have known there was anything wrong with her."

I know more than enough about my father—whoever he is. I'm never going to think about him again and I'm in no mood to argue. At least Eric is smart enough to drop it.

"No one watched out for her," I say. "Frances should have been the one in the fucking mental hospital. Why didn't anyone commit *her*? Why did they let Anna go home with her?"

"It's hard to imagine," Eric says. "Then again, if she never went home, you would never have been born."

He still doesn't get it. *"Exactly."*

———

THE BED REMAINS unmade for a week. I hardly get out of it except to make Kava tea, refill a glass of water, and, occasionally, to vomit. I spend a lot of time looking at my mother's painting, looking into it—the little cabin surrounded by tree branches bent by snow, a warm glow emanating from the windows. If God gives out houses, this is the one I want. I imagine plodding through the deep powder and knocking on the thick wooden door. Anna lets me in, puts a blanket over my shoulders, and makes a place for me next to a crackling fire. I don't imagine trying to talk. We merely cuddle up in silence, Anna rocking me gently in her arms. Baby Rubik loves to be held.

ANNA'S JOURNAL
Monday, April 17, 1972

G ulping for air, bobbing like a Moon-man, I await
rescue. Finally, someone helicopters in and escorts
me to see Dr. Abrams, again.

I don't know how long it's been since I was home last. My
visits are like dreams, and my most recent wasn't recent at all,
which makes it particularly challenging to remember the details
that Dr. Abrams is so curious about.

"Had you been taking your Stelazine when you were home?"
Dr. Abrams asked.

I said, "Yes," because that's what I knew he wanted to hear,
but the true answer was, "Probably not," since I hate how bland

and stupid they make me. But I have no idea. I can't remember what pills I took yesterday, never mind what I was taking months ago. And, when I'm at home, drinks at the beer garden have become just as good at submerging me into a milky swamp of uncertainty as any pills have ever been. (Though cigarettes seem to have the opposite effect. I should have taken up the habit long ago!)

"Do you have a boyfriend?" he asked.

My skin shrank and my hairs stiffened.

"I don't mean Stewart," he said.

I knew he didn't mean Stewart.

"Someone you see during your visits home?"

I'm sure the old pervert would love me to amuse him with the details of last Thanksgiving. Mother must have told him I went out with a man. (Did the man ever come to call on me again? If so, did Mother tell him where I went?) It infuriates me the way everyone talks about me behind my back. And the way they all question me about everything. It's tempting to make things up—to tell them only things I know *not* to be true. But to hell with all of them, they don't deserve to be told anything. Real or unreal, I'm entitled to a private life.

"There's nobody," I said to Dr. Abrams.

"Do you know how long you have been this way?"

This way? Since I was sixteen. Perhaps longer. I may have been born like this—shaken senseless inside of Mother's belly during her first seizure. But I'd misunderstood. What he meant was how long I'd been in the condition of having something trembling gently inside *me*—inside *my* belly.

"We'll contact your mother to inform her of your condition."

I'm prepared for Mother's disappointment. Contempt. Judgment. Her embarrassment, too, I hope. She deserves that much, at least. Next month I'll be thirty-eight, why should I care what Mother thinks? I have a dear and close friend growing inside me now. It doesn't matter where the baby came from or how she got there.

Yes, it's a girl.

I know because she told me.

———

ALTHOUGH I CHOSE NOT to reveal any of it to Dr. Abrams, I do remember some of Thanksgiving and I feel I should write it down while I can remember it.

The early hours of the Friday night after Thanksgiving remain the clearest—before the beer was running roughshod through my head.

I rode the Interurban trolley to the beer garden while Mother was at bingo. And why not? People have started to know me there. More than just as Frederick's sister, they say hello and call me by name. "Hi Anna!" the bartender says brightly when I walk through the door. Men will offer me cigarettes and buy me drinks if I let them. And I do.

That night I met a man—I remember his name, but I don't dare write it down—and, almost immediately, I felt an all-consuming eagerness to get to know him. It seemed a more sensible, rational, enthusiasm than what I felt toward Peter. My behavior with Peter had nothing to do with Peter as a man and everything to do with a desperate desire to fling myself toward a life that was leaving me behind. How innocent the sin of kissing Peter seems to me now.

Will I ever see this new man again? And, if I do, will he remember me? Am I memorable? Do I want to be? I can only say that at the time I met him, I felt for him the way I didn't think I would ever feel about anyone other than Stewart.

What did I see in him, exactly? He was handsome, certainly. He wore a shearling jacket over an ochre sweater like Ryan O'Neal in *Love Story*, which made him well-dressed by beer garden standards. His hair was like Ryan O'Neal's too, but darker and his face was darker, too, with the kind of finely carved features I've always liked. Dark eyebrows and intense eyes. He asked me my name and when I heard him repeat it, the sound was more lyrical than I'd ever heard my name sound before. He seemed gentle, and kind, and he looked into my eyes when he asked me questions—he seemed to care about the answers the way no one else does. Though a stranger, an aura of recognition bloomed around his face like a golden halo, which beckoned from deep within me, a sudden urge to want to know him *completely*. Awash in an ocean of both desire and desirability, I instantly believed we could give a lot to each other. Perhaps, I thought, he could teach me how to love. And how to be loved.

He told me he lived in Shadyside—*The Greenwich Village of Pittsburgh*, he said—and he was visiting family in Donora for the holidays. He introduced me to his friends, but they may as well have been empty barstools. When his two friends spoke, the sound of their voices never reached my ears. The man showed me how to play pool. I was terrible at it, but he seemed charmed by my attempt. After a while, he suggested we all go to Eat'n Park for hamburgers. I would have gone with him anywhere.

For some reason, while seated at the diner, I mentioned my time at Oakville. It's not something I usually talk about, but I was relaxed from the beer and spoke freely. The three men were curious to hear more about it. I tried so desperately to make it sound like a lovely place that I almost believed it myself. I told them about the greenhouses that grow fresh vegetables for the cafeteria, the formal rose garden with its stone benches, French hedges, and statuary. I described the piano in Jamison Cottage. (I didn't tell them that no one ever plays it.) None of them seemed to judge me for my time there, and we even traded good-natured jokes about the place, which made us all laugh. It's something I thought I had forgotten how to do. The rest of our time at the diner and afterward is lost to the blackness of a moonless night. Or perhaps I've chosen to forget it. In either case, it won't be written here. Some things will never be.

The next morning, I woke on the davenport, not sure of how I arrived there, but still dreaming of talking to this man. I started to believe he might cure me the way Frederick had cured Twilight.

By pure magic, as if willed by desire, the man arrived at my door the following Sunday and invited me for a late breakfast. His car was white, with a narrow strip of chrome running down its entire length. I ran my fingers along it.

"It's my baby," he said.

"It looks like a NASA rocket."

He opened the door and helped me into my seat. And when we pulled away, it felt like it really was a rocket, and that we were shooting skyward to where the atmosphere was so thin I could hardly breathe. I looked down on us from orbit, and watched the car sail across the Charleroi-Monessen Bridge. The Mon's deep olive water gurgled with indifference below. The man turned on the radio. I didn't pay much attention to the songs at first, the music simply blended with the hiss of tires against the asphalt, the rush of air through the open windows. But when I heard the lyrics *"Smiling faces sometimes—"* I was suddenly struck. *"—they don't tell the truth..."* Soon, it ceased to be a song at all—the singer was talking to me. He was singing about mother, and about Nurse Winthrop and Dr. Abrams. I hung on every word. Replies were pulled from my mouth—tiny yelps with question marks. *Don't let the handshake and the smile fool ya..."*

"What's that?" my date asked.

"Nothing."

I wanted this man to hold my hand and tell me everything was going to be okay. I nearly reached for his, but I was paralyzed. Motionless.

Though not exactly motionless. My heart was anxiously twittering so fast, I only appeared not to move, the way a hummingbird does. A new heaven was about to replace the hell of my life. I was sure of it.

I know better now. The singer had tried to warn me, but I'd misunderstood. Because afterward, although I continued to dream of getting to know this man, of walking along the river, playing pool, going to the movies, eating hamburgers, I never saw him again. Did Stewart creep from the depths to sabotage my life? Mother didn't seem to think so. When she saw how heartsick I was, she blamed me for scaring the man away.

"You shouldn't have told him about the hospital," she said.

But that is my life, why shouldn't I be allowed to talk about it? No one seemed upset or scared when I did. And anyway, Mother is the one responsible for sending me here—who is she to scold me for mentioning it?

Regardless, that is not the reason he disappeared, I'm sure of it. It was the marching band over the hill. The way my legs twisted and became noodles. Original sins returned and left me paralyzed on the bench seat of his car. He found out, somehow, that God had forsaken me. But that's all I know. The rest is tar-black.

"Has God been talking to you?" Dr. Abrams asked.

Yes, in His way.

My coat's zipper is stuck again. Every day it catches my scarf, and every day the struggle to free it triggers vivid fantasies of life on a tropical island. New York is such a cold city, in so many ways, and so claustrophobic, why not escape to a lazy beach town where I can focus my eyes farther than a city block? Maybe live cheap, find a kiln cheap, sell ceramics to tourists. I've made fresh starts before, why not try again? Eric, for one thing. How did I let myself become so entangled and dependent?

Without Eric's help, my options are limited in terms of escape, and full knowledge of this drags down my self-esteem. It seems my only other feasible option is to park a camper van on the property next to Dad's, hole up with an opioid prescription from a sympathetic doctor and call it a day. The swampy patch of land next to Dad's isn't much, but it was more than enough to hide upon as a child. Barefoot in the cold mud surrounded by cattails and bullfrogs. When I feel a need to hide from the world, it's still the first place that comes to mind. Maybe it's better the church owns it, now.

Wind blows from every direction. When it blasts me from the left, I turn and get blasted from the right. Barely halfway to my studio, frozen and frustrated, I step into a coffee shop to warm up. Condensation fogs the windows. It trickles down in heavy streaks. Inside, the windows glow with a bluish light from the overcast sky, and I envision a blue glaze dripping from the edge of a speckled gray mug. A blue nearly the same color as the cell phone and laptop screens illuminating all the expressionless faces. Surrounding each of the seated zombies is a mess of torn sugar packets, assorted muffin crumbs, and crumpled napkins. Coats and scarves drape the back of every chair. I've never been to a ski lodge before, but I imagine this is what they look like—a warm burrow of nesting mice.

Flyers plaster the wall beside me. Computer design services, guitar lessons, yoga classes, and so on. Among them is a post-card for a modern dance performance featuring a striking photograph of a muscular, nearly nude woman whose strength and form remind me of how badly I had wanted to be a dancer as a child. Of course, my body was all limbs and better suited to ballet than modern dance. I remember prancing around the house *en pointe,* mimicking ballerinas I'd seen on television, trying to convince Mom I showed promise. A classically trained dancer once told me I had perfect feet for ballet—strong, flexible, well-articulated. "I know people who would kill to have your feet," she'd said. I like to imagine I would have been a good dancer if Mom had allowed me to take lessons. I'll never know.

Shuffling through more postcards—one for a comedy show, another for a flea market—I come upon one promoting an art opening:

March 8 – March 29
THE JUDGMENT OF HOMER
Paintings by Eric Akers
presented by
CURIOUS 24 GALLERY
Opening March 8
6 – 9 pm

There is a painting reproduced on the postcard, the painting is of a person and to my great surprise, that person is Dad. I steady myself against the wall. Eric has captured Dad well. Too well. Sweating, I pull off my hat and unzip my coat. Dad is supposed to be sequestered in his self-contained bubble of twaddle three hundred miles away, not lurking in my everyday world, waiting to pounce. It's becoming harder and harder to compartmentalize my life.

I sweep the complete stack of postcards into my bag and zip it shut. As if that's all it will take to make it go away.

The espresso machine screeches and wails as it grinds beans for the customer ahead of me. It hisses and sputters steam into a frothy pitcher of milk. The barista wipes the machine with a damp rag. "What can I get you?"

"Never mind," I say.

Outside, I put on my hat and struggle with my stupid zipper. Do I continue to the studio, or head back to Eric's place to lie still until the waves of nausea pass? I feel too ill to have a choice.

ERIC COMES INTO THE BEDROOM, kisses my forehead, and immediately spots one of his invitations on the bedside table.

"Looks good," I tell him, nodding toward the portrait of Dad. I'm not lying. "But for some reason, I thought you were painting landscapes. I guess I wasn't paying attention. There's been so much going on lately. What else have you been painting?"

He pauses.

"Don't tell me they are *all* of my dad?" I say.

He doesn't answer.

"You're kidding me."

"It was your idea," he says, getting defensive. "Anyway, they're hard to explain. I can show you photos but I'd rather you see them in person when they're all finished. I *want* you to see them."

Seeing a single portrait reproduced on a postcard triggered such a severe anxiety attack, I'm afraid of what power the full series will hold. Pressure builds, I feel it in my ears, like a deep dive into a pool.

Eric pulls a scrap of newspaper from his coat pocket, unfolds it, and hands it to me. It's a half-page torn from the New York Times arts section about the exploding Bushwick art scene. Accompanying the article is a small map of eight galleries and a blurb about each one. Although it's not a ranking, Curious 24 is listed first. I hand it back to him, and he reads me a line about Curious 24 being a great place to catch emerging artists. "Emerging," he laughs. "Like a cicada, burrowed in the dirt for years."

"The New York Times," I say, "that's a big deal."

"Yeah, well, last week, they had a similar article listing the city's ten best food trucks, so I don't know."

"That would be a big deal, too, if you owned a food truck."

"I suppose." He folds the article with a shrug and returns it to his pocket. "Listen, there's something I need to tell you. It might influence your decision about coming to the opening."

What decision? Does he actually think there's a chance I might go?

"There's going to be a—performance." He reaches into his pocket again and pulls out a postcard similar to the one for his exhibit.

Even though they are billing *The Judgment of Homer* as a one-person show, the gallery is holding an extravaganza later the same night. *A Thousand Ways to Say I Love You* featuring poetry readings, burlesque dancers, projections, and interactive installations. It sounds like a nightmare. The crowds are bound to overlap. "I can't promise you that there won't be guys dancing in saggy underwear," he says.

"I can't believe it."

"Trust me; it wasn't my idea. Zack keeps talking about

mixing crowds, cross-promotion, all that crap. He must not think my paintings can stand on their own. Maybe they can't. I don't know. Anyway, the performance won't start until nine o'clock. If you come early enough, you can skip the nonsense."

"Even if I wanted to, I can't. It's the same day as my open studio."

"Is it?"

"I guess you'll be missing it."

"It's during the day, though, isn't it? Maybe I can swing by. And you can come to my show after your sale. Can't you? You have to come. It wouldn't be happening if it weren't for you."

"I'll think about it."

And I do think about it. I spend a whole sleepless night thinking about it. I spend the next morning thinking about it, too, as I make a second attempt to reach my studio.

AFTER COLLECTING MY PIECES, I carry them to my bench and arrange them according to style and size. Holding one up, I try to picture it with a drippy blue glaze, like the condensation on the coffee shop window, but I'm distracted by the thought of Eric's paintings. I cautiously pull one of the invitations from my bag and hold it up. *Look, Dad, this is my studio. Did you know I make ceramics? No?* An imaginary conversation with Dad isn't any more natural than a real one, and I only hear the things he always says: *The dogs won't eat. The Rapture could come at any time. The clothes you bought me are okay and all, but...* He rarely asks about my life. Barely says, *How are you doing?* Or *What's new?* I'm only torturing myself trying to imagine he ever will. "You're going to be famous, Dad," I say, turning the postcard around to face me. "How does that make you feel?" His face remains frozen mid-ramble. As usual, he isn't listening to me. "You're crazy, Dad, you know that, right?"

It distresses me to imagine a gaggle of art lovers laughing at Dad's portrait, or worse appreciating it in some ironic, hyper-critical way. What can I do about it, though? I can't tell Eric what to paint. It's too late now, anyway. He's finished the paint-ings, and his show is going to open regardless of how I feel about it. My only option is to skip the opening entirely and pretend it isn't happening. *Fuck Eric and fuck his stupid fucking paintings of my stupid fucking dad.* I wish I could be more supportive—especially considering how supportive he's been of me—but he should have told me what he was doing. He should have asked. Yes, I'm the one who suggested he paint Dad in the first place, but it never occurred to me he actually would.

I won't be getting any work done today, so I spend a few minutes cleaning and straightening up, sweeping away accumu-lated clay dust, reorganizing my tools, and so on. Before long, I can't resist wiring off a gob of clay—not to mold anything, in particular, just a little art therapy. I stay for hours.

ANNA'S JOURNAL
Monday, September 18, 1972

"Do you know where you were? Do you remember being taken to Latrobe Area Hospital?" Doctor Abrams asked. "Do you know what happened?"

Yes. A baby girl was inside of me, and now she's not—she's been held on layaway until I decide what to do.

He wants to know about the father—join the club, I thought —but I refuse to talk about him. My womb, my right, I say. It's what I have left. And the experience is all I have. It shouldn't have happened, but it did. A mistake. Or was it? I've always wanted to embarrass Mother. I mean, she's always been ashamed of me and oddly proud of it, wringing her hands about "my condition" to her friends like a badge of honor, a get-into-heaven-free card, but this is my chance to show her what real embarrassment looks like. Here's a "condition" you can't fix, especially if you're Catholic. What will she say now to the gang at bingo night? To her priest? I imagine her telling stories of an immaculate conception. Or finding a way to deny it altogether. Good luck, I say: my little Condition has ten fingers, ten toes, and an eternal soul, and she is going to outlive you all.

I told Doctor Abrams I needed to rest and clear my head, but I don't think I should have said it. Oakville's idea of clearing my head is to vacuum it out entirely. The less I understand or retain, the better they say I am. But I was exhausted and it was true that I needed to rest. He wouldn't know, but having a baby takes it out of you.

Finally, once Doctor Abrams had finished his interrogation, he had an attendant to take me to the ward. It's in the new building now, but the routine feels familiar, and nothing much has changed. Although, I noticed that many of the long-time patients seem to have finally escaped.

Henrietta became an empty rocking chair last year. Plucked from the earth by the hand of God. Olive was one of six patients given a place to stay in a transitional housing experiment. She was trained and given a job, too. I was crushed to find I wasn't chosen. They must think I'm incapable. I don't know where Nancy is. And now, even my baby is gone. No one to talk to. But that doesn't mean it's perfectly quiet here. As the attendant escorted me through the ward, the few patients who remain stopped what they were doing—which was nothing—and whispered to each other about where I'd been and what I'd done. A chamber choir of muted voices whispering like a breeze through the trees: *Sinner!*

Nurse Winthrop was pleasant enough in her way. She told me that when she, herself, had given birth to her son she had been in labor for a full day. "You need to recuperate," she said while doling out some pills.

It's hard to imagine someone like Winthrop doing what's necessary to have a baby.

I waved the pills off.

"Doctor's orders," she said, like the programmed robot that she is. "They will help you sleep."

Whatever the pills were, they didn't put me to sleep—not right away. I spent what must have been an hour lying in bed, feeling numb—almost content. There's no other way for me to describe it. I felt less consumed by depressing thoughts, less concerned with my future. I felt I was standing atop the dry crest of a turtle shell raised above my usual bog of contempt.

I don't know how long I slept, but when I woke, it took time for me to remember I had given birth. When I reached down to caress the empty nest of my belly, I heard no reassuring little voice and began to wonder if this deflated balloon had ever been home to a baby at all. When I asked one of the nurses about it, I was expecting her to tell me I'd been hallucinating.

"A woman like you can't have a baby," I expected her to say. "It isn't possible."

But it was a rare time where something I said didn't provoke a firm, condescending rebuttal.

"Don't worry," the nurse said. "Your baby is being well cared for at the nursery in Latrobe."

"When can I see her?"

"You'll have to talk to Dr. Abrams about that. Right now, you need to recuperate."

Mother told me not to name my baby yet, but I already have —Virginia. I named her after Olivia de Havilland's character in *The Snake Pit*—a mental patient, like me, who breezes out of the hospital at the end of the film. Though I may never breeze out of here, baby Virginia will do it for me—a small part of me that finally escapes. Though I miss hearing my baby talk to me— miss having an ally from within—maybe it's best if she's gone for good and never knows anything about this place. Mother made a promise to take me to Latrobe Area Hospital this weekend, so I can hold baby Virginia and decide what to do.

If they extend my stay here much longer, Mother says that she will take Virginia home and keep her there for me until I'm well enough to see her. Though I'm sure everyone would prefer me to stay at Oakville. To be tied down, sedated, shocked into a stupor. We'll see. We'll see. For now, more sleep.

OPEN STUDIO

Eric and I knock into each other in the kitchen, pulling mugs from the cupboard, spoons from the drawer. It's the big day, for each of us, and we're both scatter-brained. Eric says he doubts he'll have time to come to my open studio after all. He apologizes, again, for screwing up the dates, but says he has too much to do today. "Hope you understand."

"Too bad," I say, as sincerely as possible before using the same excuse to explain why I won't be able to attend his event either. "I'll be late packing my ceramics," I say. "And helping to clean up."

We'll miss each other's exhibits, so what? Seems fair. But he looks crushed.

"You'll be preoccupied and distracted," I say. "You won't miss me."

"Of course I will. Like I said, none of this would be happening if it weren't for you."

Isn't that enough? He must know it's an awkward situation for me, which is why he has not let me see the paintings until now. I'll see them another day.

Aside from the occasional thud of a coffee mug hitting the table or the clank of a spoon, the room is quiet. Eventually, Eric pours what's left of his coffee into mine and says he has to go. He kisses me on the cheek and pauses in front of my face, looking deep into my eyes. "Promise you'll call me later."

THE FRESHLY PAINTED showroom glows Gallery White as the early morning sun blazes through a bank of wired windows that have been scraped clean with a razor blade. My studio mates are carefully unpacking ceramics from cardboard boxes, littering the floor with crumpled pages of old newspapers. I search for my assigned spot.

A card with my name rests next to another with the name Mika Shimizu. I've seen Mika in the studio, but aside from the occasional hello, we've never spoken to each other. I've seen her work, too—delicate vases finished with painterly matte glazes that look like pale strokes of watercolor. Picturing my work next to Mika's, I feel like a heavy-handed dilettante. Who decided to put the two of us together? After reluctantly unpacking a half-dozen clunky mugs and bowls, I lift a quasi-abstract sculpture from the box and place it on the table. It looks even more amateurish than my other things, and I'm about to rewrap it and put it away when Mika arrives.

"Is that yours?" she asks, setting a box on the floor.

I tell her it is.

"I love it," she says. "Do you have more?"

When I show her the others, she encourages me to display them all.

"Ooh, so beautiful. What are they supposed to be?"

I admit I have no idea.

"Make something up," she says. "People want to hear a story. Trust me. It's the most important thing."

She unwraps her pieces and puts them on the table one by one.

"People always assume I'm from Japan," she says, "but I'm not. Watch the disappointment when I say I'm from Middlebury and see what a difference a good backstory makes."

She nudges one of her teacups to bring it into perfect alignment with the others.

"I lied once. Told a guy I came from Kagoshima. He bought four vases and stayed in touch. Told all his friends about the rare exotic objects he'd found from the Far East. Seeing his reaction tempted me to lie all the time. But I've only been to Japan once, so it's too risky. I don't even eat sushi! It doesn't hurt to keep my mouth shut, though—let people believe whatever they want to believe. *Me no speak English,* know what I mean? How about you?"

"I speak English."

"Ha, no, I mean, where are you from? Where'd you grow up?"

"Western Pennsylvania. A place called Daisytown."

"No way, that can't be real."

"Look it up."

I try to describe it—the good parts, anyway—but my mind gets clogged with the textured, complicated, confusing parts, and I begin to feel as if I'm floating above and behind my head. I love a story, too, I suppose, just not my own. Maybe I don't know what mine is. Yet.

"May I?" She picks up a wildly cockeyed piece and inspects it. She places it beside my other pieces and proceeds to experiment with their arrangement. "Looks like a family," she says. "Are you selling them as a set?"

"Hadn't thought about it."

We take turns moving pieces as if they are chessmen, dollhouse furnishings, or plastic zoo animals. A circus troupe, after Calder. I'm reminded of that circus painting I did as a child, that won me a ribbon at the Arts and Crafts show in Pittsburgh. I wonder again at the fact that my birth mother had won a ribbon, too. The characters in both our lives could definitely form a circus—we all perform in a ring at some point, and maybe this work is bringing me full circle. Literally. The figurines on the table start to make more sense to me.

I put another on the table. "Inspired by the floral hillsides and verdant valleys of Daisytown..." I say.

"Now you're getting it."

"Better yet: Inspired by the stench of fracking and the toxic waterways, the labor-union travesties and the big corporate corruption in a little corner of the world called Daisytown, where your father talks to God and your mother is not your own. A place where your loyalty is always up for grabs..."

"Ha, wow. A little dark, but okay. Dark is good."

Our playful laughter attracts the attention of a woman who has been making her way from table to table. She introduces herself and hands us each a card: Zoë Gabriel, Owner, C-World Gallery. "Mind if I snap a few photos?" Zoë says.

Mika and I look over the cards as Zoë hovers her phone above our table. She snaps some pictures with a flash, a few without.

"Are these yours?" Zoë asks, circling her finger over my figurines before looking at me with curiosity. I find myself bristling with fear as she touches them, willing her not to break them, or, worse, judge them.

"Aren't they great?" says Mika.

"There's a story behind them..." I begin, now sensing that Zoë wants one.

Zoë pauses, politely, expectantly.

"...but I can get into it later," I hastily finish, trying to pretend I'm saving her time.

"I love how these little figures seem to accept the world's natural chaos," she says, lifting her glasses, inspecting one closely, like an archeologist examining an ancient shard. "Not only accept it, they absolutely revel in it."

I feel exposed, as though she's examining my own skin, peering into my pores with a magnifying glass.

"There's a carefree naivety about them. Don't get me wrong, I mean that in the best possible way. They are so...*authentic.* It's almost as if the clay has designed itself. Beautiful."

I'm not used to such enthusiasm and am finding it hard not to question her own authenticity.

"Listen," she says. "I'm planning a show of small-scale sculptures to coincide with a Janika Smolak solo show in our main gallery—know her? She's Chechen. Draws from Eastern European folktales. Very surreal. More painterly than sculptural. Wonderful stuff. We're still working out the details, but I'd love to talk to you about including your work. Do you have a card?"

I shake my head, no. No card, no story, I don't even have prices. What an amateur.

While entering my name and number into her phone, Zoë's phone rings and she steps away to answer.

"Exciting," Mika whispers to me. "I love Janika Smolak."

"Never heard of her."

"Listen, you need to work out your story before you talk to Zoë. Trust me; it's crucial. Can I show you something?" She pulls out her phone and scrolls to a picture of an amorphous, marbled doorstop made of solid mud, of uncertain size but undeniable heft, sitting on an untreated log in what appears to be an outdoor studio. "See this? Made by a Peruvian artist named Adolpho Calapari. He hikes around his property, mines his own clay, and makes it into these biomorphic sculptures inspired by the rocky terrain of Peru. Pit-fires them in his backyard. Makes his own glazes too. His stuff sells for tens of thousands of dollars." She hands me her phone, so I can take a closer look and she waits for my reaction.

"It's beautiful," I say, handing the phone back. Other than to admit I'm envious the guy makes tens of thousands of dollars by digging around in his backyard, I'm not sure what else to say.

She puts her phone away and admits, "I lied. My five-year-old nephew made it. Who knows what it's supposed to be?"

I'm a little embarrassed at having fallen for the story about Peru. "Really? Only five years old?"

"No, actually, that's a lie, too. It's my piece. I'm experimenting with a new direction. Getting sick of being so careful and precise all the time. But this fragile watercolor stuff sells, so I can't stop making it. Not yet, anyway."

"I give up," I say, unsure of what to believe anymore, nor what sells.

"That last bit is the truth. But it doesn't matter. You get the point, right? The thing itself never changes, but your perception does."

"I get it. I'm just not good at that kind of thing. Stories. Made up or otherwise." I haven't thought about Story Time since kindergarten. Is the entire art world made up of five-year-olds waiting for a puppet show?

"Here's one: Did you know the Mona Lisa didn't become a world-renowned masterpiece until it got stolen? Seriously, it wasn't even the best-known painting in the gallery, let alone the entire Louvre. After the theft, it became world-famous overnight. But the most interesting part? Before they recovered it, people went to the Louvre to see where it had been hanging —lining up to look at a bare wall. What were they looking at? The story, of course."

She says she could talk about it all day long, and I have a feeling she might, but it doesn't change the fact I have no story of my own. But don't I? Doesn't everyone? Who knows how Eric managed to feel inspired by Dad. Damian was right that I needed to be better connected—maybe a story will do that for me, infuse not only my objects but my life with meaning. My story-less, card-less table gets less foot traffic than the others, which allows me time to look at my figurines and think about what they might mean.

As more and more visitors arrive, I begin to feel anxious and claustrophobic. I ask Mika to watch my things while I make a quick run to the bathroom. I need to pee but, more important, I need to shake off the urge to start guzzling some of the free wine I see everyone carrying. I take my time heading back, stopping here and there to see what's on display, saying hi to the people I know, cautiously circling the wine table. A glass would help me settle down, but a china shop isn't the place to risk turning into a bull.

I return to my spot in time to see Mika wrapping one of her vases for Zoë, who then carefully places it in a shopping bag, which is brimming with pieces by other artists. I congratulate Mika on her sale, but it's hard to hide my disappointment. Zoë had seemed so interested, why didn't she buy something from me? I, like a five-year-old, need a story and pronto.

"Are you kidding?" says Mika. "Zoë invited you to show at C-World. I'm so jealous."

"Who knows if it will ever happen," I say. "Maybe I'm not an artist at all."

"It doesn't matter. Everyone is an artist these days. Just keep doing what you're doing."

"I hoped to make a little money today."

"I hear you, but trust me, no one here is getting rich."

Rich is relative.

Mika, it turns out, is a lawyer. Works at an insurance company doing contracts or something. I'm sure she makes a bundle. And now she sold a vase for as much money as I earn for a full day of mind-numbingly tedious bookkeeping work. I'm desperate to quit and was hoping ceramics might offer a way out. But it won't happen at this rate.

A little later, when Mika takes a bathroom break, I watch her table and get to see, first hand, the reaction her pieces get.

"This is the Japanese artist I've been telling you about," someone says. "I read she is inspired by visits from her grandmother's ghost."

Like Mika, I keep my mouth shut. But, from my side of the table, the real, true story of a lawyer from Middlebury who, in her spare time, whips out gorgeous ceramics that sell for hundreds of dollars, is at least as impressive as a quiet and mysterious Japanese woman who channels her grandmother's ghost.

When Mika returns, she's carrying two plastic flutes of Prosecco. "Cheers," she says. Wine is hard enough to resist, but Prosecco? A small glass will rein in my jitters, so why not?

"Cheers."

Fortunately, there's not enough alcohol available to cause trouble. I have a second glass, but that's all. I relax and manage to sell a couple of bowls. I'm even reckless enough to take an order for a set of four mugs with the drippy blue glaze. Not drunk enough to take on a commission for plates, thank God. And, when someone asks about the sculptures, I say they're not for sale, which I find only makes people want them more.

———

LOOSE AND CONFIDENT from the Prosecco, I make a pit stop at home to change out of my dusty clothes before heading to Eric's exhibit. I throw on a T-shirt, notice a stain, and swap it for a different one, but it's dirty, too. I find another buried in the closet, shake it out, remind myself to do laundry, and put it on. I put on makeup and pluck one of the gray hairs I've been starting to find. When I'm ready to go, I take off all my clothes and start again. Whenever someone compliments me on my style, I laugh because my closet is so pathetically spare. Although the two small suitcases I first left home with are long gone, I've never owned more than would fit inside of them. The few things I have all come from a couple of buy-and-sell second-hand stores. I often buy something from one, keep it a while, then sell it to the other one. The salespeople must realize I do it over and over, but no one seems to care.

After trying on everything I own in all conceivable combinations, I remember a dress an old roommate gave me. It's out of rotation and isn't even in my closet—it's buried in a box still unpacked from my move. I dig it out, check for moth holes, and slip it on. It used to be too big, but it fits better now. Army boots are the most comfortable shoes I own, but how will they look? It's impossible to see myself head-to-toe in the wall mirror, so I stand on the bed and bounce a few times to get the full picture. Not bad. I take my boots off and slip on a pair of fishnets. My style hasn't evolved much—I might as well be heading to an all-ages punk show in Pittsburgh circa 1989. Am I too old to pull it off? Maybe. Probably. I don't know. Who cares? Everything will be hidden under the sticky zipper of my snorkel coat anyway.

A SMARTLY DRESSED gallery assistant greets me inside the doorway. I've met her before though I can't remember where. We say hello and kiss on the cheek. "Good turnout," she says. It's a more massive crowd than I expected—far bigger than the groups at any of Eric's self-produced studio shows. The assistant hands me a printed artist's statement, and I skim it, braced to see my family secrets exposed.

This is Homer, 77 years old, from Daisytown, PA. I met him shortly after his wife of fifty-five years passed away. He lives in a small house on 20 acres of land once owned and farmed by his father-in-law. Vegetables no longer grow there, and Zsa Zsa, the cow, is long gone. His two children have grown up and moved away. Even Jesus, to whom Homer has been speaking regularly since 1957 (the year Homer was saved), seems to have stopped answering back. ("I used to hear him as clear as I'm hearing you now," he'll tell you, "but not no more.")

Yet Homer is not entirely alone. He is visited regularly by a revolving cast of angels and demons who offer up divine visions. Among the warnings, predictions, and premonitions, they show him the beautiful new house he will get in Heaven when the Rapture comes. Each of these visions is faithfully chronicled by Homer in his notebooks.

This series began as one painting—a simple portrait of Homer's turbulent face. But a single picture didn't do him justice. The series is an attempt to capture as much as I could of Homer's obsessions and visions—as well as my own.

A story.

It goes on, but I've read enough. I stuff the statement into my coat pocket and forget about it.

Two gray-haired men, one in a plaid suit, the other in a leather Perfecto jacket, freeze mid-conversation as I pass between them and into the dense crowd. I hope they are pausing because I look good, not because I'm too old to be wearing what I'm wearing. Or worse, because they know I'm Homer's daughter. That's impossible, but it's difficult not to be paranoid. A smattering of young hipster debutantes in false eyelashes and sparkly dresses are each encircled by a group of young guys dressed identically in skinny paint-splattered jeans. They probably all work in internet marketing or something. Their strategically torn T-shirts, black-framed glasses, and beards are all identical, too. A few professional photographers— people with professional-level gear anyway—weave and bob for the right angles, holding strobes high above their heads, causing the already bright gallery to randomly pop with a blinding flash of white.

I psych myself up, elbow through the herd, and approach the first canvas—the portrait from the invitation. It's even more vibrant and striking in person. I want to step back and see it from a little further away, but the crowd makes it impossible. A pair of young lovers blocks my view of the next one. I have to wait for them to move out of the way. "My father had one of those," I hear the guy say. "Looked exactly like that." His date shudders. Once they move, I see why. It's a tightly cropped image featuring a pair of jeans falling loosely around Dad's hips. His clothesline belt is untied, and his underwear and paper towels are pulled down to his pubic line, revealing a hairy lump the size of an avocado, firm as a pregnant belly.

Dad complains about his hernia a lot, but I always manage to avoid conjuring a mental image of it. If this is what it looks like, Eric is right: he needs to see a doctor right away. I shiver before moving along, taking baby steps toward the third piece: a still life of Dad's desk covered in calendars, religious books, a bible, sympathy cards, two pill bottles, a dog leash, and a penis clamp. Nothing indicates what the clamp is used for, but I recognize it immediately. At least Eric has spared me the horror of seeing Dad wearing it. I don't notice at first, but underneath the clutter sit a few gay porno magazines. I nearly laugh.

As I turn, I catch Eric's profile through the crowd. He is talking with uncharacteristic enthusiasm to a couple of people I don't recognize, including a stylish young blonde. Immediately, I stand up straight, squint to see better. She looks to be about twenty-five, vivacious, maybe slightly drunk. Animated, at any rate, and she is staring at Eric with laser focus. Strikes me as a care-free party girl, like I used to be. I'm not used to seeing Eric laugh so hard. My jealousy surprises me. Is that what he wants? A gallerina? Because that's not me—certainly not anymore—regardless of how much Prosecco I drink. Is he what I want? Do I interrupt them and cause a scene, or watch from a distance and see what happens? Neither. I clench my fists and, with reluctant determination, bump through the crowd until they are beyond my line of sight.

Beside me is a painting called *Lawn of the Afterlife*. It's of Dad wearing a dirty white robe and a gold crown while circling his property upon a golden lawnmower. The crown and the mower are rendered in gold leaf like an illustrated manuscript. Dad's expression is fixed and determined, focused on making his already perfect lawn even more perfect. The image is precisely what I imagined when I first suggested it—except for the gold leaf. Nice touch.

Next to *Lawn of the Afterlife* is *Food of the Dogs*—a full-sized portrait of Dad looking old and crooked on the doorstep of his equally old and crooked house. Ants crawl from the crack in the stoop, stink bugs cling to the screen door. Dad wears a shapeless brown suit with a tan shirt and an orange tie, *"Like the preacher on TV."* His two dogs sit leashed together at his feet. Beside each dog lies a cornucopia overflowing with canned peaches, bananas, dog biscuits, jars of peanut butter, slices of American cheese, cans of ravioli, and so on. Dad's expression is hard to decipher. Anxious? Pained? Does anyone here, aside from me, get the joke? Is it a joke? One of the brightly colored jokes Eric said modern art is expected to be? Kind of. Maybe. I can't decide.

Noticing the blonde has left Eric's side (I promised myself I would stop looking and failed), I cut through the crowd to see him. He is engaged in conversation with the gallery owner, who is congratulating Eric on the turnout—congratulating himself is more like it. Eric looks up and appears to see me, but says nothing. Instead, he puts his head down, nodding slightly as the gallery owner informs him about another potential sale. But I can see a slow smile he can't hide creeping across his face. Why is he ignoring me? Am I invisible? Can he smell the alcohol? Who is that dumb blonde anyway? Did she take him to Daisy-town to find his muse? Could she? I don't think so. While listening in, I learn two of Eric's paintings have sold—nineteen hundred dollars for the so-called masterpiece, which I have yet to see, and sixteen hundred for the full-sized portrait with the dogs. The gallery owner tells Eric he is still negotiating with someone on the price of the still life but expects it will sell, too. From what I gather, the still life is the least expensive painting in the room. Yet, fifteen-hundred dollars is more than double what Eric ever got for any of his previous works—including the one that financed my trip to Daisytown at the start of this carnival ride. I hear Eric say he wants to let his Wall Street friend, Joe, have the hernia painting at a discount, but the gallery owner isn't thrilled about discounts. He tells Eric, "We'll talk."

Eric looks up again, does a double-take, and finally acknowledges me, a little shy, but proud. "You came!"

"Congratulations," I say into his ear as we hug. "I thought you were ignoring me."

Eric introduces me to the gallery owner, Zack. "This is my girlfriend, Rachel," he says.

Hearing him call me that—his girlfriend—takes me by surprise, but I remind myself it makes things easier. Nevertheless, after seeing him with the blonde, it feels good to hear him say it. As long as he isn't playing me, that is.

Eric promised me he wouldn't tell anyone who the subject of the exhibit is, but when Zack says, "I've heard a lot about you," I have to assume he knows what is what and who is who. It makes my cheeks itch. He asks me if I will be staying for the show. I lie and tell him I might. "You have to stay," he says. "Amy Zeker is performing. Have you seen her? She's amazing."

"I know, I'd love to." Other than having seen her name on the invitation, I have no idea who Amy Zeker is and don't care enough to find out. Zack drones on about how Amy's performance at Art Basel Miami was utterly mind-blowing, transformative, transgressive, and so on. He eventually interrupts himself when he notices someone across the room he needs to greet. "Don't go anywhere," he says.

At last, I can step back and take in the final painting: *Four Ages of Homer.* It is, indeed, a masterpiece. Ambitious, in any case. It shows the four chairs from Dad's dream—his vision. In the first chair sits Dad as a child, scruffy and poor, but smiling, innocent, with a shard of glass through his flat left foot. Next is Dad in his Army uniform, blond hair, sitting straight and tall circa 1957— the year he was saved by Jesus, as he so often declares. The third figure, paunchy in middle age, sits naked with his hands clasped over his cock—either hiding it or playing with it, it's hard to tell. And in the fourth and last chair is Dad, as he looked the last time I saw him—his thinning hair, his goatee, dirty clothes, a clothesline belt, and worn-out slippers. His wild eyes look heavenward in an expression of guilt and worry, while beams of sunlight illuminate his wispy hair like a halo. The artist's statement mentions something about the Hindu religion's Four Ages of Man, but I know what the painting represents. "Do the people here get this?" I ask.

Eric admits they probably don't. "Hopefully, it captures something more universal than just your dad," he says. "Homer is a unique character, there's no denying it, but he's still a human being. Besides, if anyone is confused, there's always the artist's statement to explain it."

"I didn't read it all."

"I don't blame you."

"I was afraid I'd see something about me."

"There's nothing."

I'm relieved at not being exposed but can't help feeling a twinge of disappointment too. I wanted to be Eric's muse, to set him on fire the way Dad appears to have done. Will it ever happen? Is it too late? I thought muses usually get to work early —before familiarity diminishes their mystique. In any case, I tell Eric he captured Dad perfectly. "But what surprised me," I say, "what I didn't expect was that—well—I guess I didn't expect to find them so funny."

"Your dad is a funny guy."

"I never used to think so." I point across the room to the painting with the dogs. "That one is my favorite—with all the crazy dog food. I laughed out loud when I saw it. His expression is spot on." Eric tells me it's been sold, but I already knew that, and I congratulate him. "It's weird to imagine my dad's face hanging on someone's wall. I've always been so embarrassed by him. I never wanted anyone to meet him. I didn't want *you* to meet him. And now look." I twirl on my heel and scan the crowd. "How much longer are you going to stay?"

"At least until nine. What time is it?"

"It's only eight. Do you plan to stay for the show?"

"I should. There are a lot of guests I haven't spoken to yet, and Zack wants to introduce me to some people. Why? Are you thinking of leaving already?"

I nod.

Eric is disappointed. Eric being Eric, he says, "I'm glad you came. I know you didn't want to."

"I was afraid, that's all."

Eric is ignoring the rest of the room. "I know."

"But I'm not afraid anymore. Maybe I could come back during the week when the crowds are gone?"

He can't hide his pleasure to hear this. "It's only open by appointment during the week, but I'm sure I can arrange a private showing for a VIP."

"I'd like that."

OUTSIDE, I'm relaxed, relieved, almost happy. Prosecco doesn't hurt, though I didn't have much. Could use another.

Despite the cold, a few people are mingling on the street, smoking cigarettes, drinking cans of cheap beer, laughing, and joking. When I call the car service, the dispatcher tells me, twenty-minutes. I'm about to argue, but who cares? It's only a ten-minute walk to the subway anyway, and I'm feeling good.

Near the station, I see my old local bar, with its sticky morass of dim memories. It's tempting to pop in for a cocktail to keep the feeling going, but, as I pass, a couple of young guys tumble out the door and onto the sidewalk.

"Hey," one of them says. "I know you. We went to the burlesque art party together."

"Right," I say. Nausea laps gently at the banks of my gut. "I don't remember your name."

"Devon."

I still don't give him mine.

"We're going to Curious 24," he says. "Want to come? They're throwing another art party. It's going to be wild."

I smile and shake my head, no.

"You'll be sorry you missed it. Amy Zeker is going to squirt paint from her ass."

Eric neglected to tell me about that. What is the name of the show again? *A Thousand Ways to Say I Love You.* I guess that's one. I know others.

ANNA'S JOURNAL
Sunday, May 13, 1973

I f I'm well enough to be home, why am I not well enough
to have my baby with me for Mother's Day? Don't they
think I can take care of her? Not even after I carried her
for so many months? Am I nothing but a spent cocoon? They
don't want us together because my daughter is the one person

in this world who would love me no matter what. They don't want anyone to love me. They want me alone in the world. Nobody trusts me. Nobody likes me the way I am.

I've been keeping a journal since I was seventeen—over twenty years now—intending to preserve my life within its pages. But when I look at what I've written, my entries are no better than the blossoms from Mother's rosebush I once tried preserving—the ones I had sandwiched within the pages of my cherished *Screenland* magazine (November 1950, sadly long gone.) The bundle lay undisturbed for weeks under my mattress and, when I finally opened it, nothing but a handful of crisp, crushed petals drifted to the floor like soap flakes. My half-filled journals are much the same—lifeless fragments—and I'm afraid my life makes as little sense on paper as it did while I lived it.

Mother's roses still clamber valiantly up the trellis. Despite dustings of soot from passing trains and mill poisons leaching into the dirt, their twisted stems strain heavenward from the earth, dotted with green nubs. Then, when the time is right, they explode into heavy blooms that hang like apples. Each rose radiates in the sun for days or weeks before it begins to wither and fade. When it does, Mother snips it off with a pair of clippers and tosses it into a paper bag propped open at her feet, saying, "The old must make way for the new." She's been doing this for decades. And when I found her pruning earlier today, I sat beside her the same way I did as a little girl. But rather than collecting discarded flowers to press, I hoped to scavenge memories.

I've been trying to fill in the gaps in my journals by asking Mother to remember things for me, hoping to leave behind something more for my little girl than just my dusty bones and disordered scribbles—a way for her to know me at least a little.

Sadly, I'm not sure I can trust Mother's answers, especially when it comes to the events of last August. But she has to understand that August 14, 1972, is an important date for me—

perhaps the most important date of them all—and it's essential I include as much about it as possible.

"Stop dwelling on the past," Mother said, tossing a severed bloom into the bag. "What's done is done."

But if Mother won't talk about it, who will? My time is running out. I'm fading, crumbling, wasting into more dry flakes. So how am I to show my little girl who I am? How is she to see that I'm not a bad person and never intended to abandon her? That I didn't—not really. I believe I am still a part of her, just as she was once a part of me. The purest part.

If you ever read this my baby, I want you to know you will always be my greatest accomplishment. Perhaps my only one. Never a minute goes by that I don't imagine what lies ahead for you. For us.

After waking Mother in the early hours one too many times, she suggested I see a doctor about my insomnia. I refused. I'm done with doctors, done with all of that now. So instead, Mother made an appointment to see a doctor herself and made up a story about having sleep troubles of her own. When Mother told me her plan, I suggested she get what they give me at the hospital—the pills that erase everything. I couldn't remember the name—proof of how well they work—and could only describe what they look like. She came home with something entirely different. Red and black capsules—each one like a tiny Mickey Mouse. A Betty Boop.

I haven't tried the Mickey Boop pills yet. Instead, I have been awake all night listening to the hiss of static, hoping Stewart might visit me for a final farewell. I still remember the first time he spoke to me through a picture in *Screenland* magazine. The future felt so certain then. So perfect. I'm sorry, Stewart. Sorry for disappointing you. For disappointing myself, as well. Too late to for me be a model now. Too late for me to be a young starlet in Hollywood. A painter. A reporter. Too late to get my baby back. It was too late to get her back before I even knew what happened—clutched from my womb by a nun from Catholic Charities while I slept. Stolen like everything else in my life.

I'm cursed to be forever sorry that I didn't have the strength to stand up for myself and my baby girl. But I don't know how I could have done it. Maybe I could have grabbed her and run away from the hospital after I delivered? I lie in bed every night with my arms wrapped around where my baby once lived, knowing that I will never hold her. I sometimes feel through my skin for her feet and hands the way I would when she moved inside me. I talk to her still and tell her that I will find her again one day, that I love her and always will.

A lifetime ago, I won a ribbon for a painting I did for the Pittsburgh Arts and Crafts show. It has hung in the same place on my wall for years and when I lifted it from the hanger, the wall behind it looked so much cleaner, brighter, and more vibrant than the dingy yellow wall that surrounds it—a reminder of how much time has passed, a symbol of how dull my life has become, the story behind the painting. The painting was professionally framed for the art show and a dust cover of Kraft paper covers its back. I have carefully sliced the paper near the frame's edge and will soon hide all my writings behind it. I will collect everything I can find—those typed onto onion skin as well as those scrawled in my barely legible hand—place them into envelopes, and tape the envelopes in place so no one knows they are there. When I finish this final entry, I will include it as well. All of the envelopes will be hidden in the space behind my painting before I carefully seal the pocket with tape. I thought of attaching a label to the painting's frame that reads, "For Virginia," but it would only stir suspicion. Instead, I'll attach a label addressed to the only person I trust: "For Esther." Who knows if Esther will ever find the pages hidden within—or if she'll have any idea of what to do with them if she does. What do I want her to do with them, anyway? What's the purpose of preserving them? Proof that I exist—or at least did so once upon a time.

Once I retrieve Mother's sleeping pills from the kitchen cupboard, I no longer will. I have given up holding on. There is nothing to hold onto. I'll do what I should have done ages ago. From this page forward, my journals will remain untouched, white, pure. Like the unwritten future of my tiny little girl.

Please don't condemn her to a life like mine. Her chance at happiness is my chance at happiness. A part of me lives inside her, now, the way she once lived inside of me.

Are you reading this? If so, I hope you'll understand and won't judge me too harshly. Trust that whatever you read in these journals isn't my whole story, and it doesn't represent the best of me. I hope your life turns out better than mine. I hope your future is perfect.

Take care, my little one. We'll meet again someday, somewhere. If not in this life, then the next.

MOTHER OF SORROWS

The rounded lumps of black snow previously lining the Brooklyn sidewalks are mostly gone now, revealing a season's worth of cigarette butts, wads of gum, and dried dog turds—all of it scattered at the curbs amid swirls of salt stains.

Eric's show is down. In the end, he sold four paintings—three for the asking price, and another at a small discount to his evergreen patron, Joe. After Zack's percentage (50%, which still sounds hefty to me), Eric walks away with close to five thousand dollars. Some art blogs mention the show—just asides within longer articles about Amy Zeker, but what can you expect? Traditional paint laid down with a brush is no match for splashes of color straight out of a woman's ass. I almost regret missing it.

"I spent over a year on those paintings," says Eric over breakfast. "The materials alone cost me a few thousand bucks. My time, the studio rental—" He eats a spoonful of cereal.

"Want to know where the paintings that didn't sell are sitting right now? In the warehouse. A year from now, and I'll be cutting them into tiny bits. If I don't do it tomorrow, that is."

Does he expect me to console him? Part of me would be happy to see them shredded.

"You sold one for nearly two grand," I say. "That's a lot of money. But it's not all about sales. You've said so yourself. I don't understand what you're complaining about."

"Postpartum depression, I guess. It would help if I didn't have to go back to work. Alongside the art I destroy are paintings worth over a hundred thousand dollars. Without knowing the artist, or the artwork's history, it's impossible to tell which is which. Sometimes I fantasize about destroying the wrong piece to make a point: Oh, that was Amy Zeker's ass painting? Sorry, I got my shit stains mixed up."

I've already tuned him out. "How about a little sunlight?" I say, raising the kitchen blinds. It looks warm outside, so I take it a step further and crack open the window.

"Our plans are still on, right? We should get going."

"Let me finish my cereal," he says.

I collect a few things and throw them into an overnight bag —not much. We won't be gone long.

"Ready?" I say as I throw on my jacket.

I HAVE a bikini in my overnight bag, but it takes so long to escape New York City, we don't arrive at the Holiday Inn until 9:45—fifteen minutes past pool hours. My disappointment escapes with a long groaning hiss.

Eric isn't a big fan of television, and the set he has at his apartment is a now-vintage portable number with a tiny ten-inch screen—no cable, and no remote. I've only ever seen him use it to watch late-night talk shows once in a while. The TV in the hotel room, on the other hand, has a larger than life flat-screen display with countless cable channels. Eric rolls his eyes when I turn on the set.

Mom and Dad had always tightly regulated my TV viewing, so having command of a gazillion channels can feel like an exhilarating luxury. Or at least a serviceable consolation prize for missing the pool. But I can't concentrate, and I circle the channels a dozen times before settling on the Cartoon Network. Preparing to be hypnotized by SpongeBob, I yank down the sheets and crawl into bed next to Eric. But the sheets and pillowcases are so clean—blindingly white and smelling of bleach—I realize how sticky and gross I am from the drive.

"Where are you going?" Eric says, disappointed, as I jump off the bed and run to the shower.

The bathroom mirror fogs up, and the walls sweat. The high-pressure showerhead is everything the motel's website promised it would be. There was a time I would have considered using the massage feature in ways in which God would never forgive me, but I haven't been feeling sexual at all, lately. Nothing to do with Eric—I don't think so, anyway. Maybe. All I know is that side of me seems to have evaporated.

I unwrap a tiny soap, lather a washcloth, and scour my grubby face. I wash my hair with a sample-sized shampoo and debate whether to shave my legs. Why bother? Instead, I stand motionless, under a thousand needles of scalding water, hoping my simmering anxiety might boil away in the heat.

THE HOTEL ROOM'S industrial-weight curtains obliterate the sun, except for a tiny blade of morning light that cuts through the room and across my face. A door slams in the hall, children laugh. I wasn't asleep in the first place, but now there's no use even pretending. I try not to wake Eric as I quietly shimmy out of bed, throw on my clothes, and head to the lobby to fetch us a couple of coffees.

The dining area is already bustling with early risers eating donuts. The pool is visible through a large window. About six kids are running around, screaming, splashing. They jump in the water, climb out and jump in again.

"Fuck that," I say while pumping coffee from the dispenser. The kids, screaming with laughter and enjoying life, trigger thoughts of my childhood and what a disaster it had been. I suppose I should want kids of my own to set things right, but, no. Not that I hate kids, but I've never experienced a burning desire to have one of my own. As Dad likes to point out, it's getting too late now anyway. Then again, it hadn't been too late for Anna and her miracle baby. Of course, you need to have sex to have a baby, so it's not a significant concern, anyway.

I cover the coffees and juggle them back to the room where Eric is out of bed, now, and pulling open the curtains.

"Looks like another beautiful day," he says.

I put the coffees down and drop onto the bed. "I thought I might get in an early morning dip in the pool, but it's teeming with urchins."

"Kids?"

"That's what I said. I'm sure the pool is half full of pee."

"What's the food situation? Anything good?"

"Pastries, rubber eggs, cold cuts, cereal and watery juice in a dispenser, waffle iron and toast on a conveyor belt—typical motel lobby stuff."

"That sounds scrumptious. I'm going to get something. Want to come along?"

"No," I say, catching my reflection in the mirror. "My hair looks like shit. I can't believe I went downstairs like this."

"Your hair looks fine," says Eric, lacing up his shoes. "Come back to the lobby with me."

"My hair is not fine. Look at it."

"Okay, whatever. Come down when you're ready, and we'll get going."

"Don't be like that."

"Like what?"

I slam the bathroom door and bend into the shower to wet down my hair. Afterward, I use the hairdryer attached to the wall. The cord is barely long enough to reach. My hair looks okay, I suppose—better than it did—but I shudder at my blueish reflection and curse the unflattering fluorescent lights.

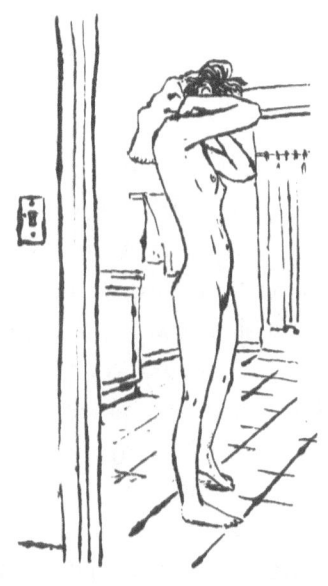

People still tell me how young I look, but I don't believe them anymore. Young for my age, maybe, but what good is that?

The mood I'm in, it could take hours to get dressed, but I was so eager to hit the road that I only brought along one set of clothes. I throw on the stale shirt and pants and ride the elevator back down to the dining area where I find Eric sitting reading a complimentary *USA Today* and eating a gummy croissant.

"What's going on in the world?" I ask. The caffeine is kicking in, and I'm feeling calmer.

"Same old, same old," he says, folding the paper and putting it aside. "What's new with you since I saw you last? Other than your fabulous hair, that is."

"I'm sorry I snapped earlier. I'm nervous."

Eric gestures over his shoulder at the pool. "I see what you mean about the urchins. The pool must be pure piss by now."

The gaggle of kids has grown to a dozen or more, none older

than ten. The ruckus echoes in the tiled pool room, only partially muffled by the glass between us.

"Remember when we were at your exhibit?" I say.

"Vaguely."

"When you introduced me to Zack, you called me your girlfriend."

"That's right, I did."

"Am I?"

"Isn't that what you told your Dad?"

"But am I?"

It wasn't long after we first met that I told Eric I was crazy about him. He'd made me dinner at his apartment and we were on a slow waltz toward the bedroom. His hands were on the small of my back, my face buried against his chest. I've always been a tactile person, maybe that's why I work with clay. Touching him hypnotized me. I used those exact words: I'm crazy about you. I immediately regretted letting it slip. I don't know what I expected him to say or do about it, but it would have been nice to hear he was crazy about me, too. To say: Let's run away together, swim to the moon, follow the sun. Instead, he said nothing, only tried to kiss me. I swatted him away, but he grabbed my wrist and hugged me. When we fell onto the bed, I kicked him and squirmed loose. He was the one who should have been saying he was crazy about me. Not sure what I'm expecting to hear now.

He reaches across the table and covers my hands with his. I turn away and watch the kids. One of them does a cannonball, but he's so small there's hardly a splash. Eric squeezes my hands and gives them a gentle shake.

"I'm crazy about you," he says, mocking what I had once said. I want to punch him. "I'm serious," he says. "Isn't it obvious by now? I love you."

After setting him up the way I did, I should say I love him, too. I think I do—I must—but I can't bring myself to say it. Not now. Not out loud. It feels too fake, forced, contrived. It's like the food behind me on the buffet counter—the pods of imitation maple syrup, the pads of margarine.

If Eric is irritated, he doesn't let on, other than to lean back in his chair. He turns away and watches the kids.

"Are we going to visit your dad while we're here?" he says.

I'd been trying to decide. I don't want to, I want the trip to be all about Anna, but I have a clawing sense of obligation.

"Doesn't matter to me," says Eric. "I figured you might want to pop in for a minute, that's all."

"A minute? That's funny."

"We'll tell him we're passing through—that we're heading to Michigan to see my mom or something. Would you like to see him before we find Anna, or after?"

Not after, I'm sure of that.

"I think I'll have a swim first." Underwater, the kids' voices don't actually sound all that annoying. They sound more like a chorus of joy, a comfort. I even toss a ball with the smallest boy.

———

ARRIVING AT DAD'S HOUSE, something looks different. The land beside his house is clear of cattails, and a backhoe sits beside a pile of dirt. I hardly have time to wonder about it before Dad calls to us from behind his screen door and begins his usual introductory small talk.

"You look good," I say. I've learned a well-placed compliment is the most effective way to derail his boring monologues.

He runs his hands over his clean T-shirt and cinches his jeans—crisp blue and held up by a legitimate belt. He appears to be dressed head to toe in our Christmas gifts.

The darker of the two dogs, Ling, is at our feet. His back legs seem fully paralyzed now as he uses his front paws to drag himself through a fresh pool of dog piss like a mop.

Dad fetches a few sheets of paper towel to swab the puddle. He kneels, rubs the floor, and stands again, all without a wince or groan.

"Glad to see your hernia's not bothering you, Dad."

"I got it fixed. A month ago—a month and a half—something like that. It got so painful I couldn't stand it no more. It only took an hour. Not even a whole day."

Beaming at us, he circles the rooms looking for the dog leash.

"I need to take Ling outside. I wasn't expecting you so soon. Let me take him out."

"Where's the other dog?" I say.

"Cheng? He's gone. He was messing all over the place. The vet said he had cancer. Like your mother. Cancer and diabetes. He couldn't see nothing and his teeth were rotted. Weren't nothing they could do. I had to put him down." His eyes grow glassy. "He was my dog, Rachel. I loved that dog. Ling, here, was your mother's dog, but Cheng was mine."

"Probably got sick from all those canned peaches."

"Peaches? I never fed Cheng no peaches."

"Oh my fucking god," I say. Eric's paintings may have given me a new perspective on Dad, but art has its limits. Thankfully I muttered it too softly for Dad to hear. "You killed him, Dad, you know that, right? And you're killing this one, too. What's wrong with him?"

"His spine has a tumor. It's cutting off his nerves and all."

"He should be put down, too. Poor thing is suffering."

"I promised Dorothy I'd take care of him. He's all I got left of your mother. He can't move his bowels no more. I have to massage him like this—"

He makes a motion like kneading bread.

"I don't want to hear it, Dad."

"Well, that's what I do."

He puts his jacket on and leashes Cheng—out of habit, I suppose, since the dog can't walk—and takes him outside.

While Dad is gone, Eric comments on how well Dad is doing.

"Are you nuts?"

"Granted, the dog isn't doing well, but it looks like your dad is taking care of himself, anyway. He's cleaned the house a bit. I noticed some nice plants outside."

"Don't get me started on those plants. My dad should be spending his money on more important things—getting his pipes fixed, hiring someone to mow the lawn, all that. Not flowers he doesn't know how to care for. Or fancy purple ties. I told you that you can't even drink the water in this house, right?

The fracking up the hill, remember? It caused Dad's well to collapse. Didn't you see all the jugs of water in the basement? You can't drink what comes from the tap."

"I've had a drink from the faucet each time I've been here. It tasted kind of funny, but I had no idea."

"Dad had it tested. The results came back with high levels of all kinds of garbage. I'm surprised you can't light it on fire. Maybe you can, I never tried. He could save money on heating oil by filling the tank with his tap water. It's probably why every living thing in this house seems to get cancer."

When Dad returns, I ask him about the backhoe and what the church is doing with Aunt Emily's small parcel of land next door.

"Peggy bought it," he says. "Reverend Furman tried to sell it to me at your mother's funeral. I wanted to buy it, but I didn't have no five-thousand dollars."

"He should have given it to you for nothing."

"Peggy bought it from him for just nine hundred dollars. I don't know how she got it so cheap, but I'm glad it's in the family again. Peggy agrees it's important to keep it in the family. She wants to buy my house, too—when I'm gone and all."

"I'm sure she does." There goes my plan of last resort. No way am I ever going to pay rent to Aunt Peggy.

"She wants to buy my house, so it stays in the family."

"But Mike and I are family, aren't we?"

"Well, on account of you two being adopted and all."

"I'm your daughter, Dad, isn't that what you always tell me? Every time I see you, every time we speak, you say, *You're my daughter. We loved you. We raised you.*' Aunt Peggy isn't your so-called *flesh and blood*. She married into the family. How is that any different from being adopted?"

"Peggy has kids is why. And her kids has kids. You don't have no kids, Rachel. You don't got no one to pass nothing down to."

"We have to go."

"You just got here."

"We just stopped in to say hi. We have to go."

"You don't want to have lunch or nothing?"

What a mistake. I should do what Mike is planning to do. Come back for the next funeral, nothing more.

I GRAB things from my bag one by one before losing patience and dumping the entire contents onto the bench seat.

"I can't believe it," I say.

Coins slip through the seat crack, lip balm rolls to the floor. An invitation from Eric's show flutters into my lap. I tear it in two and throw the pieces out the window. I'm sick of seeing my father's face and hearing his voice—in my head and out of it.

As I gather up my wallet, keys, gum, lottery tickets, and refill my handbag, I find a long-lost bottle of Chivas. It must've fallen out of my bag's little-used side pocket. It's tempting to crack it open and knock it back, but, for now, I throw it in with the rest of my things before Eric sees it.

"I can't find the directions," I say.

"Relax," says Eric. "We'll find it."

I unscrew the lid of my lip balm, scoop out a dollop, and run it over my lips.

A cluster of dogwood blooms obscures the cemetery sign, and we miss the turn. I'm furious and try, poorly, to hide it. Realizing our mistake, Eric makes a U-turn and doubles back to the secluded road. The street is cratered and pockmarked, littered with small tree branches, and shaded by a canopy of oaks. Halfway up, the road splits in two. I go with my gut and tell him to turn left. The roadway grows steeper and narrower. Even free of all the ice and snow, it's still a struggle to climb.

"I hope this is right," Eric says. "It'll be a bitch to turn around if it isn't."

Eventually, the shady trees give way to a bright open field dotted with headstones. A chipped enameled sign hangs on a rusting iron gate: MOTHER OF SORROWS.

I hop out, unlatch the gate, and swing it open. My cousins had given me vague directions to Anna's plot, but I can't get my bearings. I know it's in a corner somewhere, but the graveyard appears to be circular. What corner?

Eric drives slowly, pausing here and there, allowing me to hop out and search. When I come upon the side-by-side plots of Joseph and Frances Rubik, I know Anna must be near. I have Eric stop the car and help me look.

We get out and scan the engraved names. I pause over the final resting place of Joseph, the steelworker, and his wife Frances, the bingo addict. Do I need to say anything? No, I want nothing to do with her.

Eric calls to me: "She's over here."

ANNA RUBIK, APRIL 23, 1934 – MAY 13, 1973

"Thirty-nine," Eric says, doing the math. "Same age as you."

I already did the math and am well aware of the coincidence, but haven't been able to decide if it holds any real significance. It feels like it does, but what?

Eric assumes I need some alone time and tells me he's going to walk around and take pictures.

Two small birds flutter past, looping from plot to plot until one of them lands on Anna's headstone. Its tiny head swivels and cocks to the side with that quizzical look small birds always have. It pauses as if waiting for an answer. I don't have one. The second bird lands briefly next to the first before they each dart away. I kneel, tug lightly at the grass, and introduce myself.

"Hi Mom, it's me, Virginia. I go by Rachel now."

I pull out a few tall weeds growing at the base of the stone and run my hand along the grass as if petting a dog.

"They tell me you were trouble," I say. "They tell me I'm trouble too."

I wouldn't know what else to say, even if Anna were alive. A conversation would surely be difficult and probably disappointing. Finding her has filled a void, I suppose, but at the same time, I can feel the void gaping ever wider, stretching out in all directions. A desperate, lonely, feeling washes over me, and I want to crawl into my mother's grave and lie down beside her.

"I got your painting from Esther. The one that won the ribbon? It's beautiful—I love it. I'm going to hang it on my wall and look at it every day."

I'd like to have it cleaned. I want to keep the Kraft paper covering the back of it because it has the Art Fair entry label on it, but the backing is starting to fall apart—I'll have to do something about that.

I picture Anna smiling at me with the same smile she has in her graduation photo, before the treatments, before her thinking turned sideways. My heart aches. I hope she is finally at peace. I hope to gain some myself one day.

I pull out two clay figurines from my pocket—a mother and daughter, side by side, attached at the hands. A circus troupe of two, performing in the ring.

"I made this for you," I say, trying to dig a hole to put them in.

The ground is hard, still partially frozen. I stand up and use my boot heel to create a divot. It's not deep, but it will do. I gently place the figurines in the hole and cover them with earth and grass.

"I'm glad I found you," I say. "Now that I know where you are, I'll be back. I promise."

Eric is several yards away, hovering among the headstones, taking pictures, kneeling here and there, leaning this way and that, like a slow-motion honeybee in a garden of flowers. The birds continue to flit around, too, before perching again on a nearby headstone. Eric tries to take their picture, but they are too fast and fly away. He snaps some photos of me as I approach. I wave and smile.

"Do that again," he says.

I pull an old a pose from my modeling days and let him snap a few more.

The two of us are a lot like the birds, flitting, bobbing, circling each other, landing once in a while, and looking confused. But the birds seem happy. Maybe I can be happy, too.

"How did it go?" Eric asks. "Is everything okay?"

I nod and hug him. I pull out another small sculpture—a man and woman this time, also attached at the hands.

"It's you and me," I say.

It's rather abstract, and I'm a little shy about giving it to him, but he seems to like it.

"It isn't perfect," I say.

ACKNOWLEDGMENTS

I wish to thank Amber Qureshi for her invaluable editorial input and guidance. Also, thanks to Tom Vowler for his early editorial feedback and encouragement. Thanks to Brian Farrell, Katrina Baker, Alison Tirrell, Carlin Wragg, Brad Sprouse, and Geoff Rockwell for reading countless drafts and offering honest reactions and valuable suggestions. Thanks to Signe Yberg for allowing me into her ceramics studio. Special thanks to Riona Judge McCormack, Laura Buchwald, Ashleigh Larratt, Jerry Stifelman, Sarah Feeney, Erica Frauman, Jane & Dwight Boud. And a very special thanks to Deborah Rice for her inspiration and encouragement, without whom this book wouldn't exist in any way, shape, or form.

ABOUT THE AUTHOR

Jamie Boud was born and raised in New Jersey. After earning an illustration degree from Rhode Island School of Design, he moved to New York City, where he currently lives and works as an artist and designer. This is his second novel.